SCARY
DEAD THINGS

The Tome of Bill

Part 2

RICK GUALTIERI

Edited by Apex Editing
Cover by Mallory Rock at www.malloryrock.com

Published by Westmarch Publishing

www.westmarchpub.com

ISBN 978-1-940415-04-8

Contents

For Joey, Connor, and Raiden; the scariest things I know.

Special thanks to Alissa, Sheila, Jennifer, Sandra, Anne, and Marquel. Your encouragement helped make this book possible. I hope that one day I am able to help inspire you to reach for your dreams the way you have all inspired me to reach for mine.

Just Another Brick in the Wall

CRUNCH YEP, NO matter what way you put it, being hurled through a wall hurts. It's funny; just a few short months ago I would have argued that the dreaded *atomic wedgie* was the most common indignity I had suffered throughout my life. That's not such a bad thing, especially when one considers that the proportion of ass-crack related incidents in one's existence tends to decrease dramatically post high-school. After all, most people just won't give a wedgie to another grownup. Why? Well, my personal theory is that part of becoming an adult means that we start asking ourselves much deeper questions than when we were kids, one such question being: do I really want to put my hands where this person's dirty ass has been?

That being said, getting thrown to crash into, and sometimes through, solid objects was becoming a disturbingly common occurrence in my life as of late. Considering the overall painfulness of such experiences, I was beginning to find myself oddly nostalgic about just having my underwear bunched up my ass by some prankster.

Just in case you're taking notes, brick and concrete were easily the least fun barriers I had been smashed into; however, your basic wooden load-bearing wall – which oddly enough was what I found myself plowing into at that moment – wasn't exactly a vacation in the Caribbean either. If this kept up, I might have to consider starting a blog about all the scenic walls in the Tri-State area and what it felt like to be flung through each and every one of them.

Although perhaps right then wasn't exactly an ideal time to think about blogging. I was just starting to pull myself back to my feet when a dark angry form emerged from the shadows. It was Samuel, the leader of a coven of vampires from Queens that called themselves the HBC. This was because their home territory included the Howard Beach area. It was a stupid name, but considering my own group was known as *Village Coven* – due to being headquartered in fucking SoHo – I was probably in no position to be throwing stones.

Apparently it was tradition to name covens after their territories. Sure, you wound up with some silly names. I had even heard there was a Scotrun Coven in Pennsylvania, which was bad for them because they would forevermore be known in my mind as the *Scrotum Coven*. All things considered, though, it probably beat the alternative. If every group were given free reign for names, I have little doubt we'd wind up with dopey crap like *The Blood Brotherhood*, *The Midnight Raiders*, or maybe *The Sons of Darkness*. In short, we'd all sound like retarded local chapters of the

Legion of Doom. Trust me, I speak from experience here. My own coven had a rule not too long ago regarding taking new personal pseudonyms upon joining. As a result, we wound up with stupid shit like people calling themselves Rage Vector, Night Razor, and, of course, Dr. Death. So, taking all that into account, I could probably live with Village Coven.

Still, worrying about minor things like coven names is probably best left to moments when I'm not in danger of getting my head torn off. This was not such a time. Samuel leapt at me, no doubt going for the kill. Well, okay, maybe that's a bit obvious. After all, you typically don't fling yourself through the air at people you're having a polite conversation with. Fortunately for me, I was far from out of it. I may not be able to dish it out as well as others, but I can definitely take it. See, I'm a vampire, too (*just in case you haven't figured that out yet*). I also have a lot of aforementioned experience getting tossed around. You build up a tolerance to it after a while. Those two things combined allowed me to recover quickly enough to snatch a busted two-by-four from the rubble of the safe house wall I had just smashed through. Before Samuel could fully cover the distance, I swung the beam and connected with a solid *KAPOW*. He went flying back into the shadows from whence he came. That gave me a breather, but I didn't have any delusions that it would be nearly enough to finish him.

I had been told that Samuel was nearly two-hundred years old. As vampires tend to get stronger as they get older, that made him both a lot more powerful as well as much more experienced than me. Neither was a checkmark in my favor. Under different circumstances, I should have probably been counting my lucky stars that I was still standing. If this had been my first tussle with a vampire way out of my league, I'd probably be busy either begging for my life or kissing my ass goodbye; however, it wasn't.

Don't get me wrong. I'm no Chuck Norris, and this fight was a *long* ways from being decided in my favor; however, once you've been in a pissing match – with a monster who outclasses you in nearly every way – and lived (*sorta*) to talk about it, you start to get a little jaded about the whole thing. It's like when I was a little kid. I remember sitting there watching wrestling on the TV and listening to Mean Gene Okerlund talking about how any given wrestler on any given night could potentially become the new champ. It wasn't too different from what I was doing now. No matter how old the vampires, things weren't one-hundred percent settled until one was dust. Of course, that logic ignores the fact that wrestling is all bullshit. Unfortunately for me, I didn't have Vince McMahon off behind the scenes scripting a big upset victory. If I wanted to win this, I couldn't count on 'Stone Cold' Steve Austin running out to save my ass with a steel chair.

Fortunately, I still had a few tricks up my sleeve; one of them being that I had my wits about me. Samuel might've been much older, but he had a major weakness that I could exploit. According to the info I had been given, he was old enough to have been born a slave in the deep South before the days of the Civil War. He had been owned by an exceptionally cruel master and spent the first four decades of his life enduring a mix of excruciating labor and relentless beatings. Things like that would fuck up anybody's outlook on life, and Samuel was no exception.

From what I had been told, it was actually his owner that first had a chance encounter with a vampire. He was turned, then shortly afterwards he attacked and turned Samuel. Why? Who knows? Maybe he wanted to hold dominion over his slave forever, or maybe he was just thirsty. Either way, it's safe to say this guy was a dick sandwich and a half. He was also a complete dumbass, too. Being a brand new vampire himself, Samuel's master had no idea what he was doing. I've heard that the act of turning brings out the feral nature in some people. Samuel was the perfect poster child for this. Upon awakening as one of the undead, he completely snapped. He turned on his former master, who was too new to know how to control him. Then, when he was done, he attacked his now former owner's family. He didn't stop there either, slaughtering every living thing on his plantation and the next two over before his rage burned itself out.

Since by that time the Civil War was raging full force, nothing odd was thought of the carnage. After all, when you have an invading army with a scorched-earth policy rampaging about, most people aren't going to look at a few dozen dead bodies and immediately say,

"Hey! It must be vampires." Samuel was thus able to escape without much notice. If anyone ever did try to stand in his way, the archives make no mention of it; however, if someone did, it's a safe bet as to what happened to them.

If you're thinking that all of this caused him to spend the next century and a half nursing a massive chip on his shoulder, then bingo! Even up to the present day, it was well known in the vampire community that Samuel only accepted minorities into his coven, and even in that he was particular. Don't get me wrong, I might be just a little bit jaded, too, at the whole thing if it had happened to me; however, it also meant that it wouldn't be too hard for me, your quintessential dorky looking white guy, to push his buttons. A two-hundred-year-old vampire in a blood lusted rage was actually easier to fight than a two-hundred-year-old vampire who was thinking rationally and planning his every step. Fortunately for me, pissing people off is one of my specialties.

"Damn, *you people* have hard heads," I said in a condescending manner. I felt like a massive dick saying it, but I'd rather be a living dick than a politically correct corpse.

"What the fuck did you say!?" Samuel growled as he rose and once more began stalking me.

"Oh, I'm sorry. Forgot you don't understand proper English too well." I increased the mocking in my tone. "How's this? Yo, Nigga! You gots yourself one motherfucking hard head!" Oh yeah, I probably erased about a lifetime's worth of good karma on that one. But it worked. Samuel came right at me with little more than an inarticulate snarl. He was majorly pissed. If I didn't time this right, I was going to get a front row seat to watching my head shoved up my own ass.

As he charged me, I reached into my back pocket and pulled out my secret weapon. I was glad I'd decided to bring it. Considering this was supposed to be a peace conference, I almost hadn't. Thank goodness for paranoia. As Samuel closed the distance, I kept the fork hidden from his view, waiting for the right time to strike.

Yes, I said *fork* – not a cross, not a gun, and definitely not the holy hand grenade of Antioch. Trust me on this one. For starters, forget what you know. Crosses by themselves don't do shit against vampires. If you ever find yourself cornered by vamps and you think you're going to get out of it by holding two popsicle sticks together, you are going to be in for a *major* disappointment. Sure, maybe you'll get lucky and they'll be laughing so hard at your idiocy that you'll be able to slip away. I wouldn't count on it, though – but hey, I'm a glass is half full kind of guy.

Anyway, Samuel crossed the distance between us almost faster than I could see. I just barely had enough time to brace myself before he hit me in the side of the head with a wild backhand swing, knocking my ass to the floor. I have to admit that under normal circumstances the blow would have probably put me down for the count. But these weren't normal circumstances, and I'm not a normal vampire...if there even *was* such a thing.

You see, I was already juiced up from earlier. At the start of the fight, one of Samuel's goons had come at me first. I had stepped into his punch and sunk my teeth into his arm – managing to suck down a few mouthfuls of blood before he could pry me off.

Now this might not seem significant to you, but you need to ignore the shit on your typical late night vampire erotica – in which everyone is usually biting and sucking on everyone else. In reality, when a vamp chomps down on another, bad things happen to the biter. The effect is kind of like what you might expect if you were to drive down to Tijuana and drink your fill from the first water fountain you came across – only amplified a couple dozen times. Forget fighting; most bloodsuckers wouldn't be strong enough to *stand* for several hours after drinking another vampire's blood. But not me.

I'm what the other undead call a *Freewill*. Apparently, we're rare...as in it's been at least half a millennium since anyone has seen another. Personally, I think a good deal of what they say about me is a load of bullshit; however, it does seem to come with some perks. For starters, I'm immune to psychic domination, or *compulsion* as they call it (*hence the name Freewill, duh!*). That's one of the things some of the old Dracula movies got right. Older vampires can mentally dominate younger vampires, especially those they create. They can, more or less, force them to do whatever they want. Vampire society typically uses this to keep order within their ranks, but there are plenty of my kind who just do it to fuck around with the younger vamps.

Perhaps even cooler than that power, though, is what happens if I drink another vampire's blood. Instead of puking my guts out and lying there whimpering, I get a boost similar to Pac-Man on a handful of power pellets. Basically what happens is I somehow temporarily add their strength to my own. How? Fucked if I know. I just know it works and that it's saved my ass on more than one occasion.

I don't know how old the vampire I bit was, but I was easily running at about two-hundred percent of my normal level. Not powerful enough to engage Samuel directly, but strong enough to allow me to take blows that would otherwise turn my head concave. Thus I was able to shake his hit off and jump back to my feet. Maybe I was a little wobblier than I would've preferred (*he hit me pretty damn hard, after all*) but standing was definitely better than lying down and letting him go all ape-shit on me.

As he once more came after me, still blinded by rage, I sidestepped and plunged the fork deep into the middle of his back. Samuel was a big guy with heavily muscled arms. Normally that's a good thing, both for attracting the ladies as well as beating the tar out of flabby shits like me, but it's a bad thing for being flexible – as in nimble enough to be able to reach around and pull my meager little weapon out.

The fork itself didn't do much. I mean, I'm sure it stung *a little*. Getting stabbed wasn't fun, no matter what the weapon. But using a kitchen utensil against a vampire is a lot like using a penknife against a grizzly bear – unless, that is, it happens to be a *special* kitchen utensil. Fortunately for me, it was. After a second or two, I could smell it. Another few, and I could see it. And I'm definitely sure Samuel *felt* it.

* * *

Two weeks earlier, I had been sitting at home, sipping on a pint of refrigerated blood, just minding my own business. I was relaxing on a Monday night following a long day of coding. I work as a video game developer. I did it during my life, and I still do it during my undeath. I like my job and all, but there is a small part of my mind that likes to remind me that I'm vampire. Not only that, but I'm a legendary type of vampire, a legendary type of vampire who is also the head of his own fucking coven...and yet I was still a goddamned wage slave.

I had figured that once I took over Village Coven, it was going to be one big party after another, with maybe an orgy or two in between. But noooo. Sally, my so called *partner,* kept a tight rein on the coven's bank books. I was lucky to score cab fare from her, much less live the life of avaricious abandon I so craved. But we'll get back to her in a moment, as she definitely had a hand in the situation going on with Samuel.

So there I was unwinding when Tom came in the door. Both of my roommates, Tom and Ed, are human.

Kind of makes us a less attractive, but significantly more fucked-up version of *Three's Company*. Anyway, he had spent the weekend at his parents' home in New Jersey (*also home to his slightly underage hottie of a sister, which has really nothing to do with the present situation. I just like to mention it*) and then gone straight to his job in Manhattan, so I had no idea he had anything planned for me. If I had, I probably would have been elsewhere.

"I've got something new we can try," he excitedly said after tossing his sports jacket into the closet. I didn't even need to ask what he meant by that. I'd been turned into a vampire some six months prior, and ever since then my roommates had made it their mission in life to chart my powers and weaknesses. It was mostly the weaknesses they seemed to focus on, and thus, in addition to friends, I had to add *torturers* to the mental description I kept for both of them. Barely a week went by in which they didn't come up with some new scheme that involved stabbing, burning, or crushing me. My pain had become their hobby. Yeah, they both really needed to get laid.

"What now?" I asked in a bored tone, hoping it might dissuade him.

"This." He pulled an old fork out of his pocket.

"Let me guess, you misunderstood my previous instructions and are now going to *fork* yourself?"

"Keep trying, Bill," he dryly remarked. "In another century or two, you might grow a sense of humor that's actually funny. For your information, this here is not just a fork. It's silverware...you know, as in *silver*."

"So? You guys already tried silver. It didn't do jack-shit."

"Yeah, I know. But forget about that. That shitty letter opener was just silver plated. I didn't really think it would work anyway."

"And yet," I put an edge to my voice, "it didn't stop you from stabbing me with it...*repeatedly*."

"Sorry. All in the name of science," he continued. "But this is different, trust me. This weekend, my Mom had some friends over, and she pulled out the good stuff. She inherited it from her grandmother. This is the real deal here. Pure, solid, you-could-melt-it-down-and-shoot-werewolves-with-it silver."

"So let me get this straight: you stole your mom's prized silverware?"

"Borrowed is more like it," he replied. "Besides, I don't see anything wrong with taking a little advance on my inheritance...especially in the name of research."

"You know there's probably a special room in Hell reserved just for you, right?"

"As long as it has air conditioning, then I'm cool with it," he answered. "Now hold still. This might sting a bit."

I don't know why I let him. Maybe I *was* getting used to it or maybe I was just tired from the day's work (*vampires and normal work hours don't mesh too well under the best of circumstances*). More than likely, though, I just knew that he'd get me eventually. Even if I flat out told him "No!" now, he'd probably just wait and then stab me in the neck the second I stopped paying attention. Thus, whatever the insane reason, I held still as he jammed the damn thing into me.

"Well?" he asked, the fork sticking out the back of my hand. Small drops of blood started welling up around the tines.

"Well, it fucking hurts. Pull it out!"

"Give it a sec."

"Now...OW!" I cried as first smoke and then sparks started shooting out of the small puncture wounds.

"Holy shit, it worked! I knew it!" he exclaimed, all while watching the skin of my hand start to char and turn black.

In response I just glared and bared my fangs.

After a moment or two he finally got the hint. "Oh, sorry," he said with a sheepish smile before finally yanking the accursed cutlery out.

Goddamn, that was painful. The bleeding and burning were bad enough, but it also felt like there was a small legion of coal miners under the skin of my hand, hacking away with dull pickaxes. All in all, a dandy load of fun.

* * *

What had happened to me then was repeating itself within Samuel, albeit in a slightly more central location. As much as I had wanted to punch out Tom's lights at the time, I had to grudgingly admit that this one might be a keeper. Further (*reluctant*) testing had shown two other interesting side effects. For starters, silver was safe to the touch for me. I was able to hold and even eat with it. Yeah, that eating part took some convincing by

Tom, but he's nothing if not persistent. Whatever its effect, it apparently only happened when in contact with vampire blood – kind of like dropping a magnesium flare into a pool of water.

Even better, albeit worse for me at the time, was that something in the silver retarded my enhanced healing. Instead of a few minutes, it took all night for my hand to get back to normal. So it stood to reason that even if Samuel managed to pry loose the fork, which was rapidly turning his back into something akin to a roman candle, it was going to be a while before he felt good about it.

Blinded by both rage and pain, Samuel more or less lost it. He screamed inarticulately and began spinning around, attempting to get at the source of his pain, as his back continued to be engulfed in flames. He plowed into and through another wall, but the fork was stuck fast.

This was my chance, and I wasn't about to let it go. I picked up another plank of wood from the rubble, then snapped it in half over my knee, making sure one of the pieces ended in a nice, sharp point. It would make a dandy makeshift stake.

"Form blazing sword, motherfucker!" I shouted as I charged to finish him off. Yeah, I needed to work on my one-liners. Apparently, I still had to work on not being a cocky dickhead either. Aflame or not, my dorky catchphrase managed to catch Samuel's attention. As I closed in, stake held high, he caught me on the chin with an uppercut that sent me flying.

Time for a Recap

IT'S ONE THING to be hit; quite another to be caught square on the jaw. It's like time stops for a few moments. During those seconds, there's a disconnect between the mind and body. The mind can still be semi-rational, even a little detached. *Well, that was certainly a good shot, wasn't it? Perhaps we should respond in kind*, your brain might be thinking. Unfortunately, the body won't be quite as coherent. While the mind is carrying on a casual discourse, as if discussing last night's ball game, the body is flopping about, trying to find a comfy spot on the floor to land.

Unfortunately for me, I didn't even have that luxury. When a vampire like Samuel catches you dead center, you go flying. The hit was bad enough, but the old adage about falling applied here, too. Nobody dies from the fall itself, but the landing is a bitch. The same principle applies when you're hurtling through the air as if you've just been shot out of a cannon.

I had just enough time to register all of this when I slammed into what felt like...you guessed it...another wall. The impact was enough to scatter any rational thoughts of the battle I was currently losing and fling me into a nice, comfy little flashback regarding how I had gotten into this mess to begin with.

* * *

Things hadn't been all wine and roses since I had taken over the coven from the previous leader, Jeff, AKA Night Razor. I had defeated him in fair combat, or so the story went. In actuality, another vampire, Sally, had been the one to finish him off. She was the vamp originally responsible for luring me to my own death and subsequent turning to the *dark side*; however, soon after, she had a change of heart and decided to help me out instead. After the fight with Jeff, she had even given me credit for the deed, allowing me to take over his position.

Before you start getting all soppy over this, though, let me point out that Sally isn't exactly the altruistic sort. Everything I've ever seen her do ultimately seems to be for her own benefit. So, too, was my becoming coven leader. She quickly established herself as my partner behind the scenes. *Partner* apparently having the same meaning to her as Fidel Castro telling his fellow Cubans that they were all comrades. In her mind, she was definitely first amongst equals.

My troubles from the start were two-fold. Internally, I had to control a bunch of immortal killers in fashion model guise, all of whom were older than me. Originally, I had some delusions of trying to run a bloodless coven. Vampire or not, I'm not too big on treating normal people like they were snacks in a vending machine. Sadly, most of my undead brethren, Sally included, were not of the same mindset. I was instead forced to keep the killing contained as well as I could, which meant getting creative; however, even my best efforts couldn't lessen their bloodlust – which was partially the reason why I found myself in the middle of a vampire turf war.

The second part of my problems was the HBC. They claimed Queens as their territory, and normally there wouldn't have been an issue between our two covens. Unfortunately, within a few short weeks of being turned, I found myself number one on their to-kill list.

See, vampires have laws, too, just like everyone else. Don't get me wrong, I'm pretty sure there's no vampire statute against jaywalking, but there are rules set in place to keep our existence hidden from the general populace. The ruling counsel of vampires, known by the asinine nickname *the Draculas*, hands these dictates down to the masses. The rest of us are expected to follow them, no questions asked. In the vampire rulebook, there's no such thing as a misdemeanor. You fuck up, and you get made an example of. The HBC fucked up, and somehow I got caught up in it all.

The rumor mill had said that Samuel was recruiting in numbers above the quotas set for regional covens. The vampire in charge of *correcting* their oversight, James, had decided to disguise the culling and give me credit for it in some misguided attempt to increase my reputation as the Freewill of vampire lore.

Unfortunately, before he could do damage control and keep things from landing squarely on my head, he was called away on business. From there, things quickly deteriorated.

The HBC vampires thought I was the one responsible for killing their members. Combined with my ascension as the new head of Village Coven, it had caused bad blood to build up quickly between us. Over the next couple months, skirmishes broke out between our two groups. On the one side were vampires who hated me for a crime I didn't commit, on the other were those eager to find an outlet for the violence I had been trying to curb. All in all, it was an explosive situation.

If they were the gunpowder, though, then the fuse was named Sally. Since my dealings with the coven were mostly limited to the weekends (*due to that little job thing I mentioned earlier*), she was left in charge during the week. I had originally assumed this was for the best, as she was older than I and far better versed in vampire politics. We all know what happens when you assume; however, when you assume with regards to Sally, you can double that 'make an ass out of me' part of the deal.

It was she who had proposed the mediation between our two covens. A group from Village Coven led by us would meet with a delegation of HBC vampires led by Samuel to hash out a truce. The meeting place was set at a neutral vampire safe house close to the Brooklyn Navy Yard, which at the very least meant it was an easy commute for me.

Unbeknownst to me, though (*at least up until a short while ago*), was that Sally had purposely staffed our contingent with some of the more violent members amongst our coven. They were just looking for an excuse to do some damage. Combined with Samuel's group, who were likewise spoiling for a fight, and the talks lasted all of three minutes before the first punch was thrown.

Within the space of a few moments, at least three vampires were reduced to nothing more than ashes. After that, complete chaos descended. I quickly lost track of Sally in the ensuing melee. Then, after I spent a few minutes fighting off random Howard Beach vamps, Samuel caught sight of me.

"*THIS FUCKER'S MINE*!!" he compelled his group. Almost immediately, they all backed off and sought their mayhem elsewhere. Amusingly enough, if I were somewhat older, I probably would have sent out an opposite compulsion toward my group – instructing them to save my ass. But I'm not, and since the vamps that Sally invited from our side weren't my biggest supporters to begin with, they all had no problems letting the two head honchos battle it out *mano y mano*. Thus began our dance, which so far had consisted of Samuel bouncing me off various hard surfaces, broken up by the occasional, much less impressive return shot from me.

* * *

Oh yeah, speaking of hard surfaces, I managed to shake off the impact I had just taken and clear my thoughts. I must have only been dazed for a moment or two because I happily noticed my head was still attached to the rest of my body. Lucky me, as I looked up just in time to see Samuel's still blazing form leap across the room toward my prone self.

Just for the record, things like that may work in the movies. Hell, they still look pretty damn cool even in real life. From a practical standpoint, though, they're kind of dumb to try. I mean, I'm not exactly a Navy Seal, and even I know that while in mid-air not only are you obviously telegraphing where you're headed, but it's a bit hard to change tactics in case your intended target decides to take countermeasures.

And I was certainly going to be using said countermeasures, especially since I wasn't entirely endeared with the concept of being crushed beneath two-hundred and seventy pounds of burning vampire love. I managed to pull up my knees and get my legs underneath him as he landed on me. I kicked out and sent him back in the direction he had come from. He may not have flown as far as I had from his hit, but fly he did.

This was it. No more bullshit. No more one-liners (*sadly*). I needed to end this if I wanted to have any chance of living to brag about it. Besides, I could always make up some cool shit after the fact. I mean it's not like someone was videotaping this...hopefully.

I grabbed another beam from the rubble and started toward where Samuel had fallen. Amazingly, he was getting up again. He wasn't looking too good, what with being poisoned by silver and on fire, but he still got back to his feet. I just hoped he was out of it enough for us not to repeat ourselves. I wasn't sure I could take another hit from him without my head popping clean off.

We stared at each other across about ten feet of space. He staggered but managed to stay upright. He balled his fists defensively, and I raised my stake in return. A heartbeat passed, or it would have if either of us still had one. We locked eyes and prepared for the final charge. I couldn't help but think there should have been some Ennio Morricone music playing in the background, like in *The Good, the Bad, and the Ugly*, but sadly there's never a soundtrack when you need one.

I made my move first. I launched myself at him, and he...*exploded in a cloud of flame and dust*? What the fuck? I hadn't even touched him yet. The least he could have done was wait until *after* I staked him to do that.

I was just beginning to wonder what had happened when the smoke from his explosion thinned out, and it all became crystal clear to me. Standing directly behind where Samuel had been just a moment before was Sally, her own broken two-by-four still in hand.

"What the hell?" I stammered.

"Typically, this is the point where you would say *thank you*," she replied, smug grin etched onto her pretty face.

"I had him!" I insisted.

"Oh? Like you *had him* right before he punted your ass for a field goal?"

"You saw that?"

"Oh, I did better than that." She pulled a *Flip* camcorder from her pocket and waved it at me. Bitch!

"And you didn't help *why?*"

"I was curious to see if you'd get back up," she answered with an even voice. "Just for the record, I was actually impressed that you did."

"I'm flattered, I'm sure," I said dryly.

"Oh, don't be such a grouch. I'll give you full credit...*again*. Of course, we'll both know the truth," she said with another little shake of the camera. "By the way, is it me, or is this starting to become a habit between us?"

"I didn't need your help this time."

"Oh, really?" she countered. She bent and started rooting through Samuel's ashes. "Then why was I the one who finished him off?"

"That was a cheap shot."

"Exactly!" she replied, picking a few things out of his remains. "Thus proving my tactical brilliance compared to you both." She finished by tossing my roommate's purloined silverware back to me. "Nice fork, by the way."

Not Exactly a UN Summit

"ALL IN ALL, that went almost exactly as planned," Sally cheerfully explained as we walked back to the main meeting room where the altercation had begun. The sounds of battle could still be heard in the building, but it seemed like things were winding down.

"Whose plan, exactly?" I asked. "*My* plan was to come here, hash out a truce with Samuel, and then go home. Last I checked, *my* plan didn't include spending the last hour trying to keep him from rearranging my face."

She shook her head and replied, "Sorry to break it to you, but there's no way your little cease fire would have worked."

"It might have if you hadn't decided to bring every psycho in the coven along."

"Like I said, all according to plan," she pointed out in a tone one might've used on a particularly dimwitted child. "We killed two birds with one stone here. With Samuel gone, the rest of his gang won't want to be within ten miles of us. As for our own side of things, I'm pretty sure we managed to purge some of the less pleasant elements of our own group. That's what we like to call a win-win."

She had a point...maybe, at least minus the excessive mass murder part of it. Still, I was pretty pissed off.

"You could have told me," I growled as we entered the now deserted meeting room.

"You wouldn't have gone along with it."

"Exactly."

"Hence why I didn't tell you. Duh!" She rolled her eyes at me.

Occasionally I wished I was just a little more evil. If so, I'd have been almost tempted to make sure there was one more casualty added to the day.

* * *

We straightened up the room a little bit while Sally coached me on what to say. Once we had gotten the table and chairs set up again, she said, "Okay, you can call them all back now."

"How? This whole building is a battle zone. There's no way they'll hear me."

"Send it out as a compulsion."

"And that will do *what*, exactly? I can't control any of these vampires. They're all older than me, or have your forgotten?"

"God, you are dense sometimes," she said with a sigh. "This has nothing to do with controlling them. If you send it out as a compulsion, every vamp in the building will hear it."

"Oh. Okay, then." Yeah, I guess that made sense. Every compulsion I had ever heard (*for lack of a better term*) had been up close and personal. But since there was a psychic element to it that probably meant it could carry further than the sound of the voice making it.

"Alright, so do it then."

I went to open my mouth, then hesitated. After a couple seconds of Sally staring quizzically at me, I smiled sheepishly back at her.

As expected, her response was another eye roll. "Don't tell me you don't know how to compel. You were supposed to be practicing these things."

"I know," I stammered. "But since I haven't met any vamps I could potentially control yet...I kind of figured...what was the point?"

"And yet somehow you're still alive while a two-century old master vampire is now a pile of dust. You must have a small regiment of guardian angels looking out for you."

"No shit. I need at least half of them to protect me from you."

"Flattery will get you nowhere," she replied. "Oh well, if you want something done...*THIS BATTLE IS OVER. SAMUEL HAS FALLEN!!*"

It wasn't the loudest compulsion I'd ever heard (*or felt*), but it was apparently loud enough. The faint sounds of vampires beating the snot out of each other stopped almost immediately. As planned, I positioned myself at the head of the table, with Sally standing behind me as my subordinate. I put an expression of calm determination onto my face as best I could, which was saying something since turning my back on her was about the furthest thing I could think of to give myself a state of calm.

One by one, the various combatants began to filter back into the former meeting room. I said nothing. I merely gestured to the seats as each vampire arrived, waiting for the last of the survivors. It supposedly projected an aura of smug superiority regarding my victory, not to mention it also kept me from having to repeat myself over and over again. That was a good thing, as it lessened the chances of me saying something stupid that would just start the battle up all over again.

When a few minutes had passed since the last vampire returned, I took stock of the survivors. There was no mistaking which way the tide of battle had been turning. No matter the bloodlust some of my coven members might have been feeling, there were conspicuously less survivors on my side of things than on Samuel's. That shouldn't have surprised anyone. Jeff, the former master of Village Coven, tended to pick new members based on their looks and overall frat boy mentality. The HBC vamps, on the other hand, looked more like they had been recruited based on how many faces they had smashed in during their mortal life. If further *negotiations* went badly, it would be in our best interest to get the fuck out of Dodge as quickly as possible.

However, that possibility was still a major *if*. If I played my part well enough, there might be no need for that. Yeah, I know...another *if*.

As the last of the survivors took their seats, I reached into my pocket and pulled out the *souvenirs* Sally had dug from Samuel's ashes. I tossed his fangs out onto the table as one might toss a pair of dice in a craps game. They tumbled end over end before stopping near the far edge. I glanced around and noticed all eyes were locked on them. The expressions around the table were all nearly identical, regardless of coven allegiance...abject disbelief. I expected this from the HBC vamps – but jeez, it would have been nice if even a few of my own ranks had a little faith in me. Assholes, each and every last one of them.

Oh well, this speech wasn't going to make itself. Thus, I got things started again once the silence in the room became almost oppressive. "Who is Samuel's second?" I asked in a neutral tone.

There was no immediate answer; instead, the various HBC survivors looked back and forth at each other, confusion evident on their faces. Sally had told me to expect as much. A vampire as old, relatively speaking, as Samuel tended to run a coven with an iron fist. A succession plan or even basic hierarchy was probably the furthest thing from his mind on a day-to-day basis. If that were the case, there would be confusion enough to distract these vampires as they sorted things out amongst themselves. It was sort of like the cartoons I used to watch as a kid. If *GI Joe* shot down *Cobra Commander*, they'd still have *Destro* and the *Baroness* to worry about. On the other hand, if *He-Man* ever took out *Skeletor*, the forces of evil would be pretty well fucked, as the rest of them were a bunch of numbnuts. We were pinning our hopes that Samuel was the Skeletor of his bunch.

"I am Samuel's second!" one of the HBC vamps cried.

"The fuck you are!" another vampire immediately spat. Almost as if on cue, the rest of Samuel's group started arguing amongst themselves. I couldn't have planned it better had I tried.

The survivors of my own coven looked to me as if seeking direction. It was about fucking time. If they had bothered to do that at the beginning of things, we'd have a lot less dead vampires to vacuum up.

Oh well, there would be plenty of time to chew them out later. I motioned with my hand in a stay calm gesture, or what I hoped they interpreted as such. Fortunately, they did. Being on the losing side of a real life game of *Mortal Kombat* tends to have a sobering effect, even on a bunch of vicious nocturnal predators.

I continued to let the HBC members argue amongst themselves for a few more moments. I knew they wouldn't even come close to any conclusions in that time, but it made things seem more convincing. Finally, I raised my voice above them all. "ENOUGH!" It wasn't a compulsion, but it got their attention. Being the dude who just tossed your boss's remains in front of you tends to make one rate a few notches higher on the *people to pay attention to* scale.

Once the table had again quieted down, I resumed. "Your internal politics are not my concern. Figure it out on your own time. What I care to know is whether any of you wish to continue Samuel's quarrel with my people?" Yeah, that was total bullshit. Everyone here knew that the HBC's grudge was against me and me alone; however, as coven leader, my fight was the entire group's fight. Even I had to admit this job had a few perks.

When nobody answered, I locked eyes with the closest of Samuel's team. In as cold and dead of a voice as I could muster, I asked, "Do you still want to fight?" After a second or two of the stare-down, he slowly shook his head. I then went down the line, asking the same thing to each and every HBC vamp in the room. Now *this* part I wish someone taped because, damn, I bet it looked badass. I felt like Don fucking Corleone, I tell you.

When I had reached the last one – and received the exact same answer from him as the rest – I said, "Regardless of whichever of you is now in charge, it appears that this coven war is over. We shall go back to where we were before and respect each other's members and territory. Agreed?" When there was silence around the table for a bit too long, I repeated myself with a little more (*empty*) threat in my voice. "Agreed!?"

This time, there were nods all around the table from HBC and Village Coven vamps alike. "Very well. It is done. Only one final business remains. In accordance with the laws of our people, as the victor of this battle I may set forth further terms of my choosing."

There were a lot of ugly looks around the table at that. Sally had told me of this little clause in vampire turf wars, with perhaps a little too much eager glee in her voice. I could use this time to do something like expand our own territory, demand that the Howard Beach Coven cede some of their membership numbers to us, or any such thing so as to further weaken them. No wonder she hadn't wanted a successful treaty. Little miss hot pants behind me had herself some ambition.

I'd have to deal with that later. For now, every eye in the room was upon me. "The terms are ... this safe house is pretty trashed. Clean this place the fuck up, okay, guys?"

There was an audible gasp of relief from the HBC vamps, as well as a sharp intake of breath behind me that my sensitive vampire ears picked up on. I could feel Sally's eyes boring holes in the back of my head. Heh! Fuck you, bitch. This'd teach her to remember that I wasn't her little boy toy to screw with as she pleased. Well, okay, maybe that was a poor way to phrase it. Sally had looks that would make her seem right at home on the cover of *Cosmo*. If she and the phrase 'screw with me as she pleased' ever came up, who was I to argue?

* * *

The *peace* conference adjourned, and the HBC members left to return to their territory. I likewise ordered my contingent back to Manhattan. There had been enough misadventure for one night, and dawn was only a few hours away anyway. While most of what people think they know about vampires is total bullshit, the whole *catch on fire under the rays of the sun* thing was pretty much spot on. A few minutes of sunshine was enough to turn even the strongest of bloodsuckers into something you could pick up with a dustpan.

Once the others finally left, I relaxed in my seat and let out a huge sigh of relief. Now that the action was over and the prying eyes were off me, all of my bravado evaporated. I was once again just Bill Ryder, an online game programmer who still had no idea how he wound up neck deep in a pool of vampire shit.

"So are you really that dumb, or did you just let them off the hook as a big *fuck you* to me?" said a voice from over my shoulder, jarring me out of my reverie. It was Sally. Somehow I knew she hadn't left with the others. She was one of the few vampires who knew the real me, not the pseudo-scary '*Dr. Death*' persona I tried to make everyone else believe in. On the one hand, it was nice to have her around. I didn't have to pretend to be anyone else with her...and she wasn't exactly hard on the eyes either, as I believe I've already mentioned. Any comfortable feeling, however, was tempered by the fact that Sally was a sarcastic bitch with an attitude problem that could have spanned the Verrazano Bridge and beyond.

"Maybe a little of both," I quipped without bothering to turn around.

"Fair enough. I probably deserved it. Although you threw away a perfectly good opportunity to increase our leverage in the vampire community."

"*Our* leverage?"

"Well, you are our fearless leader," she purred, putting a little playfulness into her voice. Heh, times like that were when I trusted her least. At least you knew where you stood when she was in full-blown bitch mode. "I just keep the books in line."

"That you do."

"You're pissed, aren't you?"

"Oddly enough, no," I answered truthfully. "Don't get me wrong, I should be. Your little game almost got me killed, and you definitely got a lot of other people dusted tonight."

"Nobody who'll really be missed."

"That's beside the point. We're supposed to be partners in crime here, but it usually turns out I'm the partner while you're the one committing all the crimes."

I could hear the grin in her voice as she replied, "You've probably got me there. I suppose it wouldn't kill me to keep you in the loop a little more."

"That would be nice."

"But still, you're really not pissed?"

"No," I replied. "That's the crazy part. No matter what bullshit exploded in my face in the past few hours, I don't feel anything but relief. I'm here in the middle of a murder scene that would give the NYPD a conniption, but the only thing I can think is that this is the first time in months that I don't feel like someone is standing behind me holding a stake."

"Eh hem." Sally cleared her throat.

Sure enough, I turned around in my chair, and she was standing there holding a splintered off two-by-four.

"Et tu, Brute'?" I asked.

"Sorry." She tossed it aside. "I was holding onto it in case the premises weren't entirely clear."

"Allow me to rephrase myself," I continued. "This is the first time in months I don't feel like someone is going to try to kill me every five minutes – or are you going to pull out a shotgun and ruin that one, too?"

"Left it in my other dress."

"I thought the strip club wasn't letting you leave your laundry there anymore."

She ignored the quip and asked, "So how are you going to celebrate your newfound lease on life?"

"I'm thinking maybe a few weeks off from the vampire lifestyle. That is, if you think you can hold the fort down."

"No problem," she replied in an innocent tone. "What kind of trouble could I possibly get into?"

I probably shouldn't have, but I was tired and my defenses were down. Thus, I couldn't help but laugh.

Dating Habits of the Undead

BEFORE I WAS allowed to go on my infernal vacation of the damned, Sally wanted me to pop by *the office* the next night to take care of some paperwork. The office was a few blocks from the loft in SoHo where I had been turned and had originally associated with our coven's goings on. What can I say, you die horribly in a place, and you get a little nostalgic for it; however, the loft was ultimately little more than a hangout. The coven had space in lots of buildings in the surrounding area, not to mention the nooks and crannies below street level. One such space was an entire floor of an office building close to NYU. During Jeff's reign as coven head, the space mostly went unused. A few vamps might have squatted in it during the day, and some used it as a larder for the occasional wayward college student they caught, but that was it.

Under my leadership, that had all changed. Yeah yeah, it was mostly Sally, but I had to nod and agree to most of it...emphasis on *most*. Whatever kudos I had given her for the organizational improvements put into place were completely wiped out by one of the slimier operations she had started for the coven. It creeped the utter shit out of me. Unfortunately, considering the alternatives, it was the lesser of evils...although it was still pretty fucking evil. I didn't even like to think about it.

I passed by that section as quickly as I could, trying really hard to make 'la la la I can't hear you' noises as I did. Sally had, of course, set herself up in a comfy corner office from which to supposedly oversee the coven's paperwork. Yeah, okay, whatever she liked to call it; however, even a blind man could see she enjoyed playing queen bee. I normally wouldn't have cared, but despite my status as coven master, I didn't seem to have an executive suite here with my nameplate on it. Still, considering the business going on just a few yards away, maybe that wasn't a bad thing. I lost enough sleep over it as it was.

I approached Sally's office and saw a familiar face seated outside of it. "Hey, Starlight, what's up?" I asked as I approached. "How the hell did Sally sucker you into playing secretary for her?"

She looked up, flashed me a nervous smile, then quickly averted her eyes. "It's no problem, Bill. I don't mind helping," she answered with a little quiver to her voice.

Starlight's real name was Alice. She had been given her nickname by Jeff as part of the ridiculous pseudonym campaign that he enforced for all vampires in the coven. That rule was the first thing I'd tossed out the window, but a lot of the coven had decided to keep their 'code names' regardless. Starlight was one of them.

She was a stacked...well, Nubian goddess is probably the best term for it. She had been working on a career as a model before being turned. Despite the fact that she appeared younger than my twenty-five years, I knew she was almost twice my age. She also wasn't the sharpest tool in our shed; however, despite an outer veneer of vampire attitude, she seemed to be one of the few amongst us who genuinely cared about her coven-mates. As a result, she was also one of the few that I genuinely liked. Unfortunately, due to the outer guise I had to keep up, she was also completely scared shitless of me. I kind of felt bad about it, but not nearly bad enough to let it slip that a lot of my bravado was bullshit. The rest of the coven could smell weakness like a school of sharks. I had little doubt they'd turn on me if they suspected that I wasn't nearly the badass I tried to pretend to be.

I also had little doubt that Sally had used Starlight's fear of me to manipulate her into her current situation, but there wasn't much I could do to fix things right at that moment. Or maybe there was...

"I have business with Sally," I said with a sneer. "Go take a coffee break...a *long* one." I gave her a glare with my fangs bared, and that was all she needed to vacate the premises. As I watched Starlight run off, I heard Sally's door creak open behind me, followed by her annoyed exhale. Thanks to her vampire hearing, she no doubt knew what had happened. Heh!

"You know, I should report you for harassing my employees," she said in a dry voice from behind me.

"Take it up with the labor board." I turned toward her. "You can always hire a temp."

"True enough," she answered, showing me a smile full of fangs. "Besides, if they don't work out...well, the severance plan is a killer."

* * *

We spent the next hour or so going over various coven related business. Sally had the final tally of casualties from the fight with the HBC. Eight of our vampires were dusted. All of them were assholes, so I'd be shedding minimal tears on their behalf. She wanted to start recruiting new members immediately, but I put the kibosh on that until I got back. Since there were rituals involved with indoctrinating new members that I, as coven head, had to oversee (*stupid college-like rituals...but rituals the same*), this was one area I was confident that she wouldn't immediately set about doing the opposite of what I said.

We were finally starting to wrap up (*Ye gods, even the dead can't escape from bureaucratic red tape!*). When we were just about finished, I asked, "So what should we tell the others?"

"About what?"

"About me," I clarified.

"That you're a dumpy, four-eyed, piss-poor excuse for a vampire," she said with that sickeningly sweet smile of hers.

"About my vacation."

"Oh, that? I don't think there'll be much problem there. Word of your victory over Samuel is already starting to spread throughout the membership."

"Let me guess: you're helping that along, right?"

She smiled in response. "Well, I *was* the only witness, after all. Needless to say, I doubt too many of the coven are going to be bugging you about your personal business. Just in case they do, though, we can fall back onto some of the typical Freewill bullshit we've used before. I was thinking, if it comes down to it maybe your animalistic urges got the better of you. I could always say I was busy trying to track your feral ass down for a couple of weeks."

I thought about it for a second. "That'll work."

"Just be sure to muddy yourself up a bit before you come back."

"No prob," I replied. "We done here?"

"Almost," Sally cooed. Uh oh. "I was going to give you an update on the hotline."

I stood up, almost knocking the chair over. "I told you! I don't want to know about the hotline."

"You *need* to know about the hotline. Without the hotline, we'd be back to where we were. You were the one who forbade us from trolling the raves or luring in the uglies."

I had (*tried to*) put an end to both practices in the coven. Both groups were easy prey. The first were mostly underage, which definitely didn't sit well with me. As for the second group, that was a particular pet peeve of mine as that was how I had wound up a vampire in the first place. In years past, every few weeks the males and females of the coven would take turns on a particularly reprehensible practice. The coven members mostly consisted of people who looked like they just stepped out of an *Old Navy* commercial. They would use their sexuality to easily sway the less...err...*physically confident* into following them back to the coven lair, where they would be turned into late night snacks.

As I knew she would, Sally next reminded me of the consequences of my attempts at de-psychoing our merry little band. "Even with the assholes the HBC took care of, there's still a lot of pent up bloodlust in the coven. It's either the hotline, or you're going to have a major body count on your hands." It was a common argument from her, and one that she knew I couldn't refute.

The hotline had been all Sally's idea, but as coven head I had to pretend I'd given it my blessing. The funny thing was, since the whole idea was so insanely evil at its core, it had actually enhanced my reputation in the coven. It's a good thing I didn't need nearly as much sleep as I used to because I sure as hell wound up losing a lot of it over this.

Sally had used coven funds to purchase several 1-800 and 900 numbers. Between sundown and sunrise, coven volunteers manned the phones of what was becoming a fairly well-trafficked suicide prevention hotline. The ground rules were disturbingly simple. It was pretty much Vegas casino odds, basically a 70/30 payout. Most of the people who called would actually be given help either through talking them through their troubles or outright giving them a minor compulsion over the phone (*vampires can compel humans...just not as easily as they can other vamps*). The rest...well, as Sally put it, they were the sad statistics of the world.

I had enough sway to insist that kids were off limits. Fortunately, there were no real arguments there from anyone. Adult bodies held more blood anyway. As for the rest...generally speaking, the coven went after two types via the hotline: The first were those who were genuinely going to do it anyway, regardless of intervention. The others were your basic attention whores, those types you read about standing on the edge of a bridge, snarling up traffic for three hours with constant cries of "I'm gonna do it!" until such time as they didn't. Truth be told, this latter group didn't bother me quite as much. There were enough assholes in the city as it were. Still, this was creepy ass business, and some days I would wrack my brain trying to come up with something better. I mean, think about it: there you are depressed and thinking dark thoughts. You call up a place to discuss your problems, only for it to turn out that the voice at the other end was just sizing you up as a hors d'oeuvre. Not cool.

Sure, there was always bottled blood as a substitute. That worked for some of us. Unfortunately, a good chunk of the coven considered themselves to be active predators. They were actually blood snobs and didn't like anything that wasn't still warm and fresh. Psycho assholes! I either had to appease that need or try to stake each and every one of them. I didn't particularly favor my odds of doing the latter, thus I had to accept that part of being a vampire meant that there was a lot of shit I was going to have to toughen myself up about.

I shook my head to clear it. I had to deal with it because Sally wasn't going to let me go until I did. "Fine. How's the hotline doing?" I asked through clenched teeth.

"It's doing great!" she replied with a chipper little voice. I could tell part of it was genuine enthusiasm. Sally had benefited greatly from Jeff's demise. Upon his death, she had been pretty much instantly promoted from sex toy and part-time secretary to second in command of the coven. Behind the scenes, her position was even more powerful. I could tell she absolutely loved every minute of it. Unfortunately, I knew the other part of her cheerfulness came from knowing how uncomfortable the hotline made me. Sally derived way too much amusement from doing little things that she knew annoyed the ever not-living shit out of me.

"We got a mention in an editorial in the Post," she continued. "And guess what else?"

"What?"

"We got approved as a nonprofit. That means government grants and a huge fucking tax break at the end of the year."

"How do you sleep at night?" I sighed disgustedly.

She just kept right on beaming as she replied, "On a comfy bed, and usually next to guys much better looking than you."

* * *

On the way back home, I had at least one bright spot about the hotline to think about: Tom. I had kept both of my roommates up to date on the goings on in the vampire world, despite the fact that I wasn't supposed to. They were two of my best friends, and I used them as sounding boards·when I needed to bitch about things. Besides which, they really loved the fact that there was an actual supernatural underworld that they were amongst the few humans to know about. With regards to the hotline, Ed had been as disgusted as I. Tom's response was more practical. He made it a point to crank call them every opportunity he got. It was mostly stupid shit, but he had made one or two that would have been *Jerky Boys* worthy. I knew it pissed off Sally, even if she didn't mention it; however, there was absolutely nothing she could do. I had given specific orders amongst the coven that my friends and family were on the *do not eat* list. Considering that all the vampires in a twenty-mile radius thought I now had *two* master vampire dustings under my belt, I was fairly confident of not being crossed on that one. Tom could fuck with them to his heart's content, and he had my undying approval to do so.

Unfortunately, my blessings to crank away had to wait. I got back to my apartment in Bay Ridge,

Brooklyn, and found only my other roomie, Ed, at home.

"How'd it go?" he greeted me, momentarily diverting his attention from the TV.

"About like you'd expect," I answered. "Doesn't matter, though. I'm officially off the clock for a few weeks."

"Cool. So what are you gonna do now that you're not Dr. Death?" he replied, bringing up my old coven pseudonym. Despite my having abolished the 'superhero name rule', as I liked to think of it, my roommates still used it to refer to the persona I had to keep up around the others. The funny thing was that I did, too. In my mind, Dr. Death was the dark beast inside of me who took care of the nasty business and wasn't one to fuck with. It was all crap, of course, but sometimes it helped me think through things.

"For starters, I think I'll be happy to sit back and not worry about monsters trying to kill me or vice versa."

"Sounds like a plan," he said dismissively, turning back to his show.

"Tom out?" I asked, sitting down on the opposite side of the couch. *Iron Chef* was on. I could dig that.

"Yep. He actually has himself a date."

"Really?" I asked with some surprise in my voice. "They decide to let farm animals back into the city?"

That elicited a chuckle from Ed. He wasn't the most emotional person on the planet, but he could always appreciate a good dig.

"No, with an actual girl," he replied. "Yeah, I know, surprised the hell out of me, too. Some chick he met at work."

That could be interesting. Tom was a low level gopher on Wall Street with aspirations of brown-nosing his way up the corporate ladder. According to him, most of the people who worked there fell into two categories: the work hard, play hard types that mostly had a nervous breakdown by the age of forty, and the boring-as-all-fuck crowd, AKA the types who got into finance for the sheer *thrill* of managing budgets. So if Tom was dating a girl from work, that meant he was either tied up in some S&M dungeon getting his brains fucked right out of his head or they were sitting down somewhere discussing the finer points of well-constructed spreadsheets. Knowing Tom's luck with women, which was only marginally better than my own, I hoped his *Excel* skills were up to the task.

"Oh, yeah, your dad left a message for you," Ed said, changing the subject.

"What'd he say?"

"Do I look like your hot ass little secretary?"

"Sally's not my secretary. You know that."

"Yeah, from the sound of things, it's more like you're *her* secretary."

"Sometimes, I'm not so sure I'd disagree." I got up to listen to whatever it was my parents had to say.

"She does have a hot ass, though."

"Not arguing that point in the least," I answered, hitting play and then going to the fridge to grab myself a pint of blood.

Truth be told, I should have probably been a little more interested when my parents called me. Several months back, I had been given the scare of a lifetime when Jeff claimed to have kidnapped my mother. It had all been a misunderstanding...mostly because he was little more than a complete idiot, but it had still scared the crap out of me at the time. For a while there, I had tried to be a lot closer to my mom and dad. Jeff's scheme had given me a new appreciation for them; however, time tends to make us forget these things. By now, we were more or less back to our typical relationship, consisting of the occasional call and me more or less yessing them to death when they asked me questions about my life. I listened to the message and deleted it. I'd text Dad later to let him know it was cool.

"What's up with your folks?" Ed asked as I returned to my seat.

"They're heading to A.C. for the weekend to piss away my inheritance." I started sipping on my blood. "Their neighbors are away, so they have nobody to watch the cats."

Ed gave an amused sniff in return. "Cat sitting, huh? You vampires get all the cool gigs."

"Tell me about it. Hey, you wanna head down with me? Dad bought a sixty-inch plasma TV a while back, full HD. Got a pretty sweet sound system to go with it."

"He really *is* pissing away your inheritance."

"Yep, so I might as well get some use out of it. I figure we can throw on a few movies, maybe smoke a few blunts..."

"A few?" Ed asked skeptically.

He had a point there. Due to my vampire physiology, things like that tended to have less of an effect on me than they did normal humans. One of my roommates' more pleasant experiments had involved such. Based on our *extensive* testing, we estimated it took roughly three to four times the amount of alcohol (*or other substance*) to get me as shitfaced as it normally would. If I ever sat down to have a drinking contest with Marion from *Raiders of the Lost Ark*, I'd win...probably. The effects also tended not to last as long either. In short, when it came to better living through chemistry, I was no lightweight. The downside, though, was that it wasn't exactly friendly on the old wallet, unless I consigned myself to a night of drinking caseloads of shit beer. All things considered, I'd probably rather be staked.

"Tempting, but I might have some shit to do on Saturday," he continued. "Maybe I'll pop by on Sunday if there's anything left of you."

"Your loss."

"So what about the rest of the week?"

"Oh yeah," I answered as realization dawned. "Maybe I should have put in for a vacation from work."

Ed just sighed and shook his head. "Dude, we work from home and pretty much set our own hours. Every day is a vacation."

"There is some logic to your words. Still, it's probably too late to put in for some time off anyway. I think Jim's out of the office this week."

Jim was our boss over at Hopskotchgames.com. I was one of their lead game programmers, responsible for my fair share of hits, if I do say so myself. Ed worked as a graphic designer there, creating both in-game art as well as promotional materials. While it wasn't making either of us overly rich, it was a good place to work. Normally, the game industry is a kill-or-be-killed field, full of nonstop death marches topped off by layoffs so that the bigwigs don't have to pay out end-of-project bonuses; however, our company was pretty cool. As long as projects were finished and the money kept flowing in from users, they had a pretty laid back attitude. Give it a few years, and I'm sure they'd get big enough to adopt a corporate asshole atmosphere, but for now I enjoyed it.

Even better was that I was technically considered a permanent tele-worker.

Since a vampire and sunlight do not a wonderful pair make, after I was turned I had gotten my physician friend, Dave, to give me some bullshit excuse of a doctor's note to give to my company. I had traded my services as a guinea pig to him to do so, but so far he hadn't taken much advantage of that outside of some minor tissue samples. Thanks to him, I had been working from home for the past six months, and...and it suddenly hit me, as it always did...and that meant it had been six months since I had seen *her*.

As always, whenever I thought of her, my stomach clenched up and I felt a little light headed. I had hoped that perhaps a state of *out of sight, out of mind* would take over and make it easier for me; it hadn't. Love stinks, especially when the other person isn't aware of it. I thought about it for a few more seconds, feeling my good mood start to fade as I did; however, then I realized that perhaps now was finally the time to do something about it.

"Maybe I'll go in for a day this week," I said casually.

"Where?"

"Work, obviously."

"You do realize that there's this little thing called the sun in the sky during the day? You do remember what that does to you, right?"

"I know, *Dad*," I answered sarcastically. "It'll be okay. I can cover up, and Dave gave me this medical grade sunscreen to try out."

"It's a stupid risk," Ed rightfully pointed out.

"I know, but this is the perfect week to do it. With Jim out, nobody'll be around to give me any shit about my *condition*."

"Yeah, that's fine and all, but you don't have any reason to..." Recognition dawned in his eyes. He sighed and said, "Dude, she doesn't even know you're alive."

"Who?" I asked innocently.

"Don't act like a bigger fucking idiot than you already are. You're going to risk evaporating in the daylight just so you can see some chick you can barely work up the guts to say hi to."

"Sheila is not *some chick*," I said, more defensively than I really should have. "She's...special."

"Please tell me you did not just say that? You've said maybe ten words to the girl in the past three years."

"It doesn't matter. You don't need words to know these things. You just know."

"Much like you apparently know all about insanity?" Ed asked, an edge working its way into his voice.

"What I know is that if I have a soul mate in this world, it's her."

He made a gagging noise, and then replied, "Vampires don't have souls."

"Neither do mediocre graphic designers," I shot back.

"Probably true," he conceded. "But that doesn't change the point. You've been acting like a high school freshman around this girl for years, making all sorts of goo-goo eyes and shit at her. She hasn't responded. Time to move on."

"I'm going to finally do it," I said.

"Move on?"

"No. Ask her out."

"I'll believe it when I see your wedding invitations."

"I'm serious. Besides, you actually have a point."

"About what?"

"About it being time to move on," I said. "You're right. It's time to shit or get off the pot. I'm going to ask her out. If she says yes, then it was meant to be. If she says no..."

"You'll come home and cry yourself to sleep for the next month?"

"Probably," I admitted. "But when I'm finished doing that, I'll move on with my life."

"Like I said," he replied. "I'll believe it when I see it."

I just shook my head and sighed. "Dude, have a little faith. I've faced off against the very worst the underworld can throw at me. Asking out one girl isn't going to be an issue."

* * *

Okay, so I lied. Three days later, I finally entered the lobby of the building where Hopskotchgames resided. I'd like to say I had things to do that kept me busy, but let's not bullshit each other here. It took me until then to work up the guts to follow through with my plan. God, I am such a wuss. But that didn't matter. I was finally there. It was time to be a man.

First things first, though. I ran to one of the restrooms on the first floor. After hyperventilating for a few minutes, I peeled off the hoodie, gloves, and sunglasses I was wearing. I also washed off most of the sunscreen I had applied. No point in showing up in front of the girl of my dreams looking all greasy and smelling like rotten coconuts. Afterwards, I looked myself over in the mirror. Thank god the whole vampire reflection thing was complete bullshit! If I had even the slightest doubt that I maybe had a blemish, hair out of place, or, god forbid, a booger hanging out of my nose, the whole deal would be off before it even began.

Everything passed inspection. I looked good, or as good as I was going to get, and my breath didn't stink (*I had munched a whole tin of Altoids on the way over*). This was it. It was now or never.

I rode the elevator up to the twentieth floor, one of the two floors my company occupied. Mindful to be as discrete as possible, as I was, for all intents and purposes, technically considered *disabled*, I used my company badge to let myself in through the side entrance. I walked down a hallway past the sea of cubes, the clicking noises of many keyboards filling the air. At last it was in sight, Jim's office. Seated at a desk just outside of it was his assistant, Sheila...the girl who owned my heart, non-beating as it were.

She was slim, about five-five, with shoulder length dirty blonde hair. She had the most unusual eyes, almost a grey in color. They kind of looked like the sky on a cloudy day. Okay, enough of that. Too many of those thoughts, and I'd probably be writing shitty goth poetry next thing I knew. Anyway, suffice it to say that, to my eyes, she was truly something to behold. Hers was a different kind of beauty than Sally's. Whereas Sally would have looked at home on the cover of *Vogue*, *Playboy*...or even *Skank* magazine, Sheila was more of the girl next door type. She never would have passed as a fashion model, but she had a warm, inviting smile that said she was approachable in a "Hi, I'm really glad to see you" sort of way, as opposed to the "Please stick a twenty down my G-string" type of look I had gotten used to from my coven-mates. I tried to summon a little of my Dr. Death persona as I approached, minus of course the claws, fangs, or anything else that might scream undead demon from Hell.

It didn't work. Dr. Death was taking his vacation from the coven very seriously, it would seem. Bastard! I could feel my resolve slowly starting to crumble in the wake of her presence. My steps slowed, my knees started shaking, and that's when she looked up.

"Bill? Is that you?" she asked. Holy shit! She *did* know my name. Thank you, God!

"Hey, Sheila. Long time no see." Argh! Why did I have to sound like such a fucking douche-nozzle?

"Yeah. We haven't seen you in months. I had heard you were sick."

"Oh, not sick so much as I have a bit of a condition," I stammered. "I'm getting treatment. I actually feel pretty good today."

"I'm glad to hear it." A friendly smile spread across her face. "You look good."

"YOU LOOK LIKE A GODDESS!" I wanted to scream, but instead just replied, "Thanks...um, you too." At least I sorta managed to sputter a compliment with that last one.

"So what brings you here?" she asked, her smile still making me melt from the inside out. I wonder if getting staked felt like that...nah, probably not.

Hold on! What *was* I doing here? Motherfucker! I had spent so much time working my way up to the actual getting here part that I hadn't bothered to come up with a single simple reason to actually *be* in the office. Unfortunately, "professing my love to you," wasn't really an answer that I felt like giving out quite yet. Goddamn it! Think, stupid.

So I said the first thing that popped into my mind. "I'm here to pick up my paycheck."

"On a Thursday?" (*Shit!*)

"Well..."

"I thought you were on direct deposit." (*Fuck Fuck Fuckity Fuck!*)

"Sorry, I didn't mean *pick up* my paycheck. I needed...to...change a few things on my W2." (*that was better. The engines were reigniting. Maybe I could pull out of this death-spin.*)

"Oh. Did you get married?" (*Mayday! Mayday!*)

"NO!" I said, way too emphatically. "Nothing like that. Still single. Yep, just another eligible bachelor in the city. That's me." (*God, I want to die! Seriously, please let Sally or some other vampire be sneaking up behind me with a stake to put me out of my misery*)

"Oh," she said, looking a little confused. This was not going how I had planned. Well, okay, my plan had more or less consisted of walking coolly through the hall and her flinging herself into my arms at first sight. What? I never claimed my plan was realistic.

"I think HR usually takes care of that stuff," she finished.

"Oh, I know that. I just wanted to pop by. Check out the old homestead. You know. Say hi and all that." (*not to mention, stand around and stammer like a retard*)

"Well, I'm glad you did. It's good to see you again," she replied with that same smile. I could stare it all day. Although I had a feeling I had better not do so for more than a few seconds; otherwise, I might end the day staring at the much less friendly smiles of building security.

Hold on just one second! What an idiot I am. She just gave me an opening.

Time to man up, pussy! suddenly screamed my Dr. Death persona from somewhere deep in my subconscious. It's about time he woke up. Yeah. I could do this. It was now or never.

"I'm happy to see you again, too. Speaking of which, Sheila, I wanted to ask you a..." *RING*

"Sorry. I better get that," she said, going back into work mode and picking up the phone. Why now!? Does fate hate me so much? Don't bother answering. It was a rhetorical question.

She listened to someone speaking on the other end for a moment or two. Please let it be a wrong number. Maybe it was just some dickhead vendor making a cold call. Anyone who she could quickly get rid of before...

"It's the VP of Marketing. I should take this. Good seeing you, though," she whispered quietly to me before returning to the call.

Too late. The moment was over. I could feel whatever bravado I had spent nearly four years building up drain away in an instant. Damn you, Marketing VP! Damn you to hell! It was even worse because I knew the guy was an asshole. His name was Harry Decker. He joined the company a short while after I contracted my *condition*. I hadn't met him in person, but had been on enough teleconferences with him to know that he was useless in all areas except kissing the CEO's ass. Note to self: sic the coven on that fucker.

It didn't matter, though. I was finished. Rather than stand there and let fate continue to shit on me with the force of a thousand pigeons, I slunk away while she was still on the phone. I let myself out and got back onto the elevator. Once the doors closed and I was alone, I did the only thing I could think of...I banged my head repeatedly against the wall. I deserved it.

I looked up...okay, I didn't deserve it *that* much. Crap! Sometimes I forget the whole vampiric strength thing. There was a very visible dent in the wall of the elevator that hadn't been there a few moments ago. I quickly tossed on my daytime cover-ups so I could make a quick escape once I was back at the ground floor. I didn't need a repair bill from building maintenance to add to my shame.

* * *

Despite a nagging urge to rip off all my clothes and running screaming into the sunlight, I didn't. I managed to make it back to my apartment no worse for the wear, physically at least. Unfortunately, my pain was just beginning. Ed was in the living room waiting for me when I walked in.

"How'd it go?" he asked.

"Don't want to talk about it," I said, walking toward my bedroom / office.

"She shot you down?" Even from behind me, I could feel the grin on his face as he asked it.

"Don't want to talk about it," I repeated.

"You didn't even ask her did you?"

"You know." I spun around to face him, baring my fangs in the process, "it might not always be a good idea to piss off the *scary-ass vampire* you're living with."

"So scary he can't even ask one girl out on a date?" he asked, his grin going into full shit-eating mode.

Goddamn, I hate when he's right. My anger deflated, and I walked back to slump down onto the couch.

"You know what your mistake was?" Ed asked, sitting down next to me.

"Being born?"

"No. That was your parents' mistake. *Your* mistake was that you forgot one important rule: you *never ever* try to confess your feelings without first fortifying yourself. You should have stopped in a pub on the way for a little liquid courage, if you know what I mean."

I looked up and met his gaze squarely. "I'm fairly sure women aren't entirely impressed by guys who profess their undying love while reeking of Jack Daniels."

"I didn't say to bathe in it. I'm just saying a shot or two to calm the nerves...maybe three or four in your case."

I chuckled slightly at that. "Maybe you're right, oh wise one. At any rate, I probably couldn't have fucked it up any worse than I did."

"Fortunately for you, it's not too late," he said.

"I'm pretty sure I screwed up asking her out."

"Oh, it's too late for *that*. I meant it's not too late for some liquid fortification. You, my friend, need a drink, several of them in fact. Who knows, maybe I'll even buy one or two for you," he said, walking over to get his jacket. "And when you're finished, you're going to go to your parents' house this weekend and do it again until you are so shitfaced you don't even remember your own name. You kill off enough brain cells, and you won't be able to help feeling better about things."

Sage advice, if ever there was any.

Here, Kitty Kitty

NOTE TO SELF: don't listen to Ed's advice. Traffic was surprisingly light for a Sunday night. I was sitting in the passenger seat of Ed's two-seater piece-of-shit, watching the miles slide by. My roommate was behind the wheel. We were heading south on Route 287 toward the Outerbridge Crossing. He had been good enough to come down and give me a ride back home, which kind of made sense as it had been his counsel that had given me cause to want to flee back to the relative safety of Brooklyn. Nevertheless, I was glad for the ride. It had turned out to be a long weekend, and I was in no mood to deal with the idiocies of mass transit to get back home.

Since it was early Fall, there was no Jersey Shore traffic to contend with. Even so, considering it was only about six PM, traffic was pretty light heading toward Staten Island. Oh well, it was that lull that tends to happen around late September / early October. People were still burnt out from the summer, and the holiday rush was a good month or so off. This was one of those rare times when people just stayed put. In short, the asshole ratio on the roads was low. I liked times like this. Sadly, they were too few and far between as of late.

We had been listening to some rock music on the radio, or at least what the DJ was calling rock music. There were very few real rock stations left in Jersey. Most played either classic rock, which was mostly tolerable, or a combination of lousy ballads and pop rock (*which had just enough guitar riffs to be outside of the Justin Bieber demographic...barely*). We had been discussing how real kick-ass rock music was such a rare commodity when my cell rang.

I had been expecting it. I picked it up and answered with a "Hello."

"William, is there something you would like to tell me?" asked the voice of my Dad.

Uh oh. That wasn't a good sign. If he was calling me William, it meant he had noticed the little *mistake* I had left behind from my weekend of house sitting.

I decided to do what I did best, play dumb. "Nope. It was a quiet weekend, Dad."

"I'm sure it was," he replied in a tone that said he didn't even remotely believe me. "Your mother and I appreciate you coming down and keeping an eye on the place while we were at the beach." The *beach* in this case being some of the many casinos down in Atlantic City.

"No problem, Dad! Anyway, well I gotta..."

"Hold it!" commanded the voice on the other end. "I guess I won't beat around the bush. What the hell did you do to Angel?" At the mention of the name of

59

her favorite cat, I could hear my mother in the background. She started wailing and carrying on. It pretty much sounded like she was in the middle of a major freak-out. Not too surprising, all things considered.

"Mom sounds kind of upset."

"I noticed," my father said, sarcasm oozing out of his voice. "Do you want to know why?" he asked, despite the fact that I had a pretty good idea and he most likely knew it.

"Why?" I asked innocently.

"Because right now she's vacuuming up a pile of Angel dust."

"Angel dust? You know, she should hold on to that. I hear the street value's off the charts if it's the good stuff."

"I'm not laughing, William."

"Sorry, sir," I automatically replied, despite being an adult, having a job, living on my own, and...oh yeah...being a freaking vampire. "What happened?" I asked, genuinely curious. After all, I wasn't *entirely* sure how things had played out...especially since I'd made it a point to bug out before my parents got home, even going so far as donning a hoodie, sunglasses, and ski mask so as to brave the daylight without bursting into flames. It probably wasn't the manliest way I could have handled the situation, but I've always thought there's a fine line between bravery and idiocy. Sticking around would have definitely crossed that line.

"When we got home, your mother noticed the cat was acting a little strange," my father explained. "It was hissing and carrying on."

I again adopted an innocent tone. "They're cats. They go loopy every now and then."

"Don't be stupid. You know Angel," he chided. "You could step on the stupid cat's...sorry, dear...head, and she wouldn't bat a whisker. But not today. When we got home, she was going absolutely nuts. And there was something wrong with her eyes. They had gone all black like a shark's. That definitely was *not* normal."

"Distemper?" I unhelpfully offered.

"Not unless it was the most extreme case of distemper there's ever been," Dad continued. "Your mom was a mess. Made me go get the cat carrier so we could rush her to the vet." Oh boy, I think I knew where this was going. "I had the damnedest time getting her in it, too. Little bitch kept going after me."

"She didn't bite you, did she?" I hadn't considered that. I wasn't even sure she could pass it back to humans, but it was a risk I wasn't really willing to take...at least not with my parents.

"No, but she came damn close. I had to put on some work gloves to finally get her in. Then it got weird." (*Yeah, I bet it did*)

"I'm listening."

"Your mom got in the car, but I had left my wallet in the house. I sat the cat carrier out on the walk and went back inside to grab it, and then..."

"In the sun?" I asked, already knowing the answer.

61

"What?"

"Did you leave the carrier in the sun?" I repeated.

"I don't know. I guess so. What does it matter?" he asked irritably. "All I know is that one minute it's quiet, and the next I hear your mother carrying on like a mad woman. I ran back outside, and do you know what I found? The cat carrier was on fire. I'm not just talking a few sparks either. It was like someone doused it with rocket fuel."

I was definitely starting to get a sinking feeling in my stomach.

Dad continued with his gruesome tale. "By the time I got the hose, though, the fire was already out. The damnedest thing was the cat. I was expecting her to be all burnt up, but there was nothing left. She was completely vaporized. All that was left was a pile of ashes with her collar sticking out of it."

"Wow. That's...bizarre," I said, severely understating the whole thing.

"Yes, bizarre is one word for it. So that's why I want to know whether or not anything odd happened this weekend while you were around."

"No idea," I lied. "Like I said, Dad, it was a slow weekend. Barely saw the cat. She kept to herself. Other than that, not much going on...hello, Dad? Dad? I'm losing you. We're heading into a tunnel. I'll call..." and then I disconnected the call as I had no idea what else to say.

Ed and I drove on for a mile or so, and then he said, "I know I only caught part of that conversation..."

"I don't want to talk about it."

He ignored me anyway. "But was that about what I think it was?"

I sighed and decided I might as well confess. It was going to be a long drive otherwise. "My mom's cat, Angel..."

"Yes?"

"I kinda, might have..."

"Yes?"

"Turned her into a vampire," I finished.

"YOU WHAT!?" he yelled, just barely managing to keep the car from swerving off the road.

"Turned it into a vampire."

"Why?"

"It was an accident."

"How was it an accident?"

"Well, as you had suggested, I got pretty wrecked this weekend," I said with a guilty grin.

"And how does that lead to an immortal demon cat?"

"Well, like I said, I was pretty messed up. I guess when vampires get the munchies they don't automatically go for the nachos like everyone else."

"That's fucked up, man."

"I know."

"It's your *mom's* cat!"

"*Was* my mom's cat, anyway."

"I mean, I don't even like cats," he continued, "and I still think that's fucked."

"Yes, I get it. I didn't mean to vampirize the damn cat. It just kind of happened."

"Is that even a word?"

"It is *now*," I snapped. "And then when she woke up from it..."

"I'm listening."

"I guess I kind of fooled myself into thinking that maybe I had dreamt it all."

"I take it from your dad's call that you were wrong on that front."

"Definitely not a dream."

"Fucked up," he repeated.

We drove on again in silence for a few minutes until I heard Ed chortle. I turned to see him grinning and trying...and failing...to suppress laughter.

"What's so funny?" I asked.

"I was just thinking..."

"Yeah?"

"There is a bright side," he said.

"Do tell."

"When we get home, you at least get to tell Tom about how you got to eat some pussy this weekend," he said, finally cracking up laughing.

"Not funny," I said, but it was a lie. Put that way, it was actually pretty goddamned hilarious. I soon joined my roommate. We laughed for a good long while until my phone rang again.

"Oh shit," I said, tears still pouring down my face.

"Time to get back on the clock, my man," Ed commented.

He was right. I couldn't put this off. I just hoped I could think of something to tell my parents that sounded more convincing than, "Sorry for vampirizing your cat, Mom and Dad." I picked up the phone and answered it.

"Listen. Tell Mom I'm sorry about her cat."

"Tell her your damn self," replied Sally's voice from the other end. "I'm not your goddamned answering service."

"What?" I blurted out. "What are you doing on the line, Sally?"

"Oh, I don't know. I was lonely, what with you on *vacation* and all, and thought maybe I'd give you a buzz so you could talk dirty to me. But I'm afraid I have to draw the line at letting you call me mommy...or daddy, for that matter," she quipped.

"I can think of a few other words for you."

"I'm sure you can, but think of them while you're packing. Vacation's over," she replied.

"What?"

"You heard me," she sniffed in an impatient tone.

"Why am I packing?"

"Because that's what people do when they take a trip, unless they plan on traveling naked, and if that's your plan then please let me know so I can make sure I never have the same itinerary as you."

"Hold on. What trip?"

"The one you're taking," she said as if speaking to a moron.

"Why don't we start over, and you tell me what's going on?"

"I thought you'd never ask," she said in that annoyingly chipper tone she adopted whenever she knew she was pissing me off. "You're going to China."

"What!? Why the hell would I be going to China?"

"James's orders. He called and requested your presence."

"Why?"

"Beats me. You can ask him that in person in about two days."

"I don't even have a passport," I protested.

"Wow, that's kind of sad," she said. "Not surprising, mind you, just sad. Fortunately, you don't need one."

"Why wouldn't I need a passport to get into China?" I asked. "Pretty sure they check those things there."

"Because it's a long flight, and since commercial airlines tend to have rules against their passengers going up in smoke when sunlight hits them, I made some alternate arrangements."

"Define *alternate arrangements*."

"You, my friend," she replied, putting even more chipperness into her voice, "have been booked into a first class coffin in the cargo hold."

"WHAT!?" I screamed into the phone.

"You're welcome. By the way, you might want to pack a pillow." *click*

Bitch!

A Sandwich with a Side of Chips

I'M SURE THERE are some powers-that-be somewhere who had a good laugh at the irony. There I was looking for a vacation away from the coven, and I wound getting a vacation alright...all the way to fucking China. Why? No idea. If Sally knew, she wasn't very forthcoming, and it's not like I had James's cell phone number. Speaking of which, travel aside, the thought of running into James again produced some mixed feelings in me.

While I wasn't exactly sure of his true age, I was led to believe that he was in the neighborhood of six-hundred plus years old. Supposedly, he had been a contemporary of Marco Polo himself. That wasn't one-hundred percent relevant. What was, though, was that James was in charge of all vampire related business in the Northeast United States. All of the covens in that area, mine included, were answerable to him. He, in turn, answered directly to the Draculas, the coven of the thirteen most powerful vampires from whom all of our rules supposedly descended. I say supposedly because, aside from James, I had never met another vampire who'd ever met directly with these Draculas. Still, it was probably wise not to make too many waves with regards to them. Why? I had seen James in action.

I am told that as vampires age, their powers increase as well. James was living proof of that. When he wanted to, he could move almost faster than the eye could follow. Strength-wise, I had once seen him literally tear apart a small group of gang-bangers in less time than it takes for most of us to order a burrito at Taco Bell. I wasn't too proud to admit that he scared the bejeesus out of me. All of the Draculas, though, were older than him, some supposedly quite a bit. Therefore, it stood to reason that if a run-in with James could ruin one's day, crossing the Draculas could seriously fuck your shit up.

All that taken into consideration, I still owed the guy. If it weren't for him, my tenure as a vampire would have lasted all of five minutes. He was the one responsible for giving me a chance. He was also the one responsible for jumpstarting my reputation amongst my fellow vamps, which went a long way toward getting me to where I was now. Sure, he had also been the one to put the HBC vamps on my ass, but I was willing to believe that had all just been a case of bad timing. Before he could cool down any heat between our covens, he had been called away by the Draculas. They had sent him all the way to China, where I was now destined to follow, for whatever reason.

Speaking of China, there were mixed emotions there as well. The good being that seven thousand miles between myself and the disgust I felt at my inability to speak my mind with Sheila sounded pretty decent to me. I seriously doubted anything in the Gansu province of China would give me cause to dwell too much on her. Unfortunately, everything else fell into the bad category. The trip was a twenty-plus-hour nightmare of transfers, starting at LaGuardia (*or as I like to think of it, Satan's airport*) and ending in Beijing. However, I needn't have worried about being stuck in the middle row between two fatties or next to a screaming kid for the entire trip. No, because I was luggage.

* * *

Did I say luggage? No, luggage would be too kind. After a whirlwind packing job, including making sure my iPod was charged (*no way was I flying in the cargo hold for almost an entire day without some tunes*), I managed to convince Ed to give me a late night drop-off. This did not put him into a good mood. If you've ever driven to LaGuardia, you know what I mean. It's like the state of New York purposely decided to make one of their major transportation hubs as big of a clusterfuck as humanly possible. It was only after lots of twists, turns, and exit-only lanes, that we finally managed to crawl through traffic to our destination. Things were bad enough, and we're talking eleven PM here. I could only imagine the insanity of doing it at rush hour.

As per Sally's instructions, Ed dropped me off at a small private terminal. He gave me an annoyed growl as way of saying goodbye before driving off. The windows of the building were opaque, although whether this was purposeful or just layers of grime, I couldn't tell. The doors were also locked from the inside. I stood there looking confused for about ten minutes – getting ready to pull my cell phone out and call Sally – when finally I heard a click. The doors opened. Beyond them was a figure silhouetted by the light inside. It beckoned me forward. Creepy, but then again, I *am* a vampire. Creepiness kind of goes hand in hand with my life these days. I tried to conceal my nervousness and walked in, thoughts of all the various slasher flicks I had ever seen going through my mind.

I needn't have worried. Vampire society isn't much different than ours once you get past the 'blood-sucking eternal creatures of the night' aspect of it. Sure, they liked to put forth a mysterious atmosphere, but I think that was just to impress the newbs. Once you got past all that, it was surprisingly mundane. Case in point, once I entered the building, it became obvious that this was just another private terminal – small, spartan, and efficient. Once my eyes had adjusted to the light, I saw that my mysterious beckoning figure was another vampire, a rather bored looking one at that. He was wearing business casual and holding a clipboard.

As I entered, he said in a completely disinterested tone, "Close the door behind you and give me your paperwork." Right there and then, any creep factor dropped to zero. I was just dealing with the undead equivalent of boarding check-in. I handed him the forms Sally had emailed over to me. He took a quick look and called back over his shoulder, "I need a box, a big one!"

A few minutes later, a couple of shambling figures carried out what looked to be an oversized shipping crate. It was about seven feet long by three feet wide, and maybe four deep. The creatures carrying the crate were zombies. I had met some several months back. Apparently, they were the equivalent of general office staff to the vampires. Hmm, I wondered if they have a union. That wouldn't surprise me in the least.

Anyway, the zombies placed the crate on the floor. One of them procured a crowbar, which he used to pry the lid open. The top off, I could see the box was empty, save for some straw padding at the bottom and some black felt lining the inside – no doubt to keep the sunlight out. Looking into it, I got a distinctly sinking feeling.

"Okay, get in," said the bored vampire.

"In there?"

"You see any other box here?"

"I thought I was supposed to be traveling in a coffin." Either way, I wasn't exactly going to be traveling in style, but I was expecting a little better than this.

"Coffin, crate, what's the difference? You'll fit, and since you're flying freight, the accommodations don't need to be fancy."

"Freight?" I asked, not quite believing what I had been told.

"FedEx, to be exact. They'll be loading you up in the next hour or so. We still gotta put all the export forms onto this thing, so we don't have time for too much dicking around here. Hop on in."

"It's a box!"

"You want luxury? Next time, go first class, cheapskate."

That fucking bitch! She was mailing me to China. She was goddamned lucky that I had no interest in pissing off James. If not for that, I'd be grabbing a cab back to the loft and sticking *her* ass in a box.

"You waiting for an engraved invitation?" the vampire attendant asked impatiently.

"No, I'm going." I sighed and climbed in, trying my best to find a comfortable position to lie down in. "Just make sure my bags don't get lost."

"Won't be a problem," he started tossing them in with me. I didn't pack heavy, but still. What had merely been an uncomfortable fit was now a *tight* uncomfortable fit.

"What the fuck, man!?" I cried in outrage.

"Sorry. Your papers specify one and only one box. Take it or leave it."

Sadly, that last part wasn't really an option. Before I could say another word, the zombies placed the lid back onto the crate, and began nailing it shut.

There was a knock on the top of my makeshift tomb, and I could hear the attendant say, "Whatever you do, don't try to get out until they open it up. Once you're in China, a truck will take you to your destination, and your contacts will release you. If you try to get out beforehand...well, let's just say the Chinese can be a little trigger happy."

Great! "What if I have to go to the bathroom?" I yelled back.

"Heh! I hope for your sake you didn't drink anything before getting here."

* * *

My iPod made it about three quarters of the way through the flight before finally crapping out – not that I had much of a chance to relax and enjoy the music. The loading process was brutal in and of itself. I must have been dropped at least three times. As for the flight, aside from some brief layovers to refuel, it was a real motherfucker. The pilot was either a daredevil or an idiot, as he seemed to make it a point to head straight into whatever turbulence he could find. Even had I not been afraid of flying before, I sure as shit was afterwards. When my music finally died, I did the only thing I could think of to pass the time...mentally kill Sally over and over again. By the time we landed and I could feel my box being unceremoniously loaded onto a truck, I had come up with some pretty ingenious scenarios for her untimely demise. Ultimately, though, I kept coming back to using a wood chipper to do it. There's nothing like the classics.

The truck ride took another eternity, during which I had to assume we were either moving along unpaved roads or the driver had a serious fetish for potholes. Straw or no straw, all I knew was that my entire backside was full of splinters. I was just about to start hoping that one of them would eventually be long and sharp enough to pierce my heart when the truck finally stopped at long last.

I could feel my temporary tomb being lifted up and then dumped onto the ground. Jesus Christ! Was it too much to ask for somebody to tape a fucking '*Fragile: do not drop*' sticker onto me?

What followed was some muffled conversation. I couldn't make it out. No surprise there. I was in China after all...or at least I hoped I was. It would be just my luck to have been delivered to the wrong place. There could be some poor schmuck in Alberta, Canada, thinking he was about to unpack his new end table, when whoops...sorry, but we shipped you a pissed off vampire by mistake.

The muffled conversation started to sound like a minor argument for a few minutes; however, it finally abated, and I could hear the truck start up again and drive off. I patiently waited for what would happen next, hoping against hope that there wasn't a '*Do not open until X-mas*' sign on my new home.

For the first time in over twenty-four hours, though, luck was with me (*don't ever ask me about the whole needing to go to the bathroom thing!*). I heard the top of the crate being pried off. I just hoped that it wasn't high noon outside. The top began to move, and I could see bright light starting to stream in. Oh shit! As it was lifted off, I gave a yell of panic and reached up to shield my face with my arms.

A second or two passed, and I finally noticed I wasn't going up like wood shavings doused in gasoline. I slowly lowered my arms and realized the light was artificial. As my eyes adjusted, I made out the face of James, as well as a few others looking in at me. Most of the new faces looked bemused, no doubt at my little panic attack; however, James's expression was a bit more perplexed.

"Dr. Death?" he asked with his Bostonian accent, using my old coven name. "What are you doing here?" Despite his apparent confusion, he reached down and offered me a hand. I took it, as being wedged into a tiny box for over a day doesn't exactly leave one all that limber.

As I slowly peeled myself from my wooden prison, I replied, "You sent for me. I'm here."

"No. I didn't."

"Yeah. Sally told me you did. I just spent the last day wedged into that thing because I thought it was an emergency."

"Why didn't you just book a private charter, like we normally do?" he asked.

"That was an option?" I started to feel a different kind of smoldering going on behind my eyes.

"Of course. This isn't the eighteen-hundreds you know. We only do that vampire in a casket thing on short hops or emergencies. Ghastly way to travel."

"Yes, it is," I agreed dryly. "Let's back up for a second. You didn't send for me?"

"Why would I? I shot Sally a message asking you to contact me, but I was expecting a call or maybe an email. Certainly not you arriving all gift wrapped like this."

"But she said..."

"She must have heard incorrectly," he replied dismissively. Somehow I doubted that. "Oh well, I guess you can stay for a bit. But there's dangerous work afoot here. I'm afraid no more than a day or so, and you'll have to head back."

"Please tell me you're not stuffing me back into the box."

"Of course not. As long as you have your passport, it shouldn't be an issue." I was silent for a moment, and then averted my eyes. "You didn't bring your passport, did you?" I quickly shook my head. He chuckled, and then patted the top of my packing crate. "Well then, I'm afraid we'll probably need to hold on to this." He then turned to the others and said something I couldn't understand, probably in Chinese. A round of hearty laughter followed.

"I assume that was at my expense."

"Sorry, my friend," he replied with a smile. "But things have been fairly stressful here. I'm afraid we take our laughs when we can get them."

Speaking of here, I finally took a moment to look around. I was in what appeared to be a large circular tent. It was mostly bare except for some other crates off to the side. Apparently, this place was for storage. James was dressed warmly in what I guessed was native garb.

His three companions, all males of distinctly Asian origin, were dressed similarly.

"Care to introduce me to your friends, James?" I asked. He raised an eyebrow at that. "I abolished that rule months ago," I explained. "I didn't think you went by *Ozymandias* anywhere else."

"Oh, yes. I heard you had overthrown Night Razor. Congratulations on that, by the way. Oh well, I suppose you're right. James it is. However, I hope you don't mind if I keep calling you Dr. Death. I know it's hokey, but after a while I found myself growing used to it."

"Knock yourself out."

"Excellent," he replied, and then turned to his companions. "May I introduce you to Nergui, Bang, and Cheng-gong." I tried not to smirk at that second one. I bet he was a real hit with the ladies.

The one called Nergui turned to me and bowed. "It is an honor to meet you, Freewill Dr. Death."

"Thanks! Nice to meet you, too," I answered.

James then said, "Nergui is the only one who speaks any English. So I'm afraid you won't get much conversation out of the other two. Unless, that is, your Mandarin is up to snuff."

"I'm lucky to speak English," I replied, nodding in the direction of the other two.

"Well, why don't you wait here for a bit, and we'll see what we can do for lodgings for the night."

"Sounds good as long as you can point me toward the nearest bathroom first."

* * *

James gave me instructions to wait where I was, and then left with the two non-English speakers, leaving me with Nergui. He said it was in case I had any questions, but I had the feeling it was to keep an eye on me and make sure I didn't wander off. He needn't have worried too much. I wasn't quite up for any major exploring. Being a native of New Jersey and a current resident of Brooklyn, anything below the rating of *suburban* was more or less alien to me. I had no intention of walking around the wrong tree and winding up hopelessly lost.

In the meantime, I slowly made a circuit of the tent and tried to engage Nergui in small talk.

"So...how long have you been here?" I asked. Yeah, it was lame, but sue me. It's not often I find myself stuck in a tent in deepest darkest China, talking to what I presumed was a Mongolian vampire.

"It has been my honor to serve the Khan for these past three and a half centuries," he replied in a neutral voice. Okay, so I was dealing with another heavy hitter here. If James wanted me to stay put, there was no way I was getting away from this guy.

"That's Ogedai Khan, right?"

"We do not address him by his proper name here. He is simply the Khan," Nergui said with that same tone. I wasn't getting much of a read off this guy. Hopefully, I wasn't going to say anything to insult him. I'd hate for my first outdoor view of China to be of myself getting bashed against a rock.

"Sorry. Not trying to be insulting. I'm just curious," I said, trying to covering my ass. Nergui simply nodded at that. "Is he really the son of Genghis Khan?"

"Indeed. The Khan is the chosen son of the great Temüjin. He keeps his spirit of conquest alive in our hearts, if perhaps not in our actions."

"That is so freaking cool!"

"Explain this 'freaking cool' you speak of," he said, again without a trace of emotion. Damn, this guy could teach Ed a thing or two. He was stone cold. Of course, maybe I shouldn't have jumped to conclusions. It could just be that I was a stranger and he was speaking in a non-native language.

"It's a phrase from my country. It means it's really great to know, I guess. I mean, it's not every day you get to talk about a person straight out of the history books in the present tense." Yeah, I was rambling.

Nergui again just nodded. "You are young, Freewill. In time, these things will become common for you."

"I guess it's safe to assume you know all about this whole freewill thing."

"Many do. It has been a long time since one such as you has been seen. Our seers have spent much time trying to divine what it means."

"I don't think too much of it," I said dismissively. "I think it was just luck of the draw. I got turned, and it just happened to be a coincidence."

"No such thing," he said with an air of finality. I decided not to argue with him for obvious reasons. Time to change the topic of discussion.

"So, Nergui, right? What do you do for the Khan?"

"I am one of his assassins." Nope, forget what I said earlier about jumping to conclusions. This guy was hardcore.

"So that must be an...interesting job."

"It is what I am." Gah! This small talk thing was quickly fizzling out. Maybe it was time to do some minor wandering after all. At the rate this conversation was going, we were going to just wind up glaring at each other in silence. All things considered, I figured that was one of Nergui's specialties; however, it most certainly wasn't one of mine.

I walked over to the opening of the tent. "Is it okay if I step outside?" Figured it was safer to ask than to just try it and wind up with this guy tackling me and putting me into a chokehold.

Nergui again nodded. Damn, that was getting maddening. Not quite on the same level as Sally's eye rolls, mind you, but annoying nevertheless.

I stepped outside of the tent. I could hear quiet shuffling behind me that said Nergui had followed. No doubt about it, James had him keeping an eye on me. The question was why?

Ah, screw it – enough with the paranoia. This was the first real foreign country I had visited in in years. It was time to get a look at the place. Interestingly enough, the first thing that caught my attention was the sky. I had never seen the stars or the moon so crisp and bright. Hell, in Brooklyn you were lucky you could see the sky at all on some nights. The sight was pretty breathtaking. So this was what it was like to live in a place that wasn't constantly lit up by halogen lamps and neon. This was something you wanted to share with someone special...

Bad thought, as my mind immediately went back to *her*. Grrrr! Even thousands of miles away, my inability to ask a single simple question to her haunted me. All right, that was enough of the sky. It was depressing me now.

The area immediately around me was populated with more round tents similar to the one I had emerged from. I'm sure I learned their name somewhere in either history class or the Travel Channel, but for the life of me couldn't remember what they were called. All I remembered was that they were apparently a popular Bedouin type of dwelling. Wherever I was, this was neither a large nor permanent settlement.

I took a few more steps to get a better look. The area we were in was somewhat reminiscent of the time I had gone out to Vegas, or more specifically, the parts of the Mojave I had seen. The immediate vicinity was sparse but broken up by the occasional vegetation. To one side (*East, West, or whatever...I didn't have a compass on me*) the desert stretched as far as the eye could see. Normally in the dark, this wouldn't be very far at all; however, darkness isn't an issue for vampires. With the exception that all of the colors were heavily desaturated, I could see every bit as well as if it were broad daylight.

On the far side of the village, if you could call it that, were several large rocky outcroppings that led up to some more hilly terrain. I started wandering over to them. The whole thing was pretty damn cool now that I thought about it. Here I was in some nomadic village out in the middle of nowhere. It was like I had stepped out of my life and into the middle of an *Indiana Jones* movie...and not that lousy crystal skull one either.

I was so caught up in the fantasy of it all that I hadn't noticed that I wandered outside the edge of the settlement. I was standing close to one of the large rock formations, thinking about maybe being adventurous and attempting to scale it, when I heard a *thud* noise to my left.

I took a look around. Considering how barren the terrain was, it wasn't too hard to find what I thought to be the source. There was a large rock, nearly the size of my head, lying in the dirt no more than ten feet away from me. Maybe it had rolled down from one of the larger boulders – although, if that had happened, I probably would have heard it. The way this had sounded was if it had just dropped from the sky. Oh well. I'm sure these things were common out here. It'd take a little more than some loose rocks to scare off this city boy. I mean it's not like...*thud*

What the hell? I turned back, and there was another rock, similar in size to the first, on the ground where I had just been standing a few moments ago. If that thing had hit me, it could have shattered my skull like a chicken egg. One fallen rock was something, but two was getting a bit odd. I turned my eyes up toward the nearby hills and took a look around, scanning the area. Nope, nothing out of the...what the...

I could have sworn I had seen movement out of the corner of my eye, like something dark had just ducked out of sight.

Okay, I was probably just creeping myself out. It was time to get a grip and relax...and of course, that was when something grabbed my arm.

* * *

Let's face facts: you knew it was Nergui all along, didn't you? Well, I didn't. So I shrieked like a little girl when I felt his big, meaty fist fall onto my shoulder. The cry was cut short, though, as his other hand quickly came around and covered my mouth.

"It is not safe out here. Return with me," he said into my ear.

I tried to save whatever grace I had left, which wasn't much. I pulled out of his grip and hissed, "Jeez, dude! Did you have to sneak up on me?"

"I did not sneak. If you did not notice, then perhaps the fault lies with you," he said, and then turned back toward the ring of tents.

Grrrr! Damn him and his ninja logic.

I caught up to him, lest I stand there acting all pissy and wind up getting my brains bashed in by another of the magical raining rocks of Mongolia. "So why isn't it safe?" I asked.

"Because it is not." (*Oh Jesus Christ!*)

"Care to elaborate?"

"You are in the Wanderer's charge. If he wishes for you to know more, then he shall be the one to tell you."

"The wanderer?"

"The one you call James."

"Oh. Dude has a lot of names."

"Indeed he does," Nergui agreed.

"So where did the Wanderer wander off to?"

"The Khan is close by. He is the Wanderer's sire. Since your arrival was not expected, he is surely telling our master of the news."

"I guess that makes sense." I knew that there was some shit going down in this place. That was why James had been called away to begin with. It made sense that whenever anything happened outside of the norm, like say a packing crate full of yours truly showing up on the doorstep, that the guy in charge would need to be notified. "So is the Khan here?"

"The Khan would not dirty his steps in an unworthy place such as this."

"Oh, of course not," I replied, hoping my sarcasm didn't cross the gulf between our cultures. I got the feeling that insulting the Khan around these guys would fly about as well as pissing on a picture of Queen Elizabeth in front of the guards outside of Buckingham Palace...maybe even less so considering that most vampires I had met seemed to think that violence was a dandy solution to almost all of life's problems.

"The Khan's ger-tereg is five kilometers hence," Nergui said, pointing out toward the desert.

"Okey-doke," I answered, having absolutely no fucking idea what he was talking about. Whatever the case, though, I assumed it meant that the Khan and his entourage were a ways down the road...or sand. I mentally did the conversion in my head. Silly backwater countries and their metric system! Oh well, that would put them about three miles away. Having seen James move; however, I knew that he could probably traverse that distance in mere minutes if he so chose.

* * *

It turned out I was right. Nergui and I made it back to the supply tent, and within fifteen minutes, James and his two minions, for lack of a better term, returned. If they were out of breath from their six-mile round trip, they didn't show it.

"I'm glad to see you stayed put. Amazing how few people know how to follow instructions these days," he said as he entered.

"That's me. Mr. stay where the fuck I'm told to," I replied. If Nergui wanted to tell James otherwise, then that would be his business.

"Well, Dr. Death, you should be flattered to know a great honor has been bestowed upon you."

"Let me guess. You guys are giving me my own pet camel?"

James wisely ignored my idiocy and continued as if I hadn't spoken. "The Khan is intrigued by your presence. He wishes to meet with the Freewill."

"Cool."

James sighed at my reaction. "You have no idea how big of a deal this is, do you?"

"Not even remotely."

"The Khan is one of the *Draculas*. They are our ruling elite. They do not just grant audiences to anybody. In fact, they never speak to children...and before you say anything, yes you *are* a child, to us anyway. It's almost unheard of for the Draculas to deal with any of our kind under a century in age." He saw that I still had a fairly nonplussed look on my face. "This is kind of like the Pope just up and giving you a call to see if you wanted to do lunch."

"Oh. That makes sense then," I said, putting more enthusiasm into my voice. I still didn't care all that much, but decided I had better act like it before I started insulting a bunch of creatures with over a millennia of combined experience amongst them. "Let's get going."

"No." James stepped in front of me. "The day will be breaking in a few hours. You will meet with him tomorrow. For now, you will be his honored guest, given all the hospitality that is his to offer." When I didn't reply, James gave me a wink. "Trust me, you're going to like this part."

* * *

Since James told me they needed some time to properly prepare my lodgings, we chatted some more. I brought him up to speed on the goings on in the coven, starting with my defeat of Jeff. "You killed him yourself?" he asked dubiously. I knew he had spoken to

Sally. No doubt he'd been briefed on what really happened.

"Well, I may have had a little help," I admitted.

I then spent about an hour going over the last six months, culminating with the final fight between Village Coven and the HBC, more specifically between myself and Samuel.

"I had been meaning to apologize for all of that," James said once I had finished. "I meant to give you a little reputation boost amongst your own, not bring a full scale coven war down on your head."

"It was a bit touch and go there for a while, but since it all worked out in the end, apology accepted," I replied, which was more or less true. I had bitched enough to Sally over the past several months about the whole situation to drive her half insane (*assuming she wasn't already there*), thus I more or less had it out of my system. Besides, I preferred to stay in James's good graces.

Finally, just about when I could see the sky outside beginning to lighten ever so slightly, another vampire entered our tent and whispered something into James's ear.

"Excellent. You're all set," he said. "Monkhbat here," he gestured toward the guy who had just entered, "will carry your bags and show you to your tent."

"Are we heading over to where the Khan is?" I asked, not really looking forward to a three-mile hike.

"That's tonight. For now, you've been set up here, just across the way. I'll pop by after sundown to retrieve you. I know it may prove to be difficult, but do try to get at least a little rest." He said that last part with a wry smile.

I just gave him a confused glance as I followed my porter out of the tent and toward my destination. I was actually looking forward to some rest and relaxation. Despite spending a full day horizontal in my packing crate, I had gotten zero sleep. It wasn't exactly the most comfortable thing on the planet, and this is coming from a guy who has passed out on his fair share of floors.

We walked to the other side of the settlement. Monkhbat put my bags just outside of the door, or flap or whatever you call it, of a mid-sized tent and bowed to me before walking off. Guess I had to put my shit away myself. Fine, see if I tip the help here. Oh well. I was thinking it was time for some well-deserved shut-eye when I walked in and immediately stopped dead in my tracks.

The tent was *not* empty.

Oh boy, was it not empty.

In the center was a large pile of rugs and pillows. On top of that pile sat three attractive females. Three very *naked* attractive females. As I stood there gaping like a complete moron, they all giggled. A moment later, they got up, almost as one, and walked over to me. They removed my bags from my hands and led my still very much in shock self back to the center of the tent. Now, these were people who knew what hospitality was all about.

A Test? I Didn't Even Study!

IT WAS OFFICIAL. The Khan was by far my favorite vampire in the world. Holy shit! Forget about threesomes. Skipping all the way to foursomes is *definitely* the way to go. Not only do you have enough to make yourself a sandwich, but you get an order of chips on the side as well. If I lived to be ten-thousand, this was still going to be one of those days I bragged about. Even better, when all the *happiness* was over, they got me bathed, cleaned up, and dressed for my grand appearance with the Khan. Note to self: next time Sally tries to stuff me into a box headed for some godforsaken corner of the earth, go willingly.

As promised, shortly after sunset James appeared at the entrance of my tent. I excused myself from my little personal harem (*hmm, wonder if I should have gotten their names first...oh well*) and went out to meet him.

"I trust your day was *sunny*," he said with a bemused grin.

"Dude, these people know how to party," I replied, barely able to contain my giddiness. "I am definitely giving this resort five stars on expedia.com."

"Excellent to hear. Now if we could just..."

"I mean I don't know about you," I continued, still rambling, "but I had all kinds of freaky sex going on today."

James put up a hand. "Far too much information, thank you very much. Now if you're done gushing, you have a very important person awaiting you."

"Lead the way, my friend." I put a little swagger into my step. "Oh, and next time you need me to join you anywhere, you just say the word."

"I'll keep that in mind," he answered dryly. Before I could say anything else, he set off at a brisk pace across the compound.

"So what's the plan?" I asked as we walked.

"Very simple. We meet with the Khan, enjoy whatever festivities he has planned, and then ship you back out of here."

"Ship me out?"

James nodded. "Yes. As I told you, it's dangerous here right now. Freewill or not, you're too inexperienced to play in this league yet. Right before sunrise, another truck is coming here to take you back to where you belong. Don't worry, though; I asked my men to throw a few rugs into the crate so you're a little more comfortable on the return trip."

"Any chance of packing one of those girls in with me?"

"Alas, you'll just have to live with your memories." Oh well, fortunately I had a good memory...not to mention, a very good imagination.

We crossed the settlement in a matter of minutes. We arrived at our destination to find Nergui and James's two other companions waiting for us. They were all mounted on horseback with two additional steeds standing by. James quickly jumped up and got onto the saddle of one of them.

"I thought we were running there," I said.

"Normally, yes," he replied. "However, in times like this there are certain traditions to respect. The Mongols are expert horsemen."

"Yeah, but I'm not. I haven't even been on a pony ride since I was three."

"I'll show you what to do. Just follow my lead," he said patiently.

What followed was more or less the comedy of errors you would expect. I managed to get into the saddle on my first try. Being a vampire definitely has its perks from the physical side of things; however, the three mile trek to the Khan's settlement took several times longer than it probably should have. Bang and Cheng-gong (*get it on, bang a gong!*) thought the entire thing was hilarious. James and Nergui, on the other hand, traded glances that ranged from embarrassment to outright disgust. Finally, lest we spend all night wandering aimlessly due to my inability to control a stupid horse, Nergui grabbed the reins from me and led my horse along. Sure, it was a little mortifying. But then again, I'd like to see him try and figure out the NYC subway system on his first try. That'd show him.

* * *

I had mentioned a while back that I had felt like I had stepped into an *Indiana Jones* movie. Now I felt like I was on Tatooine from *Star Wars*. The Khan's setup looked like something you'd expect to find *Jabba the Hutt* living in. The settlement was similar, if considerably larger, than the one I had just come from, with one exception. In the middle of it, surrounded by many smaller tents, was a gigantic ornate one. It looked like a portable palace, and I really mean *portable*. The thing was on wheels as if someone had decided to turn it into its own self-contained wagon-train.

James saw my look of awe as we arrived and commented, "Even in this day and age, it's something to behold, isn't it? Takes an entire herd of oxen to pull it, but it allows the Khan's base of operations to remain mobile.

"A moving target?" I suggested.

"An apt description. The way things are going, I'd say that's probably a wise way to look at it."

We finally dismounted. Thank god! Hopefully, my vampiric healing would quickly take care of all the sores on my ass from the ride over. Nergui and his loquacious friends went ahead of us into the main tent. James held me back to help him tie up the horses, a task that I was absolutely useless at, by the way.

"They'll go in and take their seats of honor," James explained, motioning to his three companions. "You'll stay with me. As you're technically under my jurisdiction, you'll follow my lead, and in turn I'll translate for you."

"I take it the Khan doesn't speak English."

"Only a few words," he confirmed. "The Khan is not a fan of the various Western languages. He considers them crude and inelegant."

"Heh. That sounds to me like..."

"No. That sounds to *me* like you still need to watch your mouth. Everyone in there is loyal to the Khan, *absolutely loyal.* Plenty of them speak English and would be more than happy to translate any stupid comment that comes out of your mouth. I will remind you that you are in the presence of one of the thirteen ruling vampires. They are not known for either their generosity or their willingness to suffer fools."

"Noted." Seemed like the only safe answer to give. I just hoped my mouth could keep it in neutral for the time being.

"Good. Now follow my lead. Bow when I bow, and only speak to the Khan if he asks you a question first. Got it?"

"Roger that, chief," I said with a brisk mock salute.

James just sighed and said, "God help us both."

* * *

We approached the entrance to find several unfriendly looking guards blocking the way. James bowed, and I did likewise after he gave me a quick glare. He then said something in Chinese, at which the guards parted and let us through.

Gotta say, considering the guy lived in a tent, the Khan had a pretty swank setup. The entrance hall was lined in multiple layers of what looked like silk.

Ornately carved tables covered in various bits of antiquity stood against the walls. I wasn't sure what all of them were, but each and every item looked like it cost more than I'd make in my first lifetime. Gold, silver, ivory, and more gems than I could name stared out at me from statues, sculptures, and vases of varying size. If I had a little bit more skill, and slightly stickier fingers, I could have financed my parents' retirement with just one bauble.

We came to the end of the hall, where more guards awaited. They stepped aside, pulling back a heavy drapery to allow us entrance to the main area. James stopped just inside and bade me to do the same. "Wait until he calls for us," he whispered as I took it all in.

The place was larger on the inside than I thought it would be. There were two rows of tables, separated by several feet of walkway that led up the middle. Vampires, or at least so I assumed, were seated on expensive looking pillows in front of the tables. All in all, there must have been at least four dozen of them present, and they were all feasting on a variety of foods, some normal...some not so. I saw plenty of fruit, a couple cooked pigs, some goats, and a few other roasted things that I'd prefer not to think about. Suffice it to say, if any of you are missing friends or relatives who happened to be visiting China at the time of their disappearance; well, I have bad news for you...I think I found them.

At the far end of the hall, seated upon a massive pile of pillows was who I assumed to be the Khan. Heh! I had mentioned Jabba the Hutt before, but now I was reminded of him more than ever. The Khan was, to put it mildly, one big fat fuck. I mean, before I had hopped on the plane, or my box as it were, I had looked up Ogedei Khan on the Internet. A few portraits showed that he wasn't exactly a svelte fellow, but this dude...damn! Somebody was really into their Khandy (*get it!*). On the other hand, I couldn't help but feel a little bit of happiness at seeing him. At long last, I had met another vampire whom I could feel physically superior to, looks-wise at least. Seriously, this guy had to be pushing six hundred easily. I've seen sumo wrestlers who would weep at trying to manhandle this butterball.

Seated next to his royal porkness, at the head of the table, was a little midget dressed in fine robes. Hmmm, guess the Khan had his own fetishes. No. Wait, it wasn't a midget. On closer look, it was actually a little girl. She was dressed in regal finery and appeared to be not much older than ten. Oh crap. I really hoped she wasn't meant to be the Khan's personal appetizer. Not sure I could sit still and watch that.

"Who's that?" I whispered to James while we waited for the Khan to acknowledge us. I secretly hoped his answer didn't include the word dinner.

"The Khan, obviously," he whispered back.

"No. The little girl."

"Oh her? That's the Khan's daughter."

"Vampires can have kids?" I sputtered. "Damn, wish I had known that. I didn't use a condom earlier."

"Once again, more information than I *really* wanted to know," he hissed through gritted teeth. "Now please be quiet before you insult the Khan and get *both* of us killed."

Oh yeah, almost forgot about that part. From what I had been told, the Draculas were not a group to fuck around with. You stepped even an inch out of line with them, and you were dust. Forget about surviving the night; inwardly I wondered if I was going to survive the next five minutes. Pissing people off was a specialty of mine and something I tended to do whether or not I was even trying. Oh well, if things went bad, I had several dozen one-liners I could spout off to Moby Dickhead up front there. If I had to go, I might as well go out with style.

After a few minutes of pointedly ignoring us, probably some stupid ceremonial thing to remind us who was higher on the food chain, Nergui stepped forward and addressed the Khan in his native language (*I assumed, not like I could tell one foreign dialect from another*). When he was done, he gestured toward us.

"This is it," whispered James. I glanced over out of the corner of my eye and noticed a thin sheen of sweat on his forehead. Guess my reputation for being a wise-ass preceded me.

The Khan dismissed Nergui and said something in our general direction. The crowd went silent, and all eyes turned toward us. Ignoring the voice in my head that was telling me now was the perfect time to start screaming, "Yeah! It's me, the fucking Freewill, bitches!", I instead waited for James's lead. A moment later, he began slowly walking up the main aisle toward the Khan. I attempted to match his step and followed.

When we got about two-thirds of the way there, he stopped and bowed deeply. He then stepped aside, and I did the same. Nobody could say I didn't at least try to start the evening off on the right note. Once I was done, the Khan nodded his head ever so slightly. That was a good sign, I think – probably should have boned up on my ancient Mongolian vampire customs before I shipped out. The Khan then said something to James, which he, in turn, translated.

"The Khan, esteemed member of the First Coven and Shadow Lord of Asia (*oh brother!*), welcomes you as his honored guest." He then paused while giving me a look that said I was expected to answer.

"The honor is all mine, great Khan," was my reply. "Oh yeah, and Captain Kirk totally owned your ass!" Okay, I didn't say that last part out loud. I'm not *that* suicidal.

A small look of relief crossed James's face, and then he relayed my answer back to the Khan. There was another brief exchange, and James again translated.

"You are invited to enjoy the feast and all the hospitality the Khan has to offer. Once it is done, you will be called forward again."

Called forward? For what? Did he want an autograph? Or maybe he wanted to give me one. '*To my biggest fan, keep on rocking! Your bud, the Khan.*'

Before I could say anything, though, James turned back toward the Khan and again bowed. That was apparently my cue to do the same. Once it was done, the conversation amongst the vampire crowd immediately resumed, and James led me off to the side, where a space had been left for us.

We sat down, and almost immediately a servant placed a large full wine cup into my hand. Now why can't I get service like this back in the city?

"Why are they calling me back up later?" I asked James.

"Don't worry about it. Probably nothing," he said dismissively as he started to eat.

Oh well, when in Rome...I took a sip of my drink. Whoa! Good shit! Something familiar tasting about it, though. "What is this stuff?" I asked.

"Fermented blood, of course." Oh, of course.

* * *

The feast was pretty damn nice. I helped myself to plenty of the blood wine, as well as my fair share of goat and pork. I declined, however, from partaking in the roasted humans. I may be a vampire, but there are limits as to how creepy I'm willing to get. That shit definitely crossed the line. Still, aside from that one little detail, it was all good.

During the course of the meal, a few other vampires introduced themselves through James. I didn't really get a lot of names, though. For starters, I'm not good with that kind of thing, even worse when I'm being told third person. Secondly, the fermented blood had given me a pretty nice buzz. After a while, the faces just sort of became one blur after the other.

That was, until a small voice said from behind me, "So this is the Freewill? I thought he would be taller."

I turned to find the small girl from before, the Khan's daughter, staring back at me. When she grew up, she was going to be a real looker. For now, though, she was cute as a button with silky black hair and inquisitive green eyes.

"Ah! What an honor," James said, turning around to face her. He stood up and bade me do the same. "I would like to introduce her highness, Gansetseg."

The girl inclined her head to James, and then asked, "So you are the one the Wanderer calls 'Dr. Death'?"

"It's more of a nickname than anything else. My name's Bill."

"Bill..." she said, as if tasting the word in her mouth. "A simple but strong name, although perhaps Dr. Death is a more fitting title for one such as you."

"You speak really good English," I pointed out.

"Thank you. My father, though having no love of the Western world himself, has insisted that my education be thorough."

"A mind is a terrible thing to waste," I said glibly, noticing out of the corner of my eye the slight eye-roll James made. Oh crap, I was doing it again. Best to wrap this up quickly before any further stupidity escaped my lips. "Well, it was very nice to meet you, Gan."

"Gan?" she asked, a confused look on her face. "I do not understand. Is this meant as some sort of insult?"

Uh oh.

"No!" I quickly answered. "It's just a nickname. I mean, where I come from we usually shorten each other's names to something simple. It's a compliment...a form of friendship," I sputtered, hoping that I hadn't just dug my own grave with my stupid mouth.

She thought about this for a moment, and then gave what appeared to be a genuine smile. "A curious custom. We would never do that here. But yes, I think I like it. It is nice to meet you, too." She flashed me a big grin, and then walked back toward her father.

"Cute kid," I remarked to James.

"Yes, well that *kid* is three-hundred years old. You're lucky. That could have gone badly. Gansetseg is known to be *temperamental*. Instead, though, I think you actually made an impression upon her."

"Three-hundred years?" I gasped, spewing some blood wine. "Has she always looked..."

"Yes," James answered evenly. "That's the way it works with vampires. You had asked before if we can have children. The answer is both yes and no. Despite his immortality, the Khan has always kept his mortal family close. Gansetseg is actually something like his great-great-granddaughter. She was a favorite of his. When she was bitten by a poisonous snake shortly after her twelfth birthday, the Khan couldn't bear to see her die. Her turned her, and then adopted her. She's been with him ever since."

"And she'll look like that forever?" I asked, already knowing the answer.

"Yes. She is an ancient and wise woman trapped in the body of a child."

"Whoa," I said.

"Yes, *whoa* is a particularly apt answer for that."

* * *

We finished the feast. There were a lot of happy, content, and partially drunk vampires seated in the dining hall. A few more glasses of the blood, and I was going to start putting my arms around random vamps, doing the whole "I love you, man!" thing. I reflected back and realized that this had ended up becoming one hell of a fine day. Who'd have thought it? A few days ago, I was feeling at my lowest. Now, I was the honored guest of a living piece of history...oh, and did I mention the boatloads of sex I had earlier? Because if I didn't, I'd be happy to go into detail. Yeah, it was a pretty damn good day.

Which, of course, meant that it was time for the shit to hit the fan. Such is my life. Whenever the good times last too long, I know I should put on my raincoat and head into the storm cellar because some nastiness is no doubt coming my way.

Thus, as we sat around mellowing out, the Khan clapped his hands. Servants appeared from the shadows and quickly cleared the food from the tables. They then removed the tables themselves. Hmm, something about this reminded me of a scene out of *Mortal Kombat* the movie.

The Khan barked some orders, and once more the crowd fell silent. This was a guy used to getting what he wanted, although, judging from the size of him, what he usually wanted most was more pie. He then glanced at me and said something else. James turned toward me and said, "It's time. Back into the spotlight you go."

We both started to rise, but then I heard Gan's voice chime in. She said something to her father in Chinese. After a moment, he nodded back. She then said in English, "No, Wanderer. The Freewill will face his tests alone." Tests?

James bowed to her and gave me an apologetic look before sitting back down. Maybe I had insulted her after all. Oh boy.

I walked to the center of the room, aware that all eyes were upon me. If I had ever suffered from stage fright, now would be a bad time for a relapse.

The Khan turned toward Nergui and spoke a command. Nergui bowed and walked to a spot directly in front of me. He drew a large sword from a scabbard on his back. Oh crap! This guy was an assassin. No doubt he knew how to use that thing. I tried to steady my shaking knees as he leveled the sword at me...and then plunged it into the ground at my feet. He gave me a quick nod and went back to his post.

"Now we will see exactly how free your will is," spoke Gan, a mischievous smile on her face.

Before I could further wonder what she meant by that, the full force of a compulsion erupted from the Khan. Though his spoken words were unintelligible to me, I could clearly understand them inside of my head. *"PICK UP THE SWORD AND FALL UPON IT!!"* It felt like someone cracked open my skull and punched me directly in the brain. Holy shit! I wouldn't be surprised if, from that moment on, I was going to hear this guy's voice echoing in every memory I had all the way back to childhood.

My vision doubled, then blurred, and I felt myself partially double over from the force of it all. When things finally cleared a few moments later, I looked and saw drag marks in front of my feet. The sword was now a good three feet away. The force of the compulsion had physically shoved me back without my even being aware of it. Damn! And this guy was supposedly one of the younger Draculas. If so, an older one could probably cause my head to explode like a water balloon if they wanted to; however, at the end of it all, shaken as I was, the sword was left untouched.

I stood up straight, looked at the Khan, and gave my head a single shake no. The crowd erupted into shocked gasps. I turned to find James wearing a bemused grin. He gave me a quick thumbs-up. I had passed the test. I then noticed another sound. I turned toward the front of the room and saw Gan clapping her hands, a happy smile on her face. From the looks of things, I guess I hadn't insulted her after all.

Glad that was over. I looked at the Khan and gestured toward my seat. He held up his hand, the universal sign for "stop what the fuck you're doing". The crowd again went silent, except for Gan, who was still clapping. My, she was an eager little beaver. Nice to see I had a cheering section. The Khan didn't seem to be amused, though. He turned to her and said a quick word which stopped her dead in her tracks. Daughter or not, she was on as tight of a leash as everyone else there. Or maybe not, as she gave him one hell of a pouty look in return. Nepotism has some advantages, no matter where you are.

Khan and Gan (*sounds like a bad cartoon*) exchanged a few more words, and then it was apparently back to business. She turned back to me and once again spoke.

"Our legends say the gods were most generous when they created our people. Long life and strength are but a few of our gifts. However, for all of their generosity, we are still lacking in their eyes. It is said that the first Freewill was created by the gods in an attempt to address this, to bring us closer to their image. As fierce as we are, the Freewills who walked amongst us caused even our mightiest to tremble (*yeah that's right, I'm a badass!*). They led our armies against our adversaries, and with them at the forefront, our enemies were laid low. But then we did something, some transgression lost to the ages, and the gods took away our favor. The Freewills vanished, and our people were diminished (*jeez, did she pull this speech straight out of Lord of the*

Rings or what?), forever some said. Yet now, here you are. What does it mean?"

She paused. I wasn't sure if I was supposed to say something or if it was just a rhetorical thing. I was just about to shrug my shoulders (*and probably make an ass of myself in the process*) when she continued speaking. "Our seers do not yet know. All they can say is that there are dark days ahead. Will you help be the sunrise in our endless night?" Okay, this was getting a little deep. I mean, come on. I had a few extra tricks the others couldn't do. That was it. All I knew was that if I heard the words *chosen* and *one* in the same sentence, I was getting the hell out of here. They could find someone else to play *Harry Potter* for them.

On the other hand, telling a room full of vampires, all of whom were older and stronger than me, to go fuck themselves might not exactly be the best strategy either. So, for the sake of covering my own ass, I simply nodded.

That was apparently the correct answer, as Gan's face once more broke into a wide grin. The Khan spoke a few words to her, and after a brief exchange, she went on. "My father is pleased. The next test may begin."

Next test? I opened my mouth to protest, but before I could speak, it was filled with Bang's fist. At a nod from the Khan, James's errand boy had raced forward and... well, banged me. Okay, maybe that was the wrong way to put it. He came at me full speed, which in vampire terms meant he crossed the space between us in the blink of an eye, and gave me a solid punch to the face. I flew back a good dozen feet and just lay there dazed for a moment. I definitely hadn't been expecting that.

"Ow," was the best I could do as way of response.

A few seconds passed before I was able to remember my name again. I slowly pulled myself to my feet, feeling a cascade of blood gushing out of my crushed nose. The crowd again broke into murmurs, and I distinctly heard a few guffaws of laughter. I turned toward Bang to find him standing there, smirking. Assholes, all of them.

I was about to voice that opinion out loud when the Khan barked another order. This time, Cheng-gong stepped forward (*also trying and failing to suppress a grin, the fucker*). He pulled a sharp looking dagger from a sheath at his hip, held out his arm toward me, and cut open one of his veins. One guy decks me, and the other comes out to bleed all over me. Damn, these people were a pack of weirdos.

Again, though, Gan's voice rang out toward me. "Show us your power, Freewill. Show us that the legends speak true."

Okay, I had no fucking idea what she was talking about. Was she expecting me to shoot a fireball or something at these guys? What the hell power did these idiots think I was going to pull out of my ass? I turned toward James, hoping maybe there'd be a little help there. He mouthed something to me. I suck at lip reading, so I didn't quite catch it. I mouthed back

"What?", and he did it again. It looked like he was saying, "Drink and fight, stupid."

Drink and fight? What the...oh, I got it. Suck up the blood from the dude with the cutting fetish and use it to beat the crap out of the asshole who blindsided me.

Now *that* I could get behind. I walked over to Cheng-gong and grabbed his arm. When he didn't resist, I extended my fangs (*hey, might as well make a show of it*) and dug them into the wound on his arm. The crowd gave a collective gasp and went silent. I sucked down a few mouthfuls and felt Cheng's arm stiffen. He wasn't quite enjoying this. Well, fuck him. I didn't quite enjoy getting my face bashed in a few minutes earlier. I took a final draw of his blood, and then I felt it...that familiar rush I got after drinking another vampire's blood. It was like somebody hooked up a car battery to my insides. First there was an electric-like jolt, and then came the rush as my body temporarily absorbed the power from the blood and made it my own. It was time to show Bang a thing or two.

But first things first. A little show for the crowd never hurt, especially since they were here to see me. I pulled away from Cheng-gong's arm and then shoved him to the side, far more violently than warranted. He went flying into the crowd, which immediately erupted into more chatter amongst themselves. I didn't speak their language, but it was obvious from the tone that most of them had apparently not believed what they'd been told about me.

I put out my hand and did a little Bruce Lee-ish 'come over here' wave to Bang. Time to take it up a notch.

Or maybe not. A small voice in the back of my head reminded me that no matter what strength I might possess, the guy in front of me was a trained killer. He could probably take me apart piece by piece and then reassemble me backwards to do it all over again. *sigh* How the hell do I get myself into stupid situations like this?

Fortunately, though, (*for me at least*) this wasn't a UFC prize fight. This was a test of my powers as opposed to my prowess (*which was close to zero*). Bang threw another straight jab at me of about the same speed and strength as his first hit. This one I was able to see coming and catch. He threw up his other hand, which likewise locked with mine. We thus engaged in that time honored tradition of almost every schoolyard, a game of mercy.

This was apparently what the crowd was waiting for, as they suddenly got into it. There were whoops and cheers, apparently rooting for both sides of this match. I don't know what Mongolian money looks like, but judging from the paper being passed around, I'd say there was some betting going on, too. It figures. No matter how cultured the crowd may claim to be, if a fight breaks out the cash will start changing hands. Nice to see there were some universals in this screwed up world I found myself in.

Speaking of which, I almost wished I had some Mongolian cash on me because I was starting to see how this was going to play out. Cheng must have been slightly older than Bang because slowly but surely I was starting to power him back.

I could hear my Dr. Death persona awaken in my brain. *Time to end this on a high note, buddy,* my inner voice said.

Kinda figured that, I thought back. *By the way, where the hell were you when I was talking to Sheila?*

Oh that? Sorry, I was...eh...busy.

Busy? With what?

Busy with...fuck you, that's what! Now finish this thing, dickface!

Life can be so difficult when even my inner monologue is an asshole.

I pretended to give way under Bang's assault (*damn, that sounded dirty*), until I'd bent my arms enough to get some leverage. I then put all of my borrowed strength into one big shove. As I did so, I let go of Bang's hands, and he went flying. The crowd went crazy. Oh yeah, I'm the people's champion! Can you smell what Dr. Death is cooking?

The point being made (*and my nose a good way toward being healed; thank you, vampire powers*), I walked over to where Bang had fallen and offered him a hand up. This was apparently another feather in my cap because the crowd again went nuts. Over all of it, though, I distinctly heard Gan's voice yell, "Well done,

Freewill!" in that shrill tone that only a sub-teenage fangirl can achieve.

I walked back to the center and soaked up some more of the applause. Hell, I even started throwing them some poses. So this was what the roaring adoration of a crowd felt like. Okay, I take back what I was saying earlier. This was kind of worth getting punched in the nose for. After another minute of basking in my own glory, I glanced over at James to see if he was enjoying things as much as I.

He wasn't.

James's attention was diverted toward where the Khan sat. I followed his gaze and saw that the Khan appeared to be in the middle of an argument with his daughter. I couldn't hear what they were saying over the crowd, and let's face facts, even if I could it's not like I'd understand one freaking word. The argument appeared to be heating up, though. Gan kept pointing in my direction and shouting at her father. The Khan, in return, kept shaking his head and yelling back at her. What the hell? Maybe she wanted to perform some more insane tests on me and the Khan was telling her no. If that was the case, then I was definitely rooting for him. Hell, I might even take back what I said about Captain Kirk kicking his ass...maybe.

My attention was diverted from them by James. He had gotten out of his seat and grabbed hold of my arm.

"Your truck will be here soon. I think we should go," he said.

"And leave my adoring fans?" I joked, but he didn't seem to be laughing.

"I think it would be in your best interest to leave *now*." He sounded dead serious.

I was about to ask why, but, as is typical with my life, that was when all hell broke loose.

He Who Fights and Runs Away

THE FIRST THING I noticed was the screams. Initially, I assumed they were just some more wild cheers from the crowd. After all, they seemed to be loving my shit up; however, upon a closer listen, I realized they were actually screams of pain and terror. Before anyone could react with anything other than confusion, one whole wall of the palatial tent collapsed in on itself. The resulting crash kicked up lots of dust and debris...a little too much. That was when I realized some of the dust was actually smoke.

As James and I were still pretty much in the center of things, he grabbed my arm and shoved me toward the entrance. "Go!" he yelled, half pushing me along. I may be relatively inexperienced (*although not sexually so...especially after last night*), but I'm not stupid. I got my feet underneath me and rushed in the direction I had been directed. I made it to the hallway, which was still clear (*I was ahead of most of the vamps in the Khan's chamber*), and then bolted for the entrance itself. Rushing outside, I immediately noticed that the guards were nowhere to be seen. No wonder, too, as what had been a quiet settlement a few hours ago was now a battlefield.

Half the tents were burning. Vampires have excellent night vision, but smoke is another matter entirely. I could see forms running back and forth, but I couldn't tell friend from foe. Hell, I didn't even know who the foe was. What I did know was that people...err, vampires, that is...were dying. I could see occasional flashes of light from inside the smoke. I'd seen enough vampires killed to know a dusting when I saw one. The big question, though, was: were the dying vampires the good guys (*relatively speaking of course*) or not?

I'm no soldier, but I'm also not an idiot. One of the first rules of battle is don't just stand there out in the open, gaping like a halfwit. Really wish I had remembered that rule. Maybe I should revise that not-an-idiot rating. But it would have to wait because...OOF!

As I stood there looking around, something solid and heavy slammed into my chest. The next thing I knew, I was on my back with the wind completely knocked out of me. From the feel of things, there were at least a few cracked bones in there as well. I groggily glanced around from my prone position and saw the culprit. One of those head-sized rocks lay only a few feet from me. Thank god for the Khan's little tests. If I hadn't been amped on another vampire's blood, that thing could have gone straight through me. Considering the trajectory and force with which it had hit me, someone or something had thrown it...which I guess is kind of an obvious statement. I mean, rocks don't usually get pissed off at random people and hurl themselves.

That train of thought would need to wait, though, as I was roused from my introspection on the nature of angry, self-throwing stones by a bloodcurdling scream. Whatever it was, it was loud, close by, and scary as all fuck to hear. That's the type of stuff you hear in a horror movie just about the time you realize that the guns the heroes are carrying would be better served to blow their own brains out with. I didn't even have a gun with which to shoot myself, thus I felt a wee bit screwed.

That was when a shape began to take form from out of the smoke. Something was coming to finish the job. I couldn't see much detail, only a vague outline, but it was enough to tell me that it wasn't human, vampire, or a magical pixie come to grant my wishes. Whatever it was, it was *big*. Hard to tell from lying on the ground, but I'd say it was close to nine feet tall. It appeared to be humanoid in shape, and judging from its muscular outline, it could have been the poster boy for steroid abuse.

The thing raised its arms and screamed again. It wasn't quite the same as a compulsion, but it was damn loud, enough to rattle in my bones. Unfortunately for me, I was still just barely able to do more than suck in a breath. If this thing decided to fuck me over, my choices were basically limited to closing my eyes and taking it like a bitch.

Or I could rely on a convenient save. That'd work, too.

There was a quick whistling sound, following by a dull *thunk*, and the...whatever the fuck it was...screamed again and fell back from sight. I turned my head, and there stood James. Judging by the empty sheath by his side, he had just given that thing a sucking chest wound with a big-ass Bowie knife.

I'd just started to say, "Thanks," when he grabbed me by the shirt and hauled me to my feet.

"For once in your life, keep your damn mouth shut and follow me!" he barked with a tone of urgency that instantly convinced me to obey. He ducked down and headed off into the smoke. I was still barely able to breathe, but there was nothing wrong with my legs, so I followed as best I could.

More bone-chilling screams filled the night, but this time they were finally met with battle cries. From the sound of things, the vamps were attempting a counterattack. Yay for us. Go team vampire!

I had thought James would be heading toward them – after all, strength in numbers, especially when those numbers included centuries of ass-kicking battle prowess. Thus I was surprised when he started leading me away from the sounds of battle.

"We're not gonna help them?"

"That was almost a full minute of silence. A new record for you, no doubt," James hissed. "And to answer your question, no."

"But don't they need us?"

"No, they do not need *us*." He moved to the edge of a tent and looking around. The coast was apparently clear, as he gestured for me to follow.

"But we could help," I whispered back.

"Don't flatter yourself. I could help. *You*, on the other hand, would just quickly get yourself killed." I would have felt insulted if he hadn't probably been right. I wasn't exactly born and bred to battle, and considering that my intelligence on the enemy consisted of the words *big* and *scary*, there was some sound logic behind James's insult.

"But what about the Khan? What about Gan?" I nevertheless protested.

"Don't worry about them. The Khan is far more formidable than he may appear."

"But Gan's just a kid."

"Yes," he replied, continuing to lead us toward the edge of the encampment. "A kid with ten times your life experience. Trust me. They can both take care of themselves."

We reached the edge of the camp. The smoke had dissipated out here, and open desert stared back at us.

James turned back to me. "Can you move at top speed?"

My chest had come a long ways toward healing itself in the past few minutes. Even if I couldn't do my best, I could probably fake it pretty well. I nodded back.

He continued, "Good. From here, we move fast. In a flat out foot race, they won't be able to catch us."

I had just started to open my mouth to ask *who* wouldn't be able to catch us, but I stopped when I noticed that James was already a dozen yards ahead of me.

* * *

When we had covered about two-thirds of the distance back to the original camp, James finally slowed down. We were probably out of danger by now, and even if we weren't, we'd be able to see anything coming for us long before it got there.

"What the hell was that all about back there?" I finally got a chance to ask him.

"Off hand, I'd say that was a surprise attack."

Suddenly, an ugly thought occurred to me. "It didn't seem like much of a surprise to you," I said and immediately regretted it. James stopped and turned back toward me. The look on his face was so intense that I actually backed up a step (*maybe two*).

"I'm sure I didn't hear that correctly," he replied in an emotionless tone, "because that sounded vaguely like an accusation."

God, I am an idiot. I presented someone with damning evidence against them when they clearly had the advantage. I just did the same thing that would normally make me scream at the TV when the morons on some show did it. How many scenes had I watched where some plucky young woman confronted her boss alone in his office about the corruption she'd uncovered at his hands? That almost always ended badly for the would-be heroine. Yet here I was, despite knowing better, putting my plucky young ass on the line with nary any backup in sight, against a vampire I stood absolutely zero chance against. It would serve me right to get ashed.

Oh well, in for a penny, in for a pound. "Funny how you told me we needed to get moving right before we got attacked. Or does that not sound a little suspicious to you?"

I had said my piece. It was time to die, I guess. I tensed for whatever beating James was about to lay on me.

Instead, he chuckled. "*That?*" he laughed again. "Unlucky coincidence is all."

"But you..."

"I was trying to get us out of there due to the little argument going on between Gan and her father, in case you didn't notice," he said with a grin.

"What, did they have more stupid tests for me?"

"You could say that." He seemed to think about it for a moment, and then continued. "It's not important. I doubt you'll be seeing either of them again for a long time. Suffice to say, things were about to get *awkward*, and I decided it was in your best interest to leave."

We started walking again; however, I still wasn't convinced. James was definitely leaving something out. "Well then, explain why we didn't stay and help them back there. I mean, maybe I'm not the best guy to have someone's back in a fight, but *you* could have definitely helped."

"I *am* helping," he answered as we continued on our way.

"By running off?"

"By saving your ass," he snapped, the edge creeping back into his voice.

"I don't underst..."

"You really can be dense sometimes, you know. Even for a child, you are sometimes unbelievably thick." James said with a sigh. "You know that Freewills are rare. I told you as much myself. But did you hear those people back there? To them, you are a *legend*. In the States, this might make for an amusing comic book story; however, out here they pay a great deal of respect to things like that."

"Okay, I guess I follow you."

"Do you?" he asked. "Do you really? To allow you to be killed before reaching your full potential...and no, I have no idea what that might be. Well, that would be simply intolerable to them. Your mere presence gives them hope. Don't get me wrong. If they spent enough time with you, I'm sure that hope would evaporate like rain in the desert (*yep, can always count on James to make a guy feel good about himself*). However, for right now it's in our best interest for you to keep living."

"*Our* best interest?"

"Most definitely. I will admit to a certain selfishness with regards to my own wellbeing. You see, you're under my charge. If you die here, then it would be my fault."

"And your ass would be on the line?"

"Exactly," he remarked. "Perhaps you're not entirely as dense as I thought."

* * *

We arrived back at our camp a short while later. All appeared to be in order. It was quiet, but we could clearly see the guards and a few others walking around, attending to their duties. The truck that would take me back to the airport was also there waiting for us. I could see the driver lounging by the cab, looking bored.

"Thank goodness," said James with an audible sigh of relief. "I couldn't be sure until I saw it. The Alma have never been this bold before. To attack the Khan directly was an outright declaration of war."

"Who?"

"Never you mind. Ignorance is bliss. All you need care about is that New York City is not within their territory for now, so you needn't concern yourself."

"Not gonna tell me, huh?" I grumbled, probably sounding like a pouty teenager. "Wait, what do you mean *for now*?"

"Enough. You know far more about the Draculas' business already than is good for you. You're not even a year old, for midnight's sake (*yeah, definitely feeling a wee bit insulted now*). Go back to your coven. I'm sure there's plenty there to concern yourself with."

I thought back to Sally, dull anger once again filling me. There was definitely enough waiting for me back home to *concern* myself with. "Oh yeah, speaking of concerns," I replied, suddenly reminded of the whole

120

point for this trip, "what was it you wanted to talk to me about anyway?"

James stopped walking, and a look of confusion crossed his face. "That's funny. Now that you mention it, for the life of me I can't remember."

* * *

We reached the supply tent and entered it. James told me that the truck driver was a human, thus it was probably best to package me up outside of his sight. I guess some people can get a little weird if they know their cargo is a box full of grumpy vampire.

My bags were all packed and already loaded into the crate. Sure enough, James's word was good, and there were a few rugs inside to pad things out a bit. It wasn't exactly a luxury suite at the Hilton, but it would probably be at least marginally more comfortable for the return trip. Oh crap! Speaking of which, I had never recharged my iPod. Damn! Well okay, I hadn't exactly seen a lot of outlets during my adventures in Bedouin land. Guess I'd be alone with my thoughts. Fortunately, I had my memories of the day before...more specifically, *naked sweaty* memories of the day before. And if those didn't get me all the way back to New York, well then sorry, Sally, but it'd be back to the wood chipper for you.

I sighed and started to climb in. "Not looking forward to doing this again," I admitted to James.

"A necessary evil for now, I'm afraid," he replied. "However, I did bring something that should make the trip more palatable. Here." He pulled a small vial out of his pocket and handed it to me.

"What is it?"

"You know how some people are afraid to fly and they take a tranquilizer beforehand to calm themselves down?"

"Yeah, I guess."

"Well, this is kind of like that."

Oh. Okay. A little something to take the edge off might be just what the doctor ordered. I uncorked it and downed the contents, wincing as it went down. The taste wasn't great, but it was vaguely reminiscent. One summer down at Tom's house, we'd gotten shitfaced on Jagermeister and Rumplemintz...or as they're collectively known when you mix them together; *Screaming Nazis*. It's a vile concoction, but damn if it doesn't get the job done. This tasted a bit like that, albeit in a slightly more viscous sort of way.

Wow! This shit was more potent, too. Within ten seconds of quaffing it, the room started spinning around me. Within another few moments, I found I could no longer even stand. I flopped unceremoniously onto the bottom of the packing crate, managing to turn over and blearily look up at James's face. "What the hell was that?" I slurred.

"It's a poison refined from the venom of the *Mongolian death worm*," he said matter of factly. "It should keep you out for the majority of the trip. Enjoy your nap." With that said, he placed the lid back onto my crate, and I was again sealed into the darkness.

Mongolian death worm, eh? Yeah, I guess that makes perfect sense, I thought as I plunged into a much deeper darkness.

Green with Envy

WHOA! I HAVE to make it a point to get some of that stuff for my next party. I spent what felt like maybe five minutes inside of the most freaky-ass, psychedelic hallucination I'd ever experienced before I was jolted awake by the feeling of my crate being moved. I'd assumed that I was probably still in China, maybe being loaded onto the cargo plane back to the States; however, a short while later the crate lid was pried off. I found myself staring up at the faces of a couple zombies, as well as the vampire shipping clerk who had originally packed me. Yeah, definitely have to get some more of that stuff.

"Welcome back. Do you have anything to declare?" the clerk asked with a grin.

"I declare that's the last time I fly with air-vampire," I replied, taking his outstretched hand and pulling myself to my feet. I was still a bit shaky from James's Mongolian death cocktail, but damn if it hadn't done the trick. Fastest flight halfway around the world I'd ever experienced.

The zombies carried my bags to the door of the terminal. I followed and was let back outside to the gloriousness that is nighttime at LaGuardia. From the look of things, it wasn't particularly late. I turned toward the other vamp and asked, "So how do I get back?"

"There are these marvelous inventions called cabs. Have fun using them," he replied with a smirk. "Thanks for flying with us. Buh bye!" and with that, the terminal door shut and I could hear it being locked from the inside. Fucker! Some days, I just hate other vampires.

I felt bad about bugging Ed for a ride back, so I figured I'd call Sally and see if she could find it in her non-beating heart to send a car to pick me up. I was still gonna kill her, but I might kill her less severely if she could arrange for a quick pickup for me. Sadly, I pulled out my cell phone and found it to be even deader than I was. Oh yeah, hadn't had a chance to recharge that either. Oh well, guess it was time for a hike.

* * *

Fortunately, for all the indignities modern day airports inflict upon us, a shortage of cabs isn't one of them. I walked to the nearest living terminal, my baggage not really slowing my vampire self down at all, thank god, and was quickly able to flag a ride. The trip from the airport wasn't too painful; traffic was lighter than it had been when I first arrived. Sure, my Indian-accented chauffeur took a few unnecessary turns to jack

RICK GUALTIERI

up the fare, but it was still better than being crammed into Ed's junker. All in all, it was the least eventful thing I had done in several days. For that alone, I figured the cabbie had earned a decent tip.

We made it back to my place and, after sending the driver on his way, I grabbed my bags to walk up to the apartment I shared with my two friends. I let myself in and noticed the place was dark. My roommates were out. Odd. Or maybe not, as I realized I had no idea what day of the week it was. I had lost at least three or four days from my adventure in total, and taking into account the time difference with China...well, I'd be fucked if I had any idea.

Oh well, I could always check the calendar later. Right then, I needed to unpack, plug in my rechargeables (*come to think of it, my cell being dead might be a minor godsend considering the roaming charges*), and take myself a nice long shower to wash the smell of horses, rocks, and Bang off me. Thus, that is what I did.

* * *

I'd just gotten dressed and was walking into the kitchen to grab myself a nice glass of blood when I heard the apartment door being unlocked. Cool. One of my bros was home. I was all prepared to give them a disgustingly pornographic retelling of my little Asian adventure.

The door opened, and Ed walked in. I was just opening my mouth to say hi when Sally came strolling in behind him. He turned and saw me, but my gaze was

126

locked onto her. A moment later, she, too, realized I was in the apartment and our eyes met; a look of surprise on her face, a slowly spreading snarl on mine.

"You..."

"Hey, Bill," Ed greeted me. "Home already?"

"...bitch!" I finished, ignoring him. I grabbed the nearest thing to me, our toaster, and trudged into the living room.

She started to back away. "What's up, boss?" she asked with a shaky little smile.

"Come over here so I can brain you," I growled, lifting the toaster and going after her.

She ducked out of my reach and ran to the far side of our couch. "I can see you're a little miffed."

"A *little*!? You shipped me to fucking China like I was a piece of furniture!" I chased her around the couch.

"James wanted to talk to you," she said, continuing to evade me.

"On the *phone*!"

"Oh that. Yeah, I might have forgotten that detail."

"I'm forgetting little details, too," I said, again trying to cut her off, "like why I keep letting you live."

"Taking this a little hard, aren't we?" she asked, once more sliding out of my reach...nimble little minx that she was.

"I was stuck in a packing crate for two days! Maybe I should do the same thing to you and see how you like it."

"Sorry. You said you wanted a vacation. I was just trying to give you one."

I stopped my pursuit of her and stood there, fuming. "A vacation..." I started to say, and then something in my brain clicked. I took a deep breath to assess the situation.

Ed, apparently sensing that we were having a *moment,* had wisely retreated to our kitchen nook to see how things played out. I suddenly realized that he was dressed fairly nice: dress shirt, slacks, and his good shoes.

I turned to Sally, and my brain registered that she was wearing a tight maroon cocktail dress. I looked back and forth between them for a few seconds, letting this all sink in, and I was only brought back to reality by a small crash. I realized it was the toaster hitting the floor, as I had just dropped it.

"What the fuck is going on here?" I asked.

"Oh *this?*" asked Ed, sounding guilty. "I was gonna mention it."

"Mention *what?*" I inquired, a bit of attitude working its way into my voice.

"Oh Christ!" exclaimed Sally with an eye-roll. "We went out on a date. There, happy?"

A date? My roommate, friend, and colleague had just gone out with my coven-mate and psycho, hell-beast bitch of a partner. When the fuck did I leave reality and wind up in Bizarro universe?

I turned to Sally. "I thought you hated my roommates."

"Hate is such a strong word." She shrugged. "Although that other friend of yours kind of creeps me out a bit."

"And I thought that *you*," I said, turning to Ed, "were terrified of Sally."

"Oh, I am. No doubt about that," he replied. As he did so, Sally shot him a playful little grin.

"What can I say?" she chimed back in. "I like a little honesty in a man."

"This is *so* not happening," I stammered, sinking down onto the couch.

"Relax, man. It was just a little dinner and a few drinks," replied Ed in a conciliatory tone.

"Relax? *Relax*!?" I growled, getting back to my feet. "I have a whole shitload of reasons why I won't be relaxing anytime soon."

"Okay, calm down," he said and then turned to Sally. "I'm thinking maybe we'll ixnay that cup of coffee."

"No problem. I'll take a rain check." (*a rain check?*)

I stood up to get a pair of shoes, calling back to her, "I'll walk you to the train. We're not finished yet."

* * *

"You're almost cute when you're jealous," Sally purred when we stepped out into the street.

"I am *not* jealous."

"Could have fooled me."

"Besides," I continued, "I seem to recall giving clear instructions that my roommates were off limits."

"I wasn't gonna kill him, jeez. Overreacting a little, aren't we?"

"Fine. Let me amend my instructions. No killing *or* fucking my roommates. Happy?"

"I didn't fuck him...yet. Not that it's any of your business."

"Yet?"

"See? You *are* jealous," she replied in a smug little voice. God, if you're up there, please give me the strength not to kill this woman.

"Fine! You're right; probably none of my business. I'm still pissed at you for sending me to China needlessly, though."

"Maybe I *should* apologize for that," she said as we continued walking to the Eighty-Sixth Street station. "However, I really was only trying to help. I figured a few days in an exotic country might let you blow off a little steam."

She almost sounded sincere on that one...or as sincere as Sally ever sounded. Sure, I'd gotten attacked, beaten up, and almost had my head popped off by the mother of all compulsions, but then again there was the Khan's *hospitality*. I'd definitely blown off a couple years' worth of steam with that one.

"Very well," I finally replied after thinking it over for a few minutes. "Apology accepted on that one. But what about that bullshit with the packing crate?"

She turned and gave me an impish grin. "*That* part was me just fucking with you."

Bitch!

Fat Chicks versus Vampire Cake

I RETURNED HOME, a headache starting to set in, much as it often did following a conversation with Sally. Ed was still up and sitting at our table, no doubt waiting for me. I was half-expecting to have him chew me a new asshole. Maybe I even deserved it.

"Hey," I said, sitting down across from him.

"Hey," he acknowledged in return.

"So how big of a dick was I just now?"

"Pretty colossal," he replied

"Sorry about that. You pissed that I fucked up your date?"

"You didn't really fuck it up. She was just coming up for a cup of coffee."

"You sure?"

"Pretty much. You've got to work your way up to putting the moves on a chick who could snap you like a twig and enjoy every second of it," he said with a smile. "Besides, if I were in your place, I probably would have reacted the same way. So, she really freighted you to China?"

"Yep."

"Damn. I guess then I can forgive you this one time for being a little ticked off. I can see how that could ruin a person's day."

"Cool. Thanks, man," I said. It was always good to see *bros before ho's* being upheld.

We were interrupted from any further male bonding by the arrival of our other roommate, Tom. Just as well. If the conversation kept going the way it was, we'd be entering metrosexual territory pretty soon.

Fortunately, Tom was a master at killing any such mood. "S'up, guys?" he said as way of greeting, and then added, "sorry to interrupt you two staring soulfully into each other's eyes." Tom being an asshole was one constant in the universe that I could always count on.

"Ah, the wayward son returns," I said back to him.

"So sayeth the world traveler," he shot right back.

"Fair enough," I acknowledged. "So what have you been up to? My Chinese connections aside, I haven't seen you much this past week or so."

Tom grabbed a beer from the fridge and joined us at the table. It had been a busy couple weeks for all of us; thus, we hadn't been together as a team like this in a while. It felt good to have my two closest amigos by my side again.

"Been out on a date," he replied.

"Found a new glory hole at Penn Station?" Ed asked without missing a beat.

"Nah. Your mom called dibs on all the good ones. I was out again with Christy."

"She that chick from work?" I asked.

"Yep."

"How are things going with her?"

"Pretty good," he said. "She's cute, and we have fun. She's a little weird, though."

"How so? Are we talking weird as in *has a penis*?" I quipped.

"Don't confuse my dating life with your own. No, I mean she's quirky. It's hard to explain. Sometimes she gets this faraway look in her eyes. And the weirdest thing...sometimes she knows things."

"Like she's dating a virgin?" Ed chimed in.

"Only if she's seeing one of you on the side. But I'm serious. Sometimes we'll be walking down the street, and she'll just make these weird predictions out of nowhere. The other night, she pointed out this cab and said the driver was gonna be in an accident. Sure enough, ten seconds go by and we hear this crash. Some other guy ran a light and plowed into him broadside. It was freaky."

"Well, I guess she does have to be a little freaky to date you," I replied.

Ed added, "Until such time as she produces winning lotto numbers, I'm calling coincidence."

"Maybe," Tom said to him with a shrug. "Oh, speaking of winning the lottery, how did your...*thing* go tonight?"

"Bill knows."

I glared daggers at Tom. "You knew about this, too?"

133

"Knew? Who do you think put the Edster up to it? That chick was being wasted just doing your clerical work."

"For the last time, Sally's not my secretary."

"Your loss, dude. Personally, I wouldn't mind calling her into my office for a little dictation."

Ed sipped on his coffee and replied, "*Little* is an apt word to describe any dictation you'd be giving."

Tom just smiled back at him. "I'm pretty sure my date tonight would disagree."

Oh, enough of this crap! It was time to show these fuckers who was really the king around these parts. "Speaking of dates, I had one this week that puts all of your sad, pathetic little lives to shame," I said with my best arrogant sneer. Once I was sure I had their attention, I continued, "So, do you guys wanna hear about China or not?"

* * *

I filled them in on my adventures on the other side of the world from start to finish, making it a point to pay extra attention to my day of unrelenting lust. By the time I was finished, a good hour had been killed.

I concluded my tale with, "So what do you think? Pretty goddamn intense, eh?"

My roommates gave each other a glance from across the table. Finally, Tom spoke up. "Three chicks, huh?"

I nodded smugly. "And do you happen to have any proof of this holy grail of scoredom?"

"What do you mean, *proof*?" I asked.

"Exactly that," he said. "We're talking panties, interesting marks on your body, video..."

Ed jumped in, "In short, what we're trying to say is: pics, or it didn't happen."

"My cell phone was dead," I replied.

"Likely story."

"Seriously. Have you ever been to a Mongolian vampire village? We're talking *Gilligan's Island* here...like Robinson Crusoe, it's as primitive as can be."

"Uh huh."

"Oh, come on," I spat. "Don't tell me you think I'm making this shit up."

"Well, I mean, look at it from our viewpoint," Tom replied. "No pics. No witnesses. Seems a bit too convenient to me."

Ed nodded. "You gotta admit, Bill, this sounds suspiciously like the 'old girlfriend from Canada' routine."

"We're not in high school," I pointed out.

"And you have to admit you're probably a little vulnerable right now," Tom added with a condescending tone. "I've been dating Christy. Ed asked out your uber-hot sidekick. No one would blame you for feeling a little *inadequate* after your little failure to ask out that prospect from your office."

I turned to Ed. "You *told* him?"

"How could I not?" he replied with a shrug.

"My god, I'm surrounded by assholes," I said, putting my head in my hands.

* * *

They let me wallow in my own misery, standup guys that they were, for a few minutes before Ed changed the subject. "I think we're overlooking something major here. Forgetting Bill's imaginary orgies for a second, what the hell would be ballsy enough to take on a bunch of pissed off vampires? That's the part that worries me. If there's something nastier out there than your buddies, Bill, I'd sure as shit like to know about it."

"No idea," I said, eager to move away from any further mental torment, lest they convince me that the whole thing happened only in my head. Fuck them and their Vulcan mind tricks!

"Did you see whatever it was?"

"Only glimpses," I replied. "Whatever they were, they were big motherfuckers."

"Werewolves?" Tom asked.

"Nah. I don't think so," I replied. "Besides, didn't Sally say werewolves were just make believe?"

"She could've lied," he countered, a little defensively. "I don't know about you, but it just doesn't seem fair to live in a world where vampires exist and werewolves don't. I mean, if there's no war between the vamps and the lycans, then there's no reason for Kate Beckinsale to run around in skintight leather."

"Girlfriend or not, you really need to get out more," Ed said.

"And yet you both dare to pity me," I pointed out before getting back on track. "No, let's assume Sally wasn't bullshitting us...at least this once. That still leaves us with something really nasty out there. Whatever it was, it wasn't human – and it sure as shit wasn't afraid of vampires."

"Why can't supernatural monsters ever be friendly?" Tom asked.

"Tell me about it. I'd just about give my left kidney to meet *Casper* and find out he was an honest to goodness friendly ghost."

"Did this Khan guy..." Ed said, and then immediately held up his hand to Tom, "no Trek jokes. Save it for later." He then continued, "Did the Khan give you anything on them?"

"He wasn't all that talkative. Not a whole lot of deep meaningful conversation coming out of that one...unless you speak Mongolian, that is."

"What about from your buddy Ozymandias?"

"James? No. He was a little evasive. Said I didn't need to know, that I was safe in the city...oh wait! I think he called them something."

"What?"

"Not sure," I replied. "I was kind of busy shitting my pants at the time. What the fuck did he call them?" I thought about it for a second. "It was something that started with an A, I think."

"Alligator?" Tom chimed in. "Maybe the vampires are warring with the alligator people."

I sighed, turning to him. "You know, you might want to give a warning to your new girlfriend. She should avoid trying to fuck your brains out, since you already have a major deficiency in that department."

"Let's concentrate here," said Ed. "*A*...what, Bill?"

"No idea."

"Maybe we should get the dictionary. We could start going through the A's for anything that sounded threatening."

"You're out of your mind," replied Tom. "We do that, and we'll be up *all* fucking night."

"All!" I suddenly shouted. Something about that word rang a bell.

"All what?"

"It was all-something," I said, trying to concentrate. "Give me a second. It's right on the tip of my tongue. All...all...alma! I think he called them the alma."

"What the fuck's an alma?" asked Ed.

"Sounds like a fat chick name," Tom said, as usual adding nothing of value to the conversation.

"I'm pretty sure the vampires weren't attacked by a pack of fat chicks."

"Maybe they heard that vampires were made of cake," he replied with a dickheaded smirk.

I turned back to Ed. "Let's ignore him now, shall we?"

"Gladly. Well, it's not much to go on, but I guess we can look into it." Ed opened his mouth and yawned. "But maybe tomorrow. I don't know about you guys, but I'm kind of beat."

"Sally took that much out of you?"

"Heh," he chuckled. "When you're dating a girl like her, you tend to overanalyze even the smallest of things. You know, stuff like will she rip my arm out of its socket if I try to hold her hand? It makes for a slightly more stressful than average evening."

Attack of the Mighty Mongolian Monsters

THE THING ABOUT phantom, non-immediate threats is that they tend to fall off the priority list pretty quickly. Thus our research into giant vampire-hating beasts was almost immediately derailed by our normal everyday activities, be that as they may. A quick check of my email the next morning provided me with the realization that I'd missed several days of work without bothering to let anybody know. I may be an immortal creature of the night, but I was young enough that the fear of unemployment was still ingrained into my mind. I thus kicked my ass into high gear and dove straight into work, all thoughts of Mongolian mist monsters forgotten.

My roommates must have also gotten back to tending their lives because it didn't come up again in conversation, at least in the following days. Fortunately for me, I was still technically on my vampirecation, thus between my nights being free (*yeah, yeah, I don't need to be reminded of how pathetic that is*) and my enhanced vampiric typing speed, I was able to catch up to my workload in just a couple of days and maybe even push a little bit ahead of schedule.

In some ways, those few days were kind of nice. Aside from my powers and tendency to drench all my food in blood, I actually felt kind of normal. It was relaxing.

Needless to say, it didn't last.

On Thursday night, I got a somewhat frantic call from Sally. Tom was out with Christy again, and Ed was off puttering around somewhere. It was probably for the best, as they'd no doubt want to tag along on any adventures I was stupid enough to find myself in. Anyway, my phone rang, and Sally's melodious voice greeted me.

"I think you need to get over here."

"What – no hello, how are you?"

"We don't have time for this crap, Bill."

"We never just talk anymore," I said with a fake sigh and then smiled. Regardless of the urgency, it felt good to have Sally on the receiving end for a change. "Okay, so what's up?"

"There's *something* here!"

"Define something and here."

She mumbled something under her breath before continuing. I didn't catch it, but I would have bet money that there was also an accompanying eye-roll. "I'm here outside of the office. Something just burst in a little while ago, and all hell broke loose. Whatever it is, it's been calling your name."

"My name?" Oh, there came that sinking feeling again.

"Yes, *your* name."

"Did you see what it was?"

There was a pause. "No, I..."

"You *what*?"

"Fine! As soon as the ruckus started, I got out of there."

"Nice display of leadership, MacArthur," I quipped.

"Fuck you."

"I knew one day you'd beg me for it." Hot damn, I was loving this. Although if something had Sally frazzled, then perhaps it might not be the best time to enjoy rubbing it in. Ah, fuck it! I could help out *and* enjoy her discomfort at the same time. "Okay, aside from running away, have you done anything?"

"I sent Brian and Dusk Reaper in to see if they could root it out." She was no doubt swallowing whatever venom she wanted to hurl at me.

"And?"

"And Dusk Reaper came back out...or ran back out. Brian didn't."

Shit! I was kind of hoping it would have been Dusk Reaper who bought it. That guy was a serious douchebag. Yeah, I know, horrible thing to say, but well deserved – trust me on this. "Alright I'm heading over. Try to barricade the door until I get there."

"Way ahead of you, *boss*," she said and hung up.

Great! A rampaging beast was just dandy all in and of itself. A rampaging beast that knew my name – well, that was...actually, that wasn't particularly surprising. I had almost started to expect things like that to happen. Weird. That still didn't solve the mystery of *what* was causing chaos in the coven's office, but it took the edge off a little bit.

I paused for a moment before leaving, very much considering borrowing the shotgun that Ed kept stashed under his bed. He'd appropriated it back when we had to deal with Jeff. It had served him well in that ordeal, assuming you consider blowing the head off our geriatric former neighbor to be a check in the win column. Poor Mrs. Caven. Jeff had kidnapped her, wrongly assuming her to be my mother, and had subsequently turned her into a bloodthirsty monster. We attempted to rescue her but had been too late to do anything more than put her down for good.

Oh well, no use crying over spilled milk.

Considering I had half a city and several trains to traverse before reaching my destination, I decided against the gun. It was almost a pity to do so. Note to self: talk to Sally about stocking a small arsenal on coven premises. Actually, scratch that. Now that I thought about it, the words *Sally* and *arsenal* in the same sentence kind of gave me the heebie-jeebies.

I thus grabbed my jacket, and, armed only with my wits, headed off to save the day...hopefully.

* * *

I arrived at the office about an hour later, which, all things considered, was a pretty good pace – although thinking about breaking my midtown commuting record was probably something I shouldn't have been worrying about right at that moment in time. But hey, sometimes it's the little victories that really matter.

I walked up to our floor and came upon Sally, Dusk Reaper, and a few other assorted coven members standing outside the main doors.

"Where the fuck have you been?" Sally hissed. She was clearly having a bit of a stressful day. I didn't make it any better.

"Nice to see you, too. Sorry; I would have been here sooner, but I had a brief moment of sanity in which I had to question the wisdom of facing an unknown monster that's been shouting my name. Fortunately for you, it didn't last." She wasn't so stressed so as to spare me the eye-roll I knew was coming from that one. The pleasantries finished, I continued. "So did any of you see anything?"

"I did," answered Dusk Reaper.

On the train, I had some time to think about what might be after me and thus had a theory. Not sure how it would have gotten here. Then again, a few months ago I didn't even believe in vampires. So who was I to say what was and wasn't possible? "Let me guess," I said to Dipshit Reaper, "about nine feet tall, built like a bulldozer, and screams a lot?"

"No," he replied.

"*No?*" Okay, that was unexpected. Not that I should be all that sad about it. Facing off against a creature that had almost turned my rib cage into paste wasn't exactly número uno on my priority list. "What did it look like then?" I asked with a little uncertainty.

"I'm not really sure," Dusk Reaper said. "It was too fast to get a good look at. I think it was pretty small, but I've never seen anything move like that. It was like this tiny little whirlwind. It went after Brian before I could even think of doing anything, and..."

"And you ran like a pussy," I finished. Dusk Reaper had been one of Jeff's supporters, just not a particularly brave one; however, I made it a point to assert my position as alpha dog to him at every turn, just in case he ever got any bright ideas.

"So what do you think?" Sally asked.

"Tasmanian Devil?" I offered unhelpfully.

"Well, then you get to be Bugs Bunny, especially since it was calling for you," she replied.

"It knew my name?"

"Dr. Death," said a female voice from off to my left. It was one of the younger coven members (*aside from me*). Eliza, I think her name was. I didn't know her too well, other than she was one of the conscripts who helped man Sally's suicide hotline scheme.

"What was that?" I said, turning to her. I can't say I minded doing so. Much like all of the other women in the coven, she wasn't exactly hard on the eyes.

"It was calling for Dr. Death," she repeated.

Hmmm, aside from James and the occasional mocking by Sally, nobody really called me that anymore (*my subconscious aside*). James didn't exactly fit the definition of tiny, and Sally was standing right there.

"Alright, let's do this, I guess." I turned to Sally. "Are you in?"

"I've got your six," she replied.

She unlocked the door and held it open. I stepped through, trying to portray an aura of leadership for the others – one that I didn't really feel.

I had no more than crossed the threshold when it slammed shut behind me and I heard it being locked. Somehow, I wasn't surprised. Maybe I should've been nicer on the phone.

The place looked like a bomb had gone off in it. Papers were everywhere, desks were overturned, and there was a man-sized hole in the wall with a pile of dust in front of it...no doubt Brian's last stand. Dusk Reaper was right. It *did* look like a mini tornado hit this place.

Speaking of which, I should have been paying attention for the perpetrator instead of making a mental checklist for the cleanup. While I was busy observing the damage, something slammed into my back and drove me to the floor.

"FOR THE LAST TIME..." a shrill voice screamed. Strong hands grabbed me and flipped me over. Something jumped on top of me, and a small, familiar face filled my vision. "BRING ME...oh, Dr. Death. It is finally you."

"Gan!?"

* * *

"Open the fucking door, Sally!" I shouted from the other side. "I have your *monster*."

"Did you get it?" she called back.

"Yeah, I got it." And *she* was gonna get it for locking me in.

The door unlocked, and she opened it. The other vampires stood behind her, peering in with curious eyes. Goddamn, sometimes the undead can be such pussies.

"Did you kill it?"

"Not quite," I replied, gesturing to the small girl standing next to me. "Sally, meet Gan. Gan, meet Sally."

"Gan?" replied Sally, completely flummoxed.

"This is your whore, I presume?" Gan asked, looking up at me.

"What did you call me?" snapped Sally.

"A whore, obviously. A woman of status would never dress like that in my culture. What else could you be?" Gan asked matter of factly.

Sally turned beet red, which was really impressive considering her lack of a pulse. She looked like she was about to let fly with something, but I interrupted.

"Well then, now that the introductions are out of the way, what are..."

But Sally wasn't done yet. "What the hell did you think you were doing in there!?" she yelled at Gan, her courage apparently restored now that she'd gotten a good look at the big bad *monster*.

Gan ignored her, continuing to look up at me as she replied, "Your whore is insolent. You should have her whipped."

"She'd probably like that," I said, which caused Sally to turn even redder. Pretty soon and I'd be able to fry an egg on her forehead. "But Sally does have a point, Gan. Why were you wrecking the place?"

"Your servants did not immediately heed my command to bring you forth. Thus, I felt a lesson was in order."

"You killed one of my coven members," I pointed out.

"It is little matter. But I shall make you another if you wish."

"That's quite all right. Maybe some other time." I looked up and noticed that all the other vamps present were still gawking at us. I had lots of questions for her, but I neither needed nor wanted an audience. "Okay, everyone, show's over. There's a lot of cleaning to do. Get to it before I let the rest of the coven know about this."

There was some mild grumbling, but soon enough all of them, save for myself Gan and Sally, had gone back into the office to start the not-so-miniscule task of cleaning up. In at least one way, Gan was no different than any other kid; she could make a hell of a mess with very little effort.

* * *

A few minutes later, the three of us were seated in Sally's executive suite (*bitch*). I sat Gan down and got her a blood pack from the mini bar (*grrrrr*) to suck on.

"I normally prefer my food fresh," she complained.

"Maybe later. For now, just eat this, please."

She beamed up at me. "I will do it for you, Dr. Death."

"So you wanna tell me who *Wednesday Adams* here is?" Sally asked from behind her expensive mahogany desk (*goddamn it!*).

"Very well," I answered. "This is Gansetseg, daughter of the Khan...you know, as in the Khan who's a member of the *Draculas*? I hear he's kind of a big deal."

"Oh," she replied, her mouth dropping open. She hadn't been expecting that part. Anything that was even remotely connected to the Draculas got instant respect in the general vampire community. Even Sally was at a loss for words, which probably said a lot about the whole situation. "Pleasure to meet you, Gansetseg," she finally said.

"You may call me Gan, whore. I have grown to prefer it."

Regardless of Gan's station in the vampire hierarchy, her comment immediately popped the little bubble of awe that had been forming around my partner. Sally glared daggers at her, and then turned her venomous gaze toward me. "And what, pray tell, is the Khan's daughter doing here?"

"Actually, that's a good question," I remarked, realizing that I didn't know either. I figured I'd do the simplest thing...ask. "Gan, what are you doing in New York?"

"I followed you, obviously." She finished her drink and tossed the empty blood pack unceremoniously into the trash, much like any normal child might dispose of a juice box.

"Obviously," Sally mimicked with an eye-roll.

It didn't go unnoticed by Gan. "What is that expression the whore makes?"

"Oh, that? It's a...sign of respect," I said, throwing Sally a sideways glance. Hopefully, she was smart enough to realize that I had probably just saved her life. Pint-sized or not, Gan was three hundred years old. That meant she was most likely more than a match for both of us combined.

"That is good. Perhaps she knows her place after all," Gan continued.

Before Sally could open her mouth and ruin it – because believe me, she was going to – I continued with my questioning. "So why exactly did you follow me?"

Gan smiled as she answered, "Because I have chosen you as my mate."

Gan and Billy Sitting in a Tree

"WHAT!?" SALLY AND I blurted out in unison.

"I have decided you are to be my mate," Gan replied evenly. "I shall be your queen, and you shall be my consort."

I turned back toward Sally and saw that her face had gone red again (*really had no idea how she was doing that*); however, this time it wasn't anger. She looked like her head was about to explode. She quickly excused herself. The door had just barely closed behind her before I heard an eruption of laughter from outside. Good to see she had my back.

"I'm not sure I understand, Gan," I said, ignoring the guffaws still coming from beyond the closed door.

"For centuries, my father has treated me like a child; however, I am no child. I am a woman, old enough to make choices. And I have chosen you, Freewill, to be mine forever."

"*Why* exactly?"

"We are an excellent pairing. I am royalty. One day, I shall ascend to the First Coven to sit as an equal with my father. You are the Freewill that our legends speak of. Together, we will make a formidable team. Besides, you also make me smile." She grinned up at me, flashing those big green eyes of hers.

Oh boy. This was starting to look messy. "And your father agrees with this?"

"No. He is too set in his ways. He told me that he forbids it. But I am a woman. I do as my heart commands."

A thought entered my head, and with it I could feel the threat of a migraine coming on. "Your father didn't let you come here, did he?"

"I need ask no permission. I am a woman. I go where I please. It pleased me to come here for you."

Oh shit! No wonder James had wanted me to leave. He had been listening in on their argument back at my dinner/trial. I guess he figured out of sight, out of mind. He figured wrong.

"Gan, listen to me. This is important. Does the Khan know where you are now?"

"I would imagine so. I left father a letter stating my intentions as a woman."

Fuck me! I tried to hide the fact that I could feel pinpricks of sweat breaking out on my forehead. I asked with a forced cheerfulness that I wasn't feeling, "Just one more little question, Gan. What do you think your father will do once he reads your letter?"

"Father is set in his ways," she replied in the bored tone of someone who has seen this sort of thing happen many times before. "He will no doubt send his assassins to retrieve me and most likely kill you and your followers (*oh, of course*). But do not worry. Together, we will defeat them and send their heads back to him. Then we shall be together forever."

* * *

I left Gan sitting where she was and stepped out. I found Sally still wiping tears from her eyes. "Glad you find this amusing," I snarled.

"Oh, you have no idea," she chuckled back at me. "I haven't laughed that hard in decades."

"Good, because I hope you can keep your sense of humor when you learn how fucked we are."

I filled her in on what Gan had just told me, making a point to emphasize the assassins coming to kill me *and* my followers.

"How bad are we talking here?" she asked, having quickly sobered up.

"If it's what I think, then we're probably talking three vamps with about a millennium of experience amongst them."

"That's not good."

"Ya think?"

"Don't get all testy at me. You're the one that the ten-year-old she-demon finds irresistible."

"Twelve."

"What?"

"She's twelve...sorta," I replied.

"I'm pretty sure that wouldn't matter much to a jury."

"It's not the judge or the jury I'm worried about," I said. "It's the *executioners*."

"I swear, trouble just swarms to you like flies to shit."

"Maybe next time you'll just let me take my vacation in peace," I offered. "As usual, the caveat being that there *is* a next time."

"That's one of the things I admire about you, Bill, your always upbeat attitude."

"What can I say? The world needs more eternal optimists like me"

"All jokes aside," Sally said, getting back to the subject at hand. "What are we gonna do about this?"

"Not sure. From what I learned while I was there, apparently these people put some pretty big stock in my being a Freewill. You should have heard the shit they were spouting."

"Let me guess, the words *chosen one* were spoken?" Sally ventured.

"Not quite, but pretty close."

She sighed. "The world needs some new clichés."

"Tell me about it," I agreed. "But anyway, I know at least one of the guys the Khan will be sending, a dude named Nergui..."

"Nerd Gay?"

"Watch it. The juvenile humor is supposed to be my thing."

"Sorry. You must be rubbing off on me."

"We can talk about you rubbing me off another time," I said, quickly jumping out of slapping range. "For now, though, let's focus. Nergui speaks English.

Maybe we can talk him down. Hopefully, he'll be willing to listen to our side of the story."

She considered this for a moment. "A lot depends on the Khan here. If he gave a solid order...or worse yet, gave Nergui a *compulsion* to kill you, then all the flowery words in the world won't save us."

I nodded. "Yeah, I kind of figured that was the more likely scenario."

"I'll put the coven on alert."

"Good idea. What's the drill?" I was ostensibly in charge of the coven, but even I had to admit Sally had way more experience in vampire goings-on than I did. She also kept an eye on things during the week while I was off earning my sheckles as a code monkey. Thus, there was no shame in deferring to her now.

"I have a couple of ideas."

"Lay them on me."

"Okay," she started. "For now, I say we assign guards to the main coven nests. Here, the loft, maybe the warehouse. Encourage the rest of the coven to stay in those places and not go anywhere except in a group. That part shouldn't be hard."

I nodded in agreement. Jeff had run the coven much like a frat house, and a good deal of that mentality still remained. I was half-surprised whenever I saw any of our membership get up to use the bathroom without three others in tow.

"I'll also tell them to make it a point to notify us immediately in case anyone goes missing."

"I almost hate to suggest this, but what about arming the coven?" I asked.

"Stakes?"

"Guns," I corrected. Vampires are much stronger and more durable than humans, and we heal in a fraction of the time; however, from personal experience, I can attest that our nerve endings work just fine. A gun shot wouldn't do much in the way of killing a vampire, but it would hurt like hell and give the attacker an advantage. Now that I was thinking of it, maybe something like a bayonet would be ideal. Shoot 'em, then stake 'em.

"Tricky," she said, shaking her head. "You know how we have some deals in place with the human authorities?"

"To keep our messes under the rug?"

"Exactly. Well, part of those agreements include that we're not really supposed to arm ourselves with anything other than basic melee crap. I mean, haven't you wondered why you haven't seen any of us packing heat before?"

Actually, I hadn't. Now that I thought of it, the whole fracas with Samuel's group had immediately turned into a street brawl...not a single shot fired by either side. Hell, not a single gun brandished either. Damn, I really needed to start paying attention better. I shrugged and replied, "I guess I just thought you were all a bunch of luddites."

"What?"

"Basically, I figured you guys just didn't like technology because it was some kind of vampire thing. You know, maybe you all thought you were too cool for guns."

She sighed and started to open her mouth, but before she could speak the door to her office opened.

"I grow weary of your whore's sitting room," said Gan, standing there with a pouty look on her face. She might have the mind of a three-hundred-year-old vampire, but there were still some decidedly kid-like things about her.

Before Sally could say anything that would cause the rest of us to start betting on who would win in a fight (*my money was on Gan*), I stepped between them and addressed the little tyke. "Can you give us just a few more minutes? We're almost done here. Please...for me?" I asked in my friendliest tone.

Gan mimicked Sally's eye roll and did as told. After she had closed the door behind her, I turned back to my partner and said, "Awww! Isn't that cute? She's already learning something from her auntie Sally."

"Good, Bill. Because if you had called me *auntie whore*, I'd have killed you myself." From the look on her face, I didn't care to dispute that. "Although little Ms. Pain-In-The-Ass there has reminded me...what exactly are you going to do about her?"

"Me?"

"Yes, *you*. She obviously *wuvs* you," she mocked. "Unless, that is, you'd prefer to just let her, a poor helpless child, loose in the city."

I thought about that for a second before replying, "Do you think the city would stand a chance?"

"It'd be burnt to the ground inside of twelve hours," she replied.

"Maybe the coven could...ya know...watch her?" I asked hopefully.

"Can you really think of anyone in our group who you would trust to babysit?"

I thought for a moment, and then looked up. Sally had no doubt read my mind because we both said, "Starlight."

"I guess that could work," she admitted.

"Cool."

"Just one problem. I sent Starlight up to Boston. She won't be back until tomorrow night at the earliest."

"Why did you send her to Boston?" I asked, already knowing the answer. Boston was the HQ for vampire activity in the Northeast.

"I needed to file some papers up there," confirmed Sally.

"She's not your secretary!"

"But she's so good at it."

"Okay, enough. Arguing won't get her back here any sooner."

"Good, it's settled then."

"What's settled?" I asked

Sadly, I probably should have known that she was going to say, "Gan can stay at your place tonight."

* * *

Sometimes I love New York City. No matter how much of a cesspool of humanity it could be at times, I had to admit it was the only place in the world where a little Asian princess dressed in expensive silk fineries could ride the subway with a dorky companion like myself and not draw any stares. Speaking of which, though, I made a mental note to update Gan's wardrobe to something a little less conspicuous. Dressed as she was, she was practically a signal flare to the Khan's kill squad. Unfortunately, that created a whole new problem. I had no idea where twelve-year-old girls went shopping for clothes. Was *The Gap* still cool? Was it ever? How the hell would I know?

Oh well, that was tomorrow night's problem. For now, it was time to get Gan back to my place and explain to my roommates that we were now babysitters to a three-hundred-year-old spoiled little rich girl. Back when I had first told them that I'd been turned into a vampire, they'd taken it exceptionally well. I had a sneaking suspicion that asking them to help me watch over the Khan's little hellion was going to go over a whole lot less smoothly. It's kind of funny if you think about it. You tell some guys you're a vampire, a werewolf, or the freaking *Creature from the Black Lagoon*, and they'll just say "Cool" and go back to whatever they were watching on the SyFy channel; however, if you were to ask them to watch your pre-teen niece, *then* you'd be in for a freak-out.

But oh well, I figured they owed me for all the times they'd almost immolated me in the name of testing out my vampire powers. They could deal with it.

We arrived at my building and walked up to the apartment on the top floor. I unlocked the door and held it open for Gan. "Welcome to my place."

"This is where you rule your coven from?" she asked with a bit of confusion. "It does not speak well for one of your status." *sigh* Everyone's a critic. So sorry that my bachelor pad didn't conform to her highness's lofty expectations.

"It's...a disguise," I said, making it up on the spot. Yeah, that works. "So my enemies don't suspect my *true* power." (*Jeez, I sounded like Dr. Doom*)

"Ah, I see," she nodded approvingly. "My apologies, I underestimated your wisdom. You live in a den of pig offal so as to confuse your adversaries. Clever indeed."

"Yeah, whatever," I said, tossing my jacket onto the couch. "Make yourself at home."

"Where is our bed?"

That stopped me dead in my tracks. "*Our* bed?"

"Yes. As your mate, are we not expected to share such things?"

Jesus fucking Christ! All these years I've been praying that one day a girl would say something like that to me. It figures that when it finally happened, it would be from a psychotic, pre-pubescent mini-vamp. If this was going to be my eternity, I might as well just run into the sunshine right now with a big ol' smile on my face.

I was about to give Gan a long lecture on exactly why we wouldn't be sleeping anywhere even remotely in the same room when Ed's bedroom door opened and he strolled out.

"Hey, Bill," he said, and then, upon noticing Gan, added, "What's with the munchkin?"

Gan turned and smiled up at me. "You keep your own supply of food here? Excellent! I shall sample him." With that, she launched herself across the room and slammed into my roommate. He went down hard with her on top of him.

"Holy shit!" I cried, throwing myself after her. Damn, she was fast. Fortunately for me, though, I didn't exactly live in Windsor Castle. Thus, it was only a few steps until I could grab her and drag her off Ed. Or try to drag her off. She was strong for her size, too.

"What the fuck!?" he screamed at me once I'd pried her off.

"Um...Ed, meet Gan."

* * *

"Dude, put the gun away," I said to my roommate standing in the doorway to his bedroom. He was sitting at his desk, loading shells into the twelve-gauge shotgun he usually kept not-so-hidden under his bed.

"So Rainbow fucking Brite out there can try to take another chunk out of me? I think not."

"I have it under control."

"Oh yeah, real good control you got there," he said, loading another shell. "A second later, and she would have been using my head as a soccer ball."

161

"Don't you think you're overreacting?" I asked in as soothing a tone a possible, which wasn't very.

click another shell got loaded. "My apartment is now Satan's daycare. No, I don't see much overreacting here."

Okay, time to change tactics. "So says the guy who, just the other day, was putting the moves on a floozy with both a serious case of overbite and an overall lack of respect for human life."

"That's different," he protested.

"How?"

"Have you ever looked at Sally's tits?"

"Many times."

"Need I explain further?"

"No, I guess you don't." Damn, I hate sound logic. "Still, chill with the gun. You're liable to make Gan nervous."

"Bill," he replied in that tone he often used when he wished to make me feel as stupid as humanly possible, "she's the bride of Frankenstein wrapped in a pre-teen body. Her first act upon meeting me was to try to turn me into a *Slurpee*. Believe me when I say I'm not too worried about making *her* nervous."

"Point taken," I said. "But you have to..."

"Oh thank you, Freewill!" came Gan's voice from elsewhere in the apartment.

"Huh?" Before I could say more, though, her voice carried to us again.

"Such marvelous toys. I shall enjoy them thoroughly."

Ed and I both stopped what we were doing. "What the hell is Strawberry Nutcake rambling about?" he asked.

"No idea. I don't have any toys..."

Ed's and my eyes suddenly locked. A look of mutual terror crossed between us. Tom's room. Oh fuck! We both bolted in that direction.

* * *

My other roommate, Tom, was a life-long obsessive collector of old toys, baseball cards, and the like. He was convinced that one day he'd be able to retire on their collective worth. He had a ton of worthless crap, so my assumption had always been that he'd be more likely to wind up on some docudrama about insane hoarders. Then again, he also had some legitimate collector's items. Back around when I was first turned into a vampire, he'd scored a first generation *Optimus Prime* figure for next to nothing at a flea market. He'd been so enamored of it that he'd inadvertently charged it with a small portion of his life energy, thus turning it into a deadly weapon against vampires.

You see, people normally assume that crosses work on vampires because we live in fear of God's power. That's mostly bullshit. In order for a cross to work, a person has to truly believe in it. But as far as I'm aware, it has nothing to do with God. Faith, as it turns out, is actually a form a magic. Yeah, I know; I thought the same thing when I heard that magic is real. But it is, trust me on this. The same principle that applies to a cross can apply to anything a person truly believes in.

Thus, Tom wound up in possession of a junky piece of plastic from *Hasbro* that, in his hands, also happened to be the equivalent of the Ark of the Covenant against my kind.

Anyway, this magical vampire-killing toy had been broken in the final battle against my old coven master, Jeff. Tom had never let me forget it. Fortunately for me (*but much to his own chagrin*), he hadn't been able to empower any of his other collectables in quite the same way. However, just because he didn't love them all with the same fervor that he had loved Optimus didn't mean he wouldn't go completely apeshit when he so much as caught me or Ed looking at them.

Tom normally kept his room locked when he wasn't around. He tended to do that ever since our early days of living together, when he'd return home to find all of his action figures waiting for him in a variety of lewd poses. For a guy who's almost never serious, he has a surprising lack of humor when it comes to his collections.

Within moments of hearing Gan's voice, Ed and I arrived to find Tom's door wide open. A flimsy key lock isn't much protection against even the weakest of vampires. We found Gan standing in the middle of a clutter of toys. She had a big smile on her face and was busy feeding Man-at-Arms to some six-legged plastic monster.

Oh, we were so fucked.

Slumber Party of the Damned

IT TURNS OUT that Tom was the one who was fucked. Or at least that was my assumption, since he didn't return home that night. I was actually glad to see someone getting some action from a woman not associated with the supernatural world. Good for him. And also good for us once we finally managed to get Gan out of his room. Thank whatever dark gods watch over the toys of madmen that nothing was broken. We put everything back the best we could (*but knowing that a nutcase like Tom would be able to tell if his things were even a millimeter out of place*) and wedged the door shut.

You really have no idea how stressful it was. Watching Tom have a hissy fit over his toys was one of the more off-putting things I had *ever* experienced...and this from a guy whose range of non-normal experiences had gone up significantly in the past year. It just wasn't natural. Experiencing Tom rant about his toys was uncomfortable in a way that was akin to staring at non-Euclidian angles for too long. His tantrums also tended to last for a *long* time. Thus, for a variety of reasons, Ed and I wished to avoid one at all costs.

Once we'd finally finished, Ed decided to turn in. Considering the ruckus that I heard coming from his room, I assumed that not only had he locked himself in, but that there was probably a pretty good makeshift barrier constructed on his side of the door. I also had little doubt that he'd be sleeping with a twelve-gauge teddy-bear named Remington tonight. I guess I couldn't really blame him.

Unfortunately, that left me alone with Gan. I had to think quickly, lest I wind up with her wanting to get all jiggy with me. Trust me when I say that's a thought I would gladly bleach out of my brain. Maybe I'm just a product of my culture. After all, even a hundred years ago a girl of Gan's (*physical*) age would have probably already been married off. Regardless, the creepiness factor of it all made my skin crawl. This was the big joke of my existence...I was a vampire with ethics.

"Gan," I finally said, "I want you to take my bed."

"Of course," she answered.

"No, I meant that I want you to take my bed, and I'll sleep on the couch."

She looked confused. "Is it not common in your culture to share the bed of your mate?"

"Well, yeah...normally it is. It's just that..."

"Just what then?"

I figured I'd better just blurt it out. "Gan, it's the whole kid and adult thing. It's...just not right."

"In some ways, I agree," she said.

"*Really?*" I blurted out, surprised. Maybe this wouldn't end badly after all.

"Yes. There is a part of me that wonders if it is not right as well. You are just a child, after all (*huh!?*). I have lived over ten of your lifetimes. You are practically a newborn to me (*not quite what I meant*). I will admit that I almost feel...how do you say it...that I am taking advantage of you."

"Okay," was all I could say for a moment there. That was a concept I hadn't even considered. But maybe it gave me a way out. "That's good, Gan. I was...embarrassed to tell you this, but...I'm kind of...*inexperienced* with women." Never thought I'd be playing the nervous virgin card to get out of sex. Live and learn, I guess. What an odd fuckery of a world I found myself in.

Gan got a strange look on her face at my *confession*. After a moment, she replied, "What about your whore? Does she not comfort you at your whim?"

"Sally? No, trust me on that one. Not much comfort going on there."

Gan continued, "What about my father's servants? Did you not enjoy their services?"

"Oh that, well..." Shit! She *knew* about that?

"I thought so. They reported back that you were quite vigorous..."

"Yeah, I guess."

"...if a bit lacking in stamina."

"*What*!?"

"However, I am sure we could work on that problem together. My life with father and my people has taught me great patience."

"One: I do *not* have a stamina problem," I blurted out before really thinking about it. "They surprised me, is all. It had been a while since..." It was at that point that my subconscious kicked in and reminded me I was discussing my sex life with someone who would've looked more at home playing with a *Barbie* dream house. "Two: we are not having this conversation."

"I think it is important to discuss your inexperience."

"I am *not* inexperienced! What I meant was... (*think fast, stupid!*) emotionally (*yeah that'd work, I guess*). Emotionally, I'm not sure I'm ready for this. It's a big step for me. All of the *MANY* women I have been with, they've just been meaningless encounters for me. I'm not sure I'm ready to take such a big step yet." Jesus Christ, I hoped Ed wasn't eavesdropping. No way would he ever let me live this down.

"In time, you will come to love me." Argh! Talk about not taking the hint! Apparently, I needed to rent the Jumbotron in Times Square to display in thirty-foot letters 'YOU'RE TWELVE. I'M NOT SLEEPING WITH YOU!'

Okay, I had one last card to play. This chick I had briefly dated in college had used it successfully to keep me at bay. I found out later that she was more or less screwing her way through one of the frat houses on campus, but at the time it had sounded legit. Why not? Time for the Hail Mary pass.

"It just wouldn't be *right*," I said, channeling my inner female and trying to put a little emotional distress into my voice.

"Why? We are mates."

"Yes, but we're not...*married*." Ugh. I think I felt my testosterone levels drop just by saying that.

"I am not sure I understand," she replied

This was it. Time to go for the Oscar. "With all of those other women, it was just a physical thing. Two (*and sometimes four*) ships passing in the night. But this is different. I want to save myself for the *right* woman. Someone I can truly give myself to physically, emotionally...*spiritually*. If you are that woman, then you need to understand that I have to do this the right way. I need for us to wait until our bond has been sealed in the eyes of God for all of eternity."

I had thought I was maybe starting to spread it on a little thick there in the end, but when I looked down at Gan, I saw that she was actually misty-eyed. Oh yeah. I would like to thank the Academy...

"You are a good man, Bill. I have chosen wisely."

"Thank you for understanding, Gan," I said, continuing to shovel it on.

"I will respect your wishes."

"That means a lot. Really, it does." More importantly, it meant I got a reprieve until I could figure out how the fuck to stuff Prairie Dawn here into a box headed back toward China.

* * *

Sleep was a long time coming for me. Part of me wanted to keep an eye out for Gan trying to leave the apartment; however, there's also the fact that I never realized quite how uncomfortable our couch was. Our old couch had been great – old, dusty, a little musty, but comfortable as all hell. But then Jeff had trashed it (*and the rest of the apartment*) looking for me. Since then, I had never gotten an opportunity to crash (*or pass out*) on the new *IKEA* model we had replaced it with. Oh well, I imagine it's only a matter of time before I piss off some other entity and the apartment gets re-trashed. Who knows? Maybe Nergui and his fun bunch would do me a favor while they were trying to kill me and give me a reason to shop for a better one. That's me...a glass is half full kind of guy.

In the morning, I was awoken by Ed. I heard the sound of furniture being moved from behind his door, followed by him cracking it open and taking a peek around before stepping out. He gave me an annoyed glare, and then went to the kitchen to put on a pot of coffee. Oh well, no rest for the weary, I guess. I got up to join him.

"You look like you slept about as well as I did," I said, grabbing my mug.

"I kept having nightmares of Dracula's daughter trying to put me through a food processor."

"At least she didn't want to undress you like a Ken doll first," I pointed out.

"Fair enough," he replied with a bit of confused look. "Speaking of her..."

"In my room. Wanted to make sure she didn't try to leave in the middle of the night and kill everyone in the building."

"That would be hell on our rent."

"That it would," I agreed. "By the way, I'm sorry about last night."

"Probably my own fault. I guess I should be more specific whenever I wish that I was jumped by girls more often."

We shared a chuckle at that. Both of my roommates had their oddities, but no matter what dark places I found myself in as of late, it was comforting to know that they had my back. In the friend department, I'd take quality over quantity any day.

"Speaking of being jumped," he continued, "Tommy boy didn't come back last night, did he?"

"No, he did not," I confirmed. "I'm thinking that when he gets home from work tonight, it's going to be story time."

"Yep. Although there is something about living vicariously through Tom that just feels..."

"So completely wrong that you're forced to wonder whether or not you're fucked in the head?" I finished for him.

"Exactly."

It was at that point that my bedroom door opened. Ed didn't move, but I could sense him tensing up. Understandable. It's one thing to be pummeled by some big bruiser that outweighs you by fifty pounds of muscle, but getting taken down by a little girl was something that would rattle any guy.

Gan stepped out wearing one of my T-shirts.

"Oh, *this* is cute," Ed remarked under his breath, thus instantly erasing nearly all of that friendship bullshit I mentioned a second back.

"Don't start," I hissed. "Good morning, Gan," I said in a louder voice. "Sleep well?"

"I have slept on oxen that were more comfortable than your bed. It also smelled funny."

Ed wasn't quite able to conceal a laugh at that one.

However, Gan stopped his chuckle dead in its tracks by then adding, "Please have your servant open a vein so I may have breakfast. He may launder my robes when I am done."

"Gan, Ed is my friend, not my servant."

"You are friends with a human? Are they not cattle to you?"

Ed got up in a bit of a huff and walked over to wash out his mug.

"No, Gan," I replied. "In fact, Ed pays a third of the rent. That makes this place as much his as it is mine."

"A very curious thing to treat humans as equals. We do not do this where I am from."

"Equals?" Ed scoffed. "I'll put my dating history against Bill's any day."

I ignored him and continued speaking to Gan. "Ed is my *friend*, Gan. So is my other roommate, Tom. We treat each other the same." Who knows, she seemed curious enough. Maybe there was some hope of reaching through to her and not only getting myself out of this mess, but also avoiding too much bloodshed in the process.

"I think I understand." She nodded back. "You do not eat friends."

"Exactly." This was good.

"Then let us go find some humans who are not your friends so we may dine on them." Or maybe not. I put my head in my hands as I tried to think of something else to say.

"Here!" Ed said, interrupting us and placing a box in front of Gan.

"What is this?" she demanded.

"What all the cool vampire kids in America eat for breakfast...*Apple Jacks*."

* * *

Okay, so maybe giving a spoiled vampire brat a sugar rush wasn't the best of ideas. If so, then what we did next didn't exactly help either. Following her *nutritious* breakfast of cereal drowned in milk and blood (*and yes, it looked disgusting even to me*), we did the only thing we could think of...we sat Gan down and showed her how to the use the TV. I think it's safe to say that both Ed and I should consider sterilization. If that was the best we could do with a kid, neither of us should ever be allowed to breed.

But it seemed to do the trick for the moment. Gan was mesmerized by *Cartoon Network* and *Nickelodeon*, thus allowing us to retreat to our respective home offices to get some work done. Sadly, programming deadlines wait for neither man nor immortal beasts of the night.

Unfortunately, I didn't spend any real time as a teenager babysitting; otherwise, I would know that the Golden Rule of doing so is not to let the kids out of your sight. About two hours passed before I heard some loud yelling, in Chinese presumably, coming from the living room, followed by an equally loud crash. Ed and I raced out to find Gan standing there, or more specifically, Gan standing there with her fist through the screen of our TV.

Ed pretty much summed it up for both of us by yelling, "What the fuck!?"

"This box was insolent," Gan said with a pouty tone.

"What the hell does that even mean!?" again yelled my roommate.

I stepped forward to intervene. I may have explained that Ed was my friend, but I had little doubt he'd meet with the same fate as the television if she deemed him too *insolent* as well. "Gan, why did you kill the nice TV?" I asked in a patient voice.

"I demanded that it bring back the yellow one. It refused, so I punished it accordingly."

"The yellow one?" I asked.

"Yes," she replied. "The one who lives in the fruit and makes these things called patties."

"Let me get this straight," said Ed, an edge to his voice. "You smashed our television because *SpongeBob* ended?"

I shrugged and gave him a sheepish smile. "Guess I should have showed her how to use On-Demand."

Satan's Shopping Mall

THAT WAS PRETTY much the straw that broke Ed's back. Attacking him and treating him like dirt was okay – breaking the TV, not so much. He left in a huff with heavy hints that Gan should be gone by the time he got back. I really couldn't disagree with him. When I was recruited into this whole vampire thing, I accepted that I would probably face horrors beyond my imagining and endure an eternity of dealing with the darker forces of the universe. At no point did I ever think that babysitting would be included in that package; otherwise, I might have just let them stake me on that first night like they had wanted to.

Around mid-afternoon, I gave Sally a call. She would be awake by then, no doubt looking forward to another night of filling the coven's larders with the city's suicidally depressed. Well, she was going to have to change her plans. No way was I letting her or the others out of helping me with Gan. I was the coven leader, and if I ordered the rest of them to make with the Romper Room, then by God, I was going to get me some Romper Room.

"Let me guess, not a social call?" asked her voice as soon as she answered.

"Not even remotely. Starlight back yet?"

"She should be back here by sundown. I sent a car up for her."

"Good," I replied. "Assign someone else to help her." I lowered my voice so Gan wouldn't overhear. "She's gonna need it."

"None of the others are going to be happy with that."

"Ask me if I give a shit about what makes the others happy. Last I checked, none of them seemed overly concerned with my state of mental well-being."

"Okay, calm down. I'll ask around."

"Better yet, put Dusk Reaper on it. He gives you any lip, tell him he and I will be having a long sit-down to *discuss*."

There was a pause. I couldn't see her, but I knew Sally well enough to know she was probably smirking. "Can do," she replied.

"Good. I'll bring Gan over as soon as the sun goes down." I glanced over at her and noticed she was still sitting around in my T-shirt. "Oh crap." I had forgotten all about getting Gan some new clothes to wear.

"What's wrong?" Sally asked over the phone.

"Grab your pocketbook. Once I get there, you and I are going shopping."

* * *

Sundown came, and I got Gan dressed as best as I could, considering my apartment's complete lack of little girl clothes. Once done, I grabbed my wallet and told her we were heading out.

"Where are we going?" she asked. "If tonight is to be our wedding, I shall require more suitable attire."

"Uh, yeah. Sorry, the hall was all booked up for tonight," I lied. "We'll try again another day."

"Then where are you taking me?"

"I'm going to leave you with my coven. I...didn't like the way the human talked to you. My vampires will be more respectful." (*maybe*)

"Yes. That would be good. But what of you, my love? (*argh, don't call me that!*) Will you stay there with me?"

"Not tonight."

"Then where shall you be?"

"Out," I said, opening the door and leading us into the hall.

"Ah, I see!"

"You do?"

"Yes. You wish a night out to...how do they say...sow your oats."

What the? Oh, whatever. As long as it got her out of my hair. "Yeah, okay. That works," I muttered. We started to descend the stairs. All I knew was that I couldn't get to Manhattan fast enough.

As we were coming down, we ran into Tom going the opposite way.

"Hey, Bill!"

"Hey. Can't really talk, got things to do," I said, dragging Gan downstairs with me before she decided to see if I had rethought my policy on sampling my roommates.

"I need to tell you something," he called down to me.

"It'll have to wait," I yelled back, as I went through the front door.

"Dude!" his voice followed me out the door. "My girlfriend...I think she's a..."

I didn't quite catch that last part as the front door had slammed shut, but to my vampire hearing, it had sounded vaguely like *bitch*. That figured. *Welcome to the club, buddy*, I thought as Gan and I headed out toward the city.

* * *

Have I ever mentioned that there is something about being in a shopping mall that fills me with a near uncontrollable rage? No? Well, it does. Living or dead, I have always hated mall trips. I find the typical mall dwellers to be their own fetid little subspecies of humanity, maybe the result of some deranged genetic experiment to fuse man and cockroach gone awry. Vampires may be bloodthirsty monsters and zombies are disgusting walking corpses, but mall denizens...well, let's just say I'd sooner hang with the zombies. I don't know if I believe in Hell, but if it exists, it probably very closely resembles the Manhattan Mall.

Sally, on the other hand, looked like she was having a grand time. I don't think I'd seen her smile as much in total during the past several months as she was doing now, dragging me from store to store. I know it's cliché to talk about women and shopping, but she was doing her damnedest to live up to the stereotype.

I thus found myself standing in some smarmy little boutique up on the third floor, holding Sally's iced latte for her as she spritzed herself from yet another bottle of perfume that probably cost more than the down payment for a car.

"How's this one smell?" she asked, thrusting her arm into my face.

"Skanky," I replied morosely.

"You have no taste," she said with a feigned sulk.

"I also have no sense of smell. I think it burned out two stores back."

"Don't be a complainer," she said, handing the bottle back to the equally smarmy sales girl who was helping her out. "You're the one who wanted to go shopping."

"For clothes *for Gan*," I reminded her for the fortieth time.

"Relax. You can't just dive into these things. We have to work our way there."

"If you say so," I replied in a dead tone. God, this was taking forever. I glanced out the door, and then my eyes fell on the *Victoria's Secret* a few shops down. Well, that at least had potential. If Sally decided she needed to try on some lingerie, there was at least some entertainment to be had in that.

Alas, it was not to be. As we walked toward it, she saw my longing gaze wandering in its direction. "Down, boy," was the only thing she said as she strode past.

"Can't even throw me a bone?"

"I'm not touching anything that contains references to you and bones in the same sentence," she said, dragging me into a shop called *American Girl*. Considering that's exactly what I wanted Gan to fit in as, the name of the shop definitely seemed hopeful. At long last, my ordeal seemed to be nearing an end.

"Any chance we can bag the hotline and maybe just send the coven here to clean out this place?" I gestured to the mall as a whole. "Should be enough to keep them in blood for a while," I quipped while she searched through the outfits on display.

She stopped what she was doing and gave me a sigh. "Gutting this place would just be...wrong. Even I have my moral limits." I was contemplating which of the fifty or so possible answers rolling around in my head would be the best when she finally held up a little dress. "Now, this is adorable. I think we have our first winner."

I took a look. Okay, whatever; I guess it was cute. Then I happened to notice the price tag. "Holy shit! I just wanted to get her some clothes, not finance her college education."

"Don't be so stingy with your bride to be." Bitch!

"Seriously, whatever happened to jeans and a couple of tees?"

"Gan doesn't strike me as the tom-boy type. Nor does she strike me as the *Sears* clearance rack type."

"I noticed. Speaking of her *highness*, I hope she isn't giving Starlight too much trouble."

"I'm sure they'll be fine...ooh, here's another cute one."

* * *

After about another twenty minutes, during which I seriously contemplated a mall-based murder spree, we finally made it to the counter with a small bundle of outfits for Gan. The cute counter girl sized us both up as we approached. She gave Sally the smallest of sneers, but then reversed her expression when she turned to look at me. I actually got a nice, friendly smile. Come to think of it, I had noticed more than a few glances in my direction during the mall trip, but had been too irritated to put two and two together. Now it was finally clicking.

In the past, I had noticed that whenever I went anywhere with Sally, I would get stares of envy from other guys. It was obvious why. Sally was gorgeous, and they were all wondering what I had that they didn't (*fangs and an aversion to sunlight*). I knew because I had done it myself on more than one occasion. It's especially true if the guy in question with the hot babe on his arm isn't all that much to look at himself. Dudes like me just want to walk up and ask them for their secrets.

The thing is, while we guys are envious of our fellow brothers' prowess in hooking some of the hotter fish in the sea, there's usually no hatred going on there. It's more of a *'good for you, man! Hope to be there myself one day'* kind of vibe. However, judging from the looks I had been seeing, it's different for women. Let's face facts: no guy is going to be jealous of another guy who happens to be dating what appears to be a shaved ape. Women, on the other hand, seem to have this hatred for each other, no matter what they have by their side. Sally was a looker, and the other women hated her for it; however, Sally also had me walking by her side, which only seemed to increase this scorn. No matter what I looked like, they appeared to be flirting with me for no other reason than to try to take me away from her. Damn, that's cold.

On the other hand, there is the simple math of it all. Me plus Sally equals me looking more desirable. Note to self: hang out with Sally a *lot* more.

Anyway, the flirty (*toward me anyway*) counter girl rang up our order and then announced the bill. "Wow," was all I could say for a moment. "Are you sure we can't check out that clearance rack at Sears?"

Sally turned to me and gave a super slow eye-roll. Then she pulled her wallet from her purse. "Do they pay you in peanuts at that job of yours? No, don't answer that. I *suppose*, since I had a hand in this, I can help you out this one time." She pulled a card out of her wallet and handed it to the girl. Wait...was that...? The girl swiped it and handed it back. Yes it was! Holy shit, I'd never seen one of those. I grabbed Sally's hand before she could put it away again and held it up before me.

"You have a black Amex?"

"You might want to say it a bit louder. I'm sure there are one or two people on this floor who haven't heard you," she snapped back.

"I didn't even know those were real."

"They are, just not for people like you." She put it away and started to take the bags off the counter.

"Where did you get it from?"

"American Express, obviously," she quipped, starting to walk from the store.

"No shit! I meant...like...how?"

She stopped and turned toward me. "It's not exactly rocket science. I manage all of the coven's finances. It has its perks."

"Wait a second. That's a coven black Amex?" I asked, an idea forming in my head.

"Fitting color for creatures of the night, if you think about it."

"No, I mean that's attached to coven funds, right?"

"I suppose so," she replied

"And I'm coven leader, aren't I?"

She suddenly narrowed her eyes at me. "What are you getting at?"

"My turn," I said, grabbing her by the hand and leading her back into the bowels of the mall.

"Where are we going?"

"Shopping," I answered. "Dr. Death needs himself a few new toys."

* * *

So the mall was a horrific experience overall; however, I had a brand new *Playstation* and a whole bunch of new games to go with it. That should go a long way toward soothing any hurt feelings amongst my roomies regarding Gan (*and the broken TV*). It's about time I got something out of this whole vampire thing. Sure, it might be hard to play with the TV currently being busted, but I figured baby steps and all. I can't be expected to figure everything out, now can I?

Anyway, Sally and I were on our way back to the loft. "Care to stop for a coffee?" I asked while we walked through SoHo, bags full of clothes and games at our sides.

"Make it an Irish coffee, and you're on. Shopping always works up a thirst," she answered.

There was a nice little outdoor bistro that was on the way. They made some pretty decent drinks. Sure, I absolutely hated SoHo and nearly everything and everyone in it, but just this once I could make an exception and maybe pretend I was somewhere else. Having just experienced an early Christmas had put me in a surprisingly chipper mood.

Thus I should have expected something to happen to spoil it. I just never expected *her* to be the one to do it.

As we approached the cafe, Sally started talking about something else. I think it may have actually been important. I vaguely heard the words *Gan* and *assassins* mentioned, but the rest was completely burned out of my memory.

Sally took a step or two before realizing I had stopped. She turned and noticed the gaping mouthed look I was giving. I'm sure she said something or made some gesture in return, but she might as well have been invisible at that moment.

Seated at one of the bistro's tables was Sheila, AKA she who I could neither get out of my thoughts nor speak to about them – no matter how hard I tried. She was dressed in conservative business attire, but let's face facts: to me, she looked like she had just stepped out of a dream (*and not one of my nasty dreams either*). Unfortunately, that wasn't what had stopped me dead in my tracks. It was *who* she was sitting with. She was sharing a drink – and a laugh, too, by the looks of it – with Harry Decker, the fucking VP of marketing from my company. Goddamn it! Goddamn it all to hell!

Of all the women in my workplace, how dare that smug asshole put the moves on *mine*? I saw red, literally. The rage I felt at the mall was nothing compared to what I suddenly felt bubbling up inside of me. It must have been radiating off me in waves because Sally took a step toward me with actual concern in her eyes. I have never before felt such immediate anger well up inside of me. Within the space of a moment, it had consumed my being. I could feel my fangs and claws (*finally got them to work!*) extend. My eyes went black, and then it went beyond even that. I could feel myself...not even sure how to describe it. I suddenly didn't feel like me anymore. I didn't know what was happening, but Sally's eyes suddenly widened in surprise. Her concern was no matter, though. The beast that was inside of me, the one that I had been able to control for so long, was finally tearing free of its tethers.

And then Sheila looked in my general direction.

Oh shit! I panicked and did the only thing I could think of...adopt a tried a true movie cliché. I grabbed Sally, spun her around so that my back was to the cafe, and planted a big kiss on her lips.

She stiffened in surprise, but I didn't let go. I held on to her and steered us toward a little alley that we had been walking past. Once I was sure that we were out of sight of Sheila and her asshole date, I let Sally go. She had a look of utter shock on her face. I figured it was best to break the ice before things got even more awkward, so I went with my norm, meaning something smart-ass. "Sorry about that. I know you usually charge guys in advance for that sort of thing."

That snapped her out of it, and within a moment she was back to being Sally again. She replied, "Great. Now I'm gonna need a rabies shot." Having gotten out a quip at my expense, reality quickly sank back in and she took a step back and eyed me warily.

"What was that?" she asked.

"Sorry. I saw someone I know and kind of panicked."

"Not that! *You*. You...*changed*," she said in a small voice.

Guess I hadn't imagined it. I looked down at my hands; they were back to normal. Likewise, I could feel that all the other vampiric stuff had receded as well.

That was good. I had been starting to feel scary there for a second or two. I shrugged. "No idea. But looks like whatever it was is over."

I slunk over to the edge of the alley and peered around. Sheila and Harry were still seated. She hadn't seen me after all. That was good. I would never want her to ever see me like that. Sorry for all you fairy-tale love story junkies, but I just don't believe in bullshit like *Beauty and the Beast.*

A few seconds later, I could feel Sally peering over my shoulder. "What are you looking at?"

"Never you mind."

"Come on. Tell me."

"No."

"Tell me, or I'll make a scene," she insisted. "I brought my rape whistle."

I sighed. Yeah, things were back to normal. "I'm looking at Sheila."

"What's a Sheila?"

I pointed her out to Sally. She stepped out of the alley to get a closer look, at which point I immediately grabbed her arm and dragged her back.

"Do you want her to see you!?" I snapped.

"So what if she does?" she pointed out. "I don't know her." Damn, sometimes I hate logic.

"Yeah, well *I* do," I hissed defensively. A little too defensively as realization dawned in Sally's eyes.

She gave me a big, wide grin. "You *like* this girl." When I didn't answer, she added, "No. You *really* like this girl."

"I just...know her," I stammered back unconvincingly.

She took another look around the corner. "She's kind of cute...I guess." There was that female pissiness rearing its ugly head again. Men had the whole band of brothers thing going on. Women...well, without us around to stop them, I'm pretty sure they'd all happily claw each other's eyes out. Unfortunately, though, I had too much of my own pissiness going on at the moment to worry about that.

"She is not *kind of cute*!" I snapped. "She is absolutely beautiful." Okay, maybe that wasn't exactly as subtle as I had meant it to be. I saw the look Sally was giving me back. "*Fine*. Maybe I do sort of like her a bit."

"No shit, Romeo," she replied, looking again. "Who's the guy she's with?"

"Some asshole VP from my company."

"He's not exactly hard on the eyes," she purred.

"You're not helping."

"Good for her, though. Climbing the old corporate ladder."

"*Really* not helping!" I hissed.

"Sorry," she said, backing off. "So what are we doing standing here?"

"I'm trying to think of what to do," I peered back around the corner again. I looked hard at Decker and could feel that rage starting to build up inside of me again.

"What do you mean?"

"About *him*."

"What about him?"

"I think we need to kill him," I said flatly.

"Excuse me?" she asked, a tone of surprise in her voice.

"You heard me," I growled, continuing to look. I could feel that my fangs had extended again. "You have your cell on you?"

There was no answer, so I continued. "Give the coven a call. Get a few of them over here. Actually, call in Dread Stalker and Victor. They love this kind of shit. Those two will tear him apart limb by fucking limb before they let him die. I can dig that."

The only response was silence for a moment, followed by a sound behind me, a familiar one. I turned, and there stood Sally about three paces back, giving me a slow clap with her hands.

"Congratulations," she said with no emotion.

"On what?"

"You're finally one of us."

"What the hell are you talking about?"

"That guy. His only transgression is that he's dating a girl you like, and you just condemned him to death without a second thought. That's very *vampiric* of you," she said in that same flat tone, and again gave me a slow clap.

There was a pause just long enough for a heartbeat, if I still had one, and then her words sank in. Oh God! She was right. All this time, I had been looking down my nose at the other vampires, thinking that they were little more than well-coiffed animals. The truth was they *were*, but I was kidding myself that I was any better than them. I had become the thing that preys on the weak and hides under little kids' beds at night. I was no better than some rabid dog. I was *a monster*.

My knees buckled, and I leaned back against the wall. I took several deep breaths to clear my head. When I felt like I was in control of myself again, I looked back around the corner one last time. Sheila and Harry had gotten up and were leaving the bistro together.

All I ever really wanted for her was that she be happy. I had hoped it would be with me; however, I saw now that whatever future we might have shared had been irrevocably altered on the day I was made into this *thing* that I was. If Harry was the one who gave her the happiness that I could not, then so be it. I wouldn't stand between that. I couldn't live with myself if I did.

I sighed and turned back toward Sally, my eyes damp. "Let him go," I said softly.

She actually walked up to me and put a hand on my shoulder. It was by far the most tender thing I had ever seen her do. "Keep your humanity for a little while longer, Bill," she said. "It's one of your more endearing traits."

Our eyes met, and we shared what was probably our first genuine moment.

And that's when a voice from above spoke to us. "Yes. It is endearing. That is why I will kill him for you."

* * *

Both our heads immediately shot up toward the voice. There, about twelve feet above us, standing on a fire escape, was Gan.

"What are *you* doing here?" I asked, still trying to process this latest development.

"Following you, my beloved."

"You were supposed to stay with Starlight," Sally said.

"Ah yes, the simple one. I quickly grew tired of her."

"What did you do to Starlight, Gan?" I said, a note of warning in my voice. I was still pretty screwed up in the head and in no mood for this shit.

"Do not worry, my love. She is unharmed. She wished to play this silly game with me...what did she call it...hide and seek. While she stood there counting into her arms for whatever reason, I left."

"How did you find us?" I asked.

"I have your scent. I can track you *anywhere*," she replied, tugging at the sleeve of her shirt. Before heading to the loft, I had given Gan one of my old T-shirts and a pair of shorts that no longer fit me. She was absolutely swimming in the outfit, but a little creative cinching had made it passable until we could get her some new clothes. I saw now that it had been a mistake. Sally had once alluded to me that vampires could sense other vampires, but it was something I hadn't given much thought to before now, mainly because I didn't seem to be able to do it very well. I hadn't considered that Gan, being several hundred years older than I, might be both a lot more experienced and sensitive to these things than I was. Shit! I *so* didn't need this.

"Gan, you need to go back to the loft," Sally said.

"I need do nothing you tell me," Gan replied in a tone that suggested her statement was a mandate handed down by the heavens.

"How about if I ask you to do this...for me?" Ugh! I could almost feel the smirk that must be trying to escape from Sally's face at that one. Safe to say, our moment was over.

"No. I heard the things you said. I believe you need for me to do this."

"Gan..." I started, but she interrupted me.

"His life shall be my gift to you. Perhaps then you shall consider kissing me with as much passion as you kissed the whore."

Now it was Sally's turn to start fuming. I could practically feel it coming off her. I turned to say something, but it was a mistake. There was a flash of movement in the periphery of my vision, and I looked up to see that Gan was no longer there. All I saw was a quick flash of T-shirt disappearing over the rooftop of the building. Fuck me, but she was fast.

"We need to stop her," I said to Sally.

"Define *we*. I'm not entirely sure that *the whore* is interested in having anything to do with little Ms. Muffett right now."

"Come on, Sally. Don't do this. Didn't you just give me the whole 'don't lose your humanity' spiel?"

"Yeah, but that was *you*. If I get my hands on that little bitch right now, I'm going to do some decisively non-human things to her." She bent down to pick up her shopping bags and started walking in the direction of the loft. "Have fun finding your fiancé. If you need to kill her to stop her...oh well."

sigh Bitch...no, make that *two* bitches!

The Scent of a Woman

I HAD ABSOLUTELY no chance of catching Gan. She was too fast. It also wasn't helping that Sally had conveniently left the game system bag behind for me (*and no, I wasn't leaving that!*). My best bet was to try to catch up with Sheila and Harry before Gan did. She wouldn't hesitate to tear him apart like a paper bag and then bring me his heart as a trophy. On second thought, maybe I didn't need to hurry *that* much. No! Those were bad thoughts. Needed to keep them out of my head...no matter how tempting they might be.

Gan had a huge edge in speed, but the home turf advantage was definitely mine. I set out in the direction that the couple (*ugh, that word tasted awful even in my brain*) had, in the hopes of tracking them down before Gan did. I could use a little bit of my vampiric speed to help me along, but not much. The streets were far too crowded for me to go full out without being noticed; however, that was also another advantage in my favor.

Despite Gan's insistence on being a little murder monkey on my behalf, she no doubt knew the rules. Hell, I imagine she had it fully ingrained into her head that she couldn't exactly announce her existence to the world. Her father was one of the Draculas, and as far as I had been told, one of their edicts was that the general public couldn't know about us. Yeah, yeah, I know I've broken that rule all to hell a couple of times already...but then I don't have a father sitting on the board of directors for the infernal hellions of the world. So give me a break. Considering the rigid world she came from, I had little doubt that Gan couldn't help but have a bit more respect for these things than I did. She'd wait for them to be relatively alone before striking...hopefully.

The only problem was, where the hell were they? If they had ducked into another establishment, I would never find them; however, I also didn't see them anywhere on the street. Jeez, they didn't have *that* big of a lead on me. This was the city, though. Everyone who walked its streets was more or less a rat in a maze, and considering the size of the maze, it wasn't too hard to get lost.

I started ducking down less crowded side streets so as to make better time, but it still didn't appear to be helping. It wasn't like I wouldn't notice her, even in a crowd. I knew what she looked like. I knew how she walked. I knew how she dressed (*hmm, now that I thought of it, it sounded a bit creepy, even to me*). I knew what perfume she...that was it! She always wore the same scent, the same heavenly scent...err, sorry. Easy to get distracted by thoughts like that. Anyway, if one vampire could track another by smell, then maybe I could use my enhanced senses to find her. Hey, it works in the comics for *Wolverine*.

I moved out of the crowd and closed my eyes. I took a deep breath through my nose and concentrated on the smell of her perfume.

Nothing.

I needed to try harder, block out everything else around me. Gah! That was hard. Even on my best days, I'm not exactly known for a Zen-like state of concentration. Right then, my entire being was in turmoil. How was I supposed to focus when my main reason for doing so was to save some douchebag I had no interest in helping cross the street, much less rescuing? And that was when a thought hit me.

What was to stop Gan from killing Sheila after she was finished with Harry? Nothing, really. She didn't have any feelings toward humans. What was one more sheep to the slaughter for her? In fact, if she had really overheard everything I said, she might consider doing it just to remove the competition. Oh shit! That did it. The girl of my dreams in potential danger gave me the focus I needed. I concentrated. I imagined her scent. I breathed deep once, twice...and there it was. Faint, but I got a sense of the direction to go in. Thank you, vampire powers!

Wasting no time, I immediately bolted from my spot. I raced down a few side streets and then finally turned a corner I sensed she had gone down and...and of course, I collided head-on with another fast-moving figure.

* * *

We both went down in a tangle of arms, legs, and shopping bags. Considering the speed I had been moving at, if I had collided with a normal person there would definitely have been the accompanying sounds of breaking bones. As there was not, I had to conclude that my personal tackling dummy was thus not human. Great! Just my fucking luck to run into the Khan's assassins when I was trying to do the right thing.

However, as I untangled myself I realized that the Khan's assassins probably never looked this good, not even on their best day. I stood up and found myself face-to-face with Starlight, a look of surprise on her face that was quickly giving way to abject terror.

"Oh my God, Bill!" she shrieked.

"Star," I replied, dusting myself off.

"I'm so sorry, Bill. She got away. Gan, I mean. I turned my back for one second, and she was gone. I'm trying to find her. Please, please, don't be mad," she rambled. There was more, but it was increasingly becoming a panicky blur of sound. One of these days, I really needed to undo the fear of God I had instilled into her months back. For now, though, there was no time. I held up my hand, and she immediately stopped talking. Sometimes it's good to be king.

"Enough, Starlight. I know. I'm not mad. But I need to find Gan, too. If I don't, someone is going to die who doesn't deserve to (*mostly, I guess*). Can you help me?"

She nodded. "I've been tracking her."

"Good," I replied in as patient of a voice as I had, which wasn't very. "I'm tracking her intended victim. Let's split up (*and get hacked to death by Michael Myers...oh wait, wrong story*) and hope one of us gets there before it's too late."

She again nodded, the panic slowly starting to seep out of her face as she saw that I wasn't going to chew her any new orifices (*figurative or otherwise*).

"I appreciate the help. Now get going."

She didn't hesitate. She took off again, hot on Gan's trail I hoped. She apparently had no qualms about going all out, speed-wise. Guess that makes sense for her. I doubt too many New Yorkers would be all that big on giving the police a report on a leggy super-model running through the streets at a gallop that would make a race horse weep.

I resumed my concentration and attempted to pick up the scent of Sheila's perfume again. It was easier this time, as she had probably only passed this place a few moments before Starlight and I collided. Good thing she hadn't been around to see us...that would have just looked embarrassing.

* * *

Finally! I turned another corner and spotted them further down the street. This was a residential neighborhood, and considering the time of night, it was a lot emptier than where I had chased them from. I also happened to know from...ahem...some *research* that Sheila lived pretty close by. The question was, was Decker walking her home, or had she invited him up?

That latter thought again brought the outer twinges of blinding anger back into my brain. I needed to cut this crap out; otherwise, I'd wind up cheering Gan on instead of stopping her. I tried to focus on the saving aspect of things and not so much on any possible sweaty aftermaths of their date...grrrr, I was doing it again. Focus, stupid! Unfortunately, my little mental back and forth cost me precious seconds. I was closing in on them, but as it turns out, so was Gan.

I was still maybe a dozen yards away when I realized I had no idea what the hell I was going to say once I caught up to them. Hopefully, I'd think of something more clever than "Get your arm off my girl before I rip it out of your socket!", but hey, who knows. Anyway, I was closing fast when there came the most god-awful shriek. We *all* stopped dead in our tracks at that. Holy crap, was someone strangling a bobcat?

But no, it was Gan. She emerged from a side street and screeched again, a look of pure animalistic rage on her face. Whoa, she looked pissed. With my enhanced vampire night-vision, I could also tell she was armed for battle, claws and teeth at the ready. She spotted the two I had been tracking and went straight after them.

This was it, only one chance. I put on all the speed I could and launched myself on an intercept course with the little she-devil. As I accelerated, time seemed to slow down. Sheila appeared rooted to the spot, a cross between confusion and fear on her face. Mr. VP of Marketing, though, wasn't quite so frozen. He gave a shout of surprise and actually jumped behind Sheila,

SCARY DEAD THINGS

raising his arms in some sort of gesture as he did so. Jesus, what a fucking pansy!

But I didn't have (*much*) time for name calling. As Gan closed on them, I launched myself and caught her, full bore, on the side.

"Gotcha!" I yelled as we tumbled head over heels into a pile of garbage on the side of the street.

"Let me go. I do this for you!" she hissed at me, struggling to get up.

She was a lot older, and in a fair fight could easily have taken me; however, I had a pretty good adrenaline rush going on, and had the advantage of size and leverage. I managed to wrap my arms around her and drag her to her feet.

"You need to knock this crap off now," I said.

"Bill?" a heavenly voice suddenly called to me. Oh, yeah. The woman who held my heart in her hands was standing not fifteen feet away, watching me manhandle a little girl. This had the potential to be a bit *awkward*.

I thought fast. Nothing good came to mind. Oh well, time to wing it. But first things first. I whispered in a barely audible voice, but one that I knew Gan would hear just fine, "Whatever you do, please just be quiet for now." Then it was show time.

"Sheila? Is that you?" I asked, turning toward her with a big, sunny smile on my face. "Funny running into you here. Wow, small world."

The look on her face was absolute confusion. "What are you doing?" escaped from her (*luscious*) lips in a small voice.

"Oh, *this*? Yeah, probably looks pretty whacky," I said in an overly chipper voice. "I was just...playing with...my *niece*, Becky."

Gan had put away her fangs for now; however, she was still giving Harry a look of murder. Fortunately, for once she did as told and kept her mouth shut; otherwise, this could have ended badly.

"Your niece?" Sheila asked, looking between myself and the little Asian girl in my arms.

"Yeah. What can I say? We're one big *diverse* family. Fun on the holidays, I can tell you."

She still had a doubtful look on her face, but at least the fear had drained out of it. She opened her mouth to speak again, but that's when Harry stepped back up next to her (*guess the pussy was done with his cowering*) and growled, "What the hell do you think you're doing?"

Sheila gave him a not-so-kind look (*yes!*) and said, "Harry, this is Bill Ryder. You know, from the Games Department."

"I know *him*," he said in a slow, malicious voice...something cold sparkling in his eyes. However, then he apparently realized his tone as he lightened it considerably. "You're one of Jim's boys, right?" (*Jim's boys? Fuck you, you brown-nosing cocksucker*)

"I work for Jim. I'm pretty sure we've met," I said in an even tone, locking eyes with him. He stared back. Yeah, well screw you, pal. I've stared down centuries-old predators. No way was I backing down from some marketing drone. Before things could heat up, though, Sheila spoke and ended our little pissing match.

"Harry has a point, Bill. What *were* you doing?"

"Oh, you know," I said, again adopting an innocent tone. "We were just horsing around. I took Becky here to a movie tonight. Afterwards, we went and got some ice-cream. I guess I sugared her up a little too much (*God, this sounded awful*). She decided she wanted to play...a game of tag, and I've been stuck chasing her, the little scamp," I said cheerfully, giving Gan's shoulders a playful shake. She continued to say nothing, which was a minor godsend, although she still kept staring at Harry like he was a side dish on the dinner buffet. "Sorry she scared you back there," I said to him, a big ol' grin on my face. "Guess I shouldn't have taken her to see that zombie flick."

Harry just glared daggers at me. I couldn't help but notice that Sheila gave him another minor look of disapproval as he was doing so. Oh, yeah. Whatever moves he had put on her earlier had just gone down the drain. Take that, limpdick!

I was trying to think of an appropriate out before any of the parties present wised up and realized that my story made absolutely no fucking sense when I heard another voice shout, "Gan!"

I turned my head to see Starlight come running down the street toward us. Upon seeing that we weren't alone, she quickly slowed down to a more normal speed as she approached. Oh crap! Just what I needed, more complications.

"Gan?" asked Sheila.

"Oh...that's just our little *nickname* for Becky here," I sputtered as Starlight came up to us. I thought fast. "Oh hey, Alice!" I said to her, using her real name. "Sorry we missed you at the ice cream shop. Just playing a bit with my favorite niece...*your daughter*...here," I said, throwing her a wink. I hoped she was bright enough to pick up on things. Even if not, hopefully she was scared enough of me to just play along without questioning.

"This is your sister?" asked Sheila. My, she was an inquisitive little thing.

"Yes," I said. "This is my...*sister*, Alice." It was then that I realized that together we probably all looked like a workplace poster for diversity training, so I quickly added, "She's adopted...so is Gan...err Becky. Yep! That's my family. Almost too much love to go around."

"Oh. I'm sorry, I didn't mean to pry. I think that's wonderful, by the way," Sheila quickly replied after pausing for a few moments. Thank goodness for politically correct politeness. There was still confusion in her eyes; she certainly wasn't stupid, but I think she figured it might be rude to probe more.

"Yeah, isn't it?" I said, continuing with the smiles. "Well, will you look at the time? Way past Becky's bedtime here, wouldn't you say, *sis*?" I nudged Starlight with my foot.

"Oh...yes. Time for little growing girls to be put to bed," she stammered unconvincingly. An actress, Starlight was not.

Fortunately, Gan was our out here. Despite the fact that I was sure that they, or at least Harry, wanted to put me under a lamp and grill me until I cracked, the old 'I need to put the kids to bed' routine was a surefire escape route. Trust me on this. I've seen more than one of my now married college friends use that excuse.

"I guess it *is* getting late," replied Sheila. The tone of her voice suggested that she was saying it to everyone present, Decker included. So maybe this whole debacle didn't turn out to be such a clusterfuck after all.

"Goodnight," I said to her fondly before turning to the asshole by her side. "Good to see you again, Harry." My tone hopefully implied I didn't feel anything of the sort.

"Likewise," he replied dryly and then added, "I'll see you again *soon*," in that creepy tone he had used earlier. This was a guy in desperate need of a personality transplant.

Sheila said goodnight to me (*oh, to only hear those words in a different context*) and did a quick "Nice to meet you," to Gan and Starlight, and that was our cue to exit stage left.

Starlight and I started walking away with Gan tucked closely in between us. She was fast, but probably not so fast as to be able to bolt without one of us getting a hold of her first.

"You should have let me kill him. The world would not miss *his kind*," said Gan, sensing that it was now okay to break her silence.

"I know you think humans are less than us, Gan. But that doesn't make it right to kill them for no reason," I replied.

"You are angry?" she asked in a slightly disappointed tone.

I thought about it for a few seconds and then smiled at her. "Actually I'm not as angry as you might think. In fact there's a small part of me that's pleased."

"I do not understand. I did not kill him as you had earlier wished."

"No, you did not, and that's a good thing. On the other hand, you sure as shit guaranteed that he'll be sleeping *alone* tonight. And that, believe me, is a pretty damn good happy ending if ever I heard one."

Heads Up

I DECIDED TO accompany Starlight and Gan back to the loft, mostly to keep an eye on the latter. Along the way, I tried to think of a way to explain to her why she needed to stay with the coven. Considering my previous failures in doing anything to get her to stay put or listen, I decided to change tactics. Gan wasn't from our society, and thus our normal ways of getting someone to comply (*please, or the ever popular 'do as I tell you or I'll kick your ass*) wouldn't make any sense to her. I wasn't very well versed in Asian culture, but I had seen enough anime (*and not just of the tentacle porn variety*) to be able to make an educated guess.

"Despite your motives, what you did tonight was very...*disrespectful*, Gan," I said in a stern but otherwise emotionless voice.

She turned to face me, but then actually averted her eyes. Yes! She had no doubt been read this riot act before. No matter her age or station, I was learning that there were still some kid parts in her brain. And regardless of the attitude, most kids know when they've done wrong, especially when they get called out on it. I remembered this very well from my own childhood. The thing with parents is they know which buttons to push on a child. If I was right, and Gan's reaction told me that I probably was, she'd been ingrained to react like Pavlov's dog at any mention of disrespect from any person in authority. Since I was technically one such person and she was on my turf, I was hoping I could instill a similar reaction in her. Thus I pressed onward.

"When I first arrived in your land, James...the Wanderer, asked me to stay where I was. I was new to the land, and there were dangers about. I did as I was asked (*sorta*) because it would have been both foolish and disrespectful to do otherwise." I glanced over and saw that her eyes were downcast. Oh yeah! Every fish just needs the right bait to be caught.

"Think about that, Gan," I continued. "The same is true of you. You don't know this city. Trust me when I say there are many dangers here (*her being one of the biggest*). I didn't ask you to stay with Starlight as a punishment. I asked you to do it because this is my land, those are my rules, and (*time for another Oscar moment*) ...because I care about your safety. You *disappointed* me tonight, Gan."

Her eyes were still downcast, but I could have sworn my sensitive vampire ears picked up a small sniff from her. She finally said in a very small voice, "I am sorry, Bill. You are right. I have acted shamefully. I will not do so again."

Wow, I gotta remember to browbeat kids more often. Now the question was whether or not she meant it. That was a big *if*, as I was sure that, sooner or later, she was going to remember who was who on the vampire food chain. But for now at least I could let out a nice, long sigh of relief.

Then, as we neared our destination, a thought hit me. "Starlight, speaking of disrespect, where the hell is Dusk Reaper? Wasn't he supposed to be helping you?"

She hesitated for a few seconds, no doubt debating between the lesser of the two evils of covering for him versus ratting him out. Once upon a time, it wouldn't have been much of a choice; however, these days I was holding a lot more cards than he was. I just waited for her to make the decision I knew she would.

"He...wasn't very helpful," she finally said.

"I gathered that."

"He pretty much just went down to the bar." Not too surprising. The loft was located in the third floor of its building. The second story was kept bare for the purposes of a little extra noise insulation, as well as storage. The ground floor was home to a small but fairly popular lounge. It provided both enough sound to cover some of the nastier goings on in the loft, as well as occasionally served, in times of need, as a convenient hunting ground for the coven.

"What about after Gan left?" I asked.

"I went to get him. But he told me that he'd stay behind. You know, just in case Gan came back."

"How *noble* of him," I remarked. Unfortunately for Mr. Nobility, I still had just enough anger in me from the events of the past hour to ensure that I was going to enjoy having a little *talk* with him when we got back.

* * *

We entered the loft, and Dusk Reaper's visage was waiting there to greet our return. Unfortunately, any talk I planned to have with him probably needed to be postponed...indefinitely, due to the *oddities* of the situation – those oddities mostly consisting of his head staring up at us from the floor, minus any sign of his body.

Just so that I don't come across as getting overly desensitized to this sort of thing, I should probably point out that my immediate reaction was to yell, "HOLY FUCKING SHIT!"

Starlight's reaction was even worse. I had mentioned before that she was no actress. Well, judging by the way she was screaming, she might have actually made a pretty good extra in a *Friday The 13th* movie.

Gan, of course, had to put both of us to shame by keeping her shit together. In an almost bored voice, she remarked, "I see the assassins have arrived. I would have expected them sooner."

* * *

After I had gotten Starlight to stop screaming, no easy feat, I led her into the kitchen. There, I sat her down at the table with a fifth of tequila I had procured from one of the cabinets. I ordered her to take a few shots to calm her nerves. That would keep her out of my hair for a few moments until I could clear my mind.

I returned to find Gan examining the crime scene.

"Be careful with that, Gan. It could be dangerous," I said lamely, not really knowing what danger a disembodied head posed. But hey, it was the best I had at the moment.

"Do not fear, Dr. Death," she responded without looking up. "They are no longer here. If they were...you would know."

If that was meant to reassure me, it failed badly. However, just to make myself feel a bit better, I closed and locked the front door anyway. It wasn't much, but if they came back, it might give me just enough time to kiss my ass goodbye before they broke in.

That being done, I turned back toward Dusk Reaper's head. I had seen enough dead bodies by this point, so the shock didn't last too long. There was also the fact that any mourning period I might've had for him ended about ten seconds after finding his remains. He was a douche, no two ways about it. I would miss him about as much as I missed having crabs (*not that I ever had them, mind you*). Still, there was something odd about his death. It took me a moment, but then I realized what it was.

"How come he's not dust?" I asked no one in particular.

"His body is," Gan answered. "Look over in the corner." She pointed into the living room, and sure enough there was a small pile of ash lying there.

"Yeah, but his head..."

"Father's assassins are well trained in this. There are times when an enemy's fangs are simply not enough to send the correct *message*."

"Yeah, but how?" I asked. "Every vamp I've ever seen get dusted...well, it was kind of a package deal."

"Your inexperience shows, my love," she answered, again going back to that *my love* bullshit. I guess we were past the whole disrespect thing already. "They would have removed it in one quick strike with a sharpened silver blade coated in a special poison. The body immolates, but the head remains."

"Oh. That's pleasant to know."

"That is not the worst," she continued.

"No? Sounds pretty much like *the worst* to me."

"Your friend was lucky. They let him die."

"Not really following you here, Gan."

"If they had placed his head immediately into blood, they could have kept it alive," she explained. "That is a fate reserved for the worst offenders."

I gulped. "How long could they keep it alive?"

"For an eternity, if so desired. Imagine an existence such as that. Unable to do anything but tolerate the whim of your captor. Unable to even die unless granted mercy."

Whoa. Considering that the elder vampires weren't particularly known for their mercy, that didn't sound like much fun.

"Do you think your father has that in mind for any of us?" I asked, really hoping that the answer that was popping into my mind wasn't the one she was going to say.

"If father is angry enough, then that fate would be reserved for you as the leader of your coven."

"I was afraid you'd say that."

"Yes. Thus, it is in your best interest to avoid that fate."

Talk about stating the obvious.

* * *

Oh crap! I had forgotten about Sally. She was supposed to drop Gan's clothes off at the loft. Not good. I could feel panic settling in as unwanted thoughts started filtering into my head. Okay, calm down. Freaking out wasn't the most productive thing to do. I pulled out my cell phone. It was at least one action I could do, rather than stand there in a state of confusion. However, it rang before I could even start to dial.

"Hello?" I answered, half-expecting a heavily accented voice to state, "We have your whore."

Instead, Sally replied from the other end, "Bill? Are you all right?"

"Yeah, I'm fine. You?" Wow, two whole sentences without a barb at each other. That's almost a record.

"I'm not quite sure I'm what you'd call okay. Whatever you do, don't go back to the loft."

"Too late."

"What's there?" she asked, although the tone of her voice suggested she already knew.

"Dusk Reaper's smiling face. Unfortunately, the rest of him decided to skip town."

"Same here. I decided to stop off at the office first."

"How bad?"

"Three severed heads, and at least four other members of the coven seem to be missing."

Goddamn it! I had thought the office would be safe, considering it was usually staffed pretty heavily with vamps. If these guys had just turned a good chunk of my coven into confetti, it meant they were even better than I thought.

"Are you still there? At the office, I mean?" I asked.

"Are you fucking retarded?" Ah yes, we were back to normal again. "I'm standing right in the middle of the busiest street I could find."

"Good. Any idea how they found us?"

"Public records...for vampires, at least."

"What do you mean?"

"Boston. They have most of our addresses on file," she said.

"You think they'd rat us out?"

"If one of the Draculas asked?"

"Yeah. Sorry, stupid question," I replied. "Wait, you said *most*."

"Exactly. Covens are supposed to report all of their holdings, but it's kind of an unwritten rule to tolerate a few off-the-books safe houses."

"Alright. Don't say anything over the phone."

"This isn't *Mission Impossible*," she said with a sniff. "I'm pretty sure they aren't tapping us."

"You have an office full of beheaded vampires, and you're telling me that a little paranoia isn't warranted?"

"Point taken," she answered.

"Okay, let's meet up at that espresso shop James likes. We can talk then."

* * *

The four of us met up as planned about a half hour later. Sally was already there, and I saw that she brought Gan's clothes with her. Good idea. In all the chaos, I had forgotten that Gan was still dressed like something a blind man would cobble together from the Goodwill box.

"Hey," I said by way of greeting. Sally nodded back at me and Starlight then gave Gan a sour glance. "So how are we looking?"

"Not good," she said. "Between the brawl with the HBC and tonight, we're down to half a coven."

"The others?"

"I got a few of them on the phone, told them to spread the word."

"So what about those places you told me about, the ones off the grid?" I asked.

"Three come to mind. As far as I know, the warehouse where we dusted Jeff should be safe. That leaves..."

"Um, I don't think so," said Starlight in a small voice.

"What are you talking about?" Sally turned toward her.

"I may have mentioned it to Colin while I was up there," she squeaked in return. Colin was normally James's assistant in overseeing the Northeastern covens. However, since James was out of country, that left Colin in charge. Unfortunately for us, he was a little suck-up of a weasel. If he had information that any of the Draculas wanted, you can bet he handed it over to them on a silver platter.

"What the hell were you thinking?" Sally growled.

Starlight shrank back and immediately started rambling. "Well, you called me when I was up there. After you told me what was going on, it might have..."

"Might have *what*?" Sally got in her face.

"Slipped."

"How does the location of our secret safe house slip?" Sally hissed. I could see tinges of black starting to work their way into her eyes. She was not a happy camper.

"It just did!" Starlight pleaded. "Colin was there when you called, and he started asking me questions..."

"Okay, enough," I said, getting between them. "What's done is done, Sally. At least we know the warehouse isn't safe. We need to get the word out to not use it."

"Fine," she replied through gritted teeth, still glaring at Starlight.

"So what else do we have?" I asked, trying to get us back on track. Normally I'm all for a good chick fight, especially when the chicks in question look like Sally and Starlight. Throw in some tight T-shirts and a vat of

Jell-O, and we'd have ourselves a party to remember. But now was probably not the time to indulge in twisted little fantasies like that. The last thing I wanted was to be distracted by some wet dream and then wake up to discover the Khan was going to be skull-fucking my dismembered head for the rest of eternity.

"It's not great," replied Sally. "There's the place where we met with the HBC."

"Boston doesn't know about that?"

"No, but the Queens vamps obviously do," she confirmed. "If word gets out that we're using it and they decide to fuck us over..."

"Gotcha. What's left?"

"Your apartment," she said.

"*My* apartment?"

"Yes. As far as I'm aware, only a few vamps in the coven know where you live."

"The Brooklyn safe house it is, then," I said.

"But what about..."

I cut her off. "We'll deal with the HBC if we need to. I'm not hosting a vampire slumber party."

"God forbid you ever do anything to add some class to that place," she quipped.

"I'm serious, Sally. Get the coven into Brooklyn. Arm them with every stake you can find, and then have them lay low. If need be, I'm not too far away. But there's no way you're all staying at my place. Not gonna happen. Besides which, I only have one bathroom."

"Fine. I'll send most of them there with instructions to stay put, stay vigilant, and only open the doors for someone they know," she said.

"I couldn't help but notice that *most* part again," I pointed out.

"Good to know you pay attention to something other than my chest on occasion," she replied. "I hope you enjoyed spending quality time with Gan because she's going back with you. Oh, and in case you're wondering, I'll be joining her."

Toked-up Television

I MUST BE such a repressed closet homosexual that even I don't know it because I never thought in my life that I'd be arguing *against* a woman of Sally's looks shacking up at my place for a few days. But yet, there I was. One night with Gan had been bad enough. Potentially several nights with both Gan and Sally sounded like a disaster waiting to happen. In close quarters, they'd no doubt be at each other's throats constantly, and that didn't even count my two human roommates and their tasty, blood-filled selves. I wasn't sure I had enough sanity in me to referee that kind of nonstop cage match.

Yet, Sally's words did have some logic to them. As usual, it was just enough to make me question my course of action.

"These guys are after Gan," she pointed out. "Therefore, it stands to reason that Gan should be kept away from the others."

"And why does that mean my place?"

"Because the assassins are after you too, stupid," she continued. "If both of their main targets are together, that's even better for the rest."

"Okay. I can see your *Star Trek* logic here."

"What the hell are you talking about?"

"Your whore is being insolent again," Gan cut in.

"Not now, Gan," I said, and then turned back to Sally. Oh yeah, those two in the same apartment together. Hoo-boy! "And as for you, I believe the phrase is '*The needs of the many outweigh the needs of the few.*' That's from *The Wrath of Khan*, just in case you were wondering."

"I do not believe I have ever heard my father say that."

"Different Khan, Gan," I said. "Anyway, logical or not, how do *you* play into this?" I asked Sally.

"It's pretty simple, really. I've gone stark raving insane," she answered cryptically.

"I'm not doubting you, but that's not quite the answer I was looking for."

"I've obviously gone bonkers," Sally explained, "because rather than the safety of numbers that the coven offers, I've decided to stick with you. Two reasons: You get ashed, and I probably go back to being some other vampire's chew toy; and secondly...and Lord help me for this, but I actually believe in you. Yeah, I know, sounds crazy to me, too. But you just keep beating the odds, Bill."

Wow, that almost sounded like a compliment. "I may beat the odds occasionally, but..."

"Most of the time, it's only because I'm there with you," she interrupted. "I know. So I can't help but think, against all logic, that the absolute safest place for me to be is plastered next to your imbecilic side."

I actually smiled at that. It was kind of sweet in an insulting sort of way. I held up a fist in front of Sally. "Partners?"

"Partners," she confirmed with a fist-bump.

"Do not get any ideas, whore," added Gan. "When this is over, he is still mine."

* * *

We decided to first accompany Starlight to the safe house. From there, she could coordinate making sure the others arrived safely as well. Gan's senses were the most acute amongst us, and we periodically had her checking to see if she could sense whether the assassins were close by. She didn't catch wind of them, which was good. A few subway stops later, and I felt better about that. As I said before, good luck with a bunch of yak herders trying to negotiate the NYC tubes successfully.

We gave the building a once over, making sure no non-coven vamps were hiding anywhere, and then helped to secure the exits. Once we were relatively sure of the building's security, Sally, Gan, and I grabbed a cab back to my apartment. We then wound up hoofing it the remaining mile or so after Gan insulted the driver and got us thrown out. Can't tell you how *glad* I was that I got to spend some more time with the pretty little princess. Every hour with her felt like ten.

Unfortunately, she was only part of the problem. I had a trio...or what I assumed were a trio, nobody had actually seen them and lived to give a tally yet...of assassins in the city, gunning for my ass. There had to be some way both to keep them from killing me and convince Gan to go back home with them. Unfortunately, for the life of me I had absolutely no clue as to how to do that. If I somehow, through some miracle, lived long enough to join the Draculas, I was going to institute a policy of talking through our troubles. Maybe start each of our meetings out with a group hug. Yeah, that could work...maybe.

Oh well, hopefully all of that could wait until the morning. Most vampires were strictly night people. For those keeping score, I was, too but, since I had a job to do, I had trained myself to be able to function during daylight hours...minus maybe any sunbathing. If we could make it until then, I could be relatively sure of a few hours of peace, during which the assassins would be sleeping and I could maybe think of something to do.

Speaking of sleeping, I was also wondering what the arrangements were going to be. I had given Gan my bed the night before, and I would probably do so again; however, that left Sally. I was pretty sure she wasn't going to be all that enamored with sharing a bed with the little girl who called her a whore with every other breath. Maybe Tom would be out again, and she could take his room...after getting *extensive* instructions of what not to touch. Yeah, this was going to be a disaster.

Before stopping at my building, we did a quick circuit of the block to allow Gan to sniff out whether

Nergui and his buddies were anywhere close by. After a few minutes, she stopped and wrinkled her nose.

"They are not here...but there *is* something," she said.

"Define 'something'," I replied

"There is something...unnatural in the air."

"But no vampires?" Sally asked.

"No. There are no other vampires near. But there is..."

"Listen, honey," said Sally. "This is New York. Pretty much everything smells unnatural here. If there're no vamps, I say we're golden."

I shrugged and replied to Gan, "Sally's got a point. You're probably just getting a whiff of the streets in general. Tomorrow's garbage day, after all."

* * *

I unlocked the front door, and we went in. I led the way up, Gan took middle, and Sally brought up the rear. We reached my door, and I let us in. I was a little surprised to see that the lights were all still on, considering the late hour. However, it wasn't unheard of. I soon saw why. Tom and Ed were both up. They were seated on the couch, facing the...still broken TV?

"Hey, guys!" I said. "Hope you don't mind, but we have guests." I waited for a moment, expecting a tirade from Ed, since I imagined he was still pretty pissed about the whole Gan thing, but neither of them said a word. I continued, "Sorry for the late notice, but there's some shit going down. Sally and Gan need to stay here for maybe a few days. Oh yeah, Tom, this is Gan."

There was still no acknowledgment from either of them. They both sat in the same place, quiet and unmoving. Odd. Even with Tom not knowing Gan and Ed not liking her, I would have expected them to have bolted around fast enough to cause whiplash at the first mention of Sally. When this continued for a few more seconds, I began to get an idea of what was going on.

"Are you sure they are still living?" asked Gan with casual indifference. Alive or dead, humans were pretty much the same thing to her.

Sally gave a puzzled look. "Yoo-hoo, guys! I'm here...so are my breasts if you want to stare at them," she said in their direction, and then turned toward me. "I agree with Gan. You might want to check them for a pulse."

I shook my head and smiled. "I've seen this before."

"You have?" asked Sally, her tone dubious.

"Yeah. A couple of years ago, our old TV went out. Cash was kind of tight back then. So, until we could replace it, we used to get completely shitfaced stoned in the evenings, then sit there and watch the TV *in our minds*." Ah yes, the good old days.

"That is probably the most *pathetic* thing I have ever heard in my life."

"I do not fully understand what you are saying," Gan likewise commented, "and even I find myself agreeing with the whore."

"Will you *stop* calling me that!?" Sally snapped.

"Perhaps when you stop acting like one," Gan replied. "Besides, that is unimportant right now. What matters is that Dr. Death is *wrong* about his friends."

"What are you talking about?" I asked.

Gan gave me a look as if to say one of us here was a stupid child and it wasn't her. "Your friends are obviously bewitched."

"Bewitched?"

"Yes...magic," she continued. "Can neither of you smell it? It is as plain as the..."

Unfortunately, if Gan was able to finish her sentence, I never knew. As she spoke, a bright white light flashed in the room. Before I could even begin to wonder what happened, it had engulfed me. As it did, all rational thoughts immediately scattered to the wind.

Magically Delicious

I WAS BACK in the tent with my three clothing-impaired female companions. We were picking up, with great enthusiasm, where we had left off. Why I had ever left this place was beyond me. Actually, maybe I hadn't left after all. I mean, here I was. Maybe I had just dozed off and dreamt all of that crap. Yeah, that made sense. Now it was time to show these babes the true meaning of vigorous.

We were all rolling around, having a good time, when I finally wound up on my back. I turned my head to the side and saw Ed lying there just a few feet from me. He had his own female companionship busy nuzzling his neck while grinding away on top of him.

"S'up, bro?" I called to him.

"Hey, Bill," he called back, a big grin on his face.

"What? No 'hi' for me?" the girl on top of him said, turning around to face me.

"Hey, Sally! What are you doing here?" I cheerfully inquired.

"Oh, just fucking your roommate like a good little whore."

"Good for you," I answered back.

"When your other buddy gets here, do you want me to take care of him, too?" she purred, running her nails down Ed's chest.

"Entirely up to you, babe. Personally, I say you snooze you lose."

"Whatever you say, Bill. You're the boss."

Yes, I am, I thought, getting back into my own groove.

"Bill! What are you doing?" asked a voice from my other side. I turned my head and met Gan's accusing eyes.

"I'm kind of busy, Gan. Can you come back later?"

"No, I cannot," she said with a pouty tone. "Our wedding is now. You will be late!"

"Don't worry," I assured her. "I'll be finished here soon enough, thanks to my lack of stamina."

"Bill..." she called again.

"Bill!"

"BILL!"

* * *

"*BILL, WAKE UP!!*"

Let it be known that a vampiric compulsion makes one hell of an alarm clock. I snapped out of the dream with a jolt. A part of me was sad to see it go, but the rational part of me that neither wants to see my roommate naked nor wishes for Gan to watch me having sex was fairly relieved to see it go back to the realm of my fucked up subconscious.

227

I lifted my hands to rub my eyes...correction, *tried* to lift my hands. They didn't seem to be making much headway. For a moment, I had an intense feeling of panic that maybe my hands didn't move because I didn't have them, or for that matter, a body anymore. Living forever as the equivalent of a talking bowling ball did not particularly appeal to me; however, it quickly passed as I looked down and saw I was still properly attached to my favorite parts. I just couldn't move any of them.

I was sitting upright in a chair. That much was obvious. However, I didn't seem to be restrained by anything. I tried again to move...nothing. Okay, it was time to force the issue and put a little of that vaunted vampire strength to use. I struggled again, and this time...OUCH!! Suddenly, it felt like both my arms were on fire. I glanced down and saw they were actually smoking. What the fuck?

"I was just about to warn you not to try that," said Sally.

I turned toward her voice and saw that she was seated about two feet to my left. She must have been the one who compelled me to wake as I saw that Gan, a little further down and seated in her own chair, was apparently still out cold. Sally likewise appeared to be unbound in any way. Yet, like me, she was unmoving.

"Are you okay?" I croaked at her.

"I'd say we're a bit closer to fucked than we are to okay," said a voice to my right. I turned my head to see my roommates. They were seated like me with the exception that they were actually tied up with rope. Tom was the one who had spoken. Ed's eyes were open, but he looked like he was still out of it.

I craned my head to look around. We were definitely not in our apartment. But where? It seemed kind of familiar...

Wait, it seemed familiar because it *was* familiar, as in I had been here just a few short hours ago.

"Are we at the loft?" I asked Sally.

"Looks like it."

"I guess the question is, why?"

"Christy," said Tom.

"What?"

"Christy...you know, my girlfriend? The one I *tried* to tell you about earlier when you just blew me off."

"What about her?" I asked. "You said she was a bitch or something."

"I said she was a *witch*."

"Aren't all women?" slurred Ed.

I ignored that and asked, "So why do you think she's a witch?"

"Well, for starters she told me," Tom said. "Secondly..." he glanced around at us all, "Duh!"

"Point taken," I conceded. "Sally, what do you know about witches?"

"They like ruby slippers?"

"Not particularly helpful."

"Sorry. What do you want me to say? I've never met one aside from a few of those Wiccan hippies. All I know are stories."

"Well, since we all seem to be gathered 'round the campfire, why don't you tell us one?"

"I don't know much," she replied. "Supposedly we've tangled with them in the past. But we're talking *King Arthur and Knights of the Round Table* timeframes here."

"I guess the question then is, why is one tangling with us now? How would she even know we're vampires?"

At that, Tom made a slight coughing noise.

"What the hell did you do, dipshit?" Sally hissed at him.

"I might have kind of told her Bill was a vampire," he replied sheepishly.

"Kind of?"

"Well, she seemed to already suspect it...no idea how, but I guess she needed me to confirm it."

I gritted my teeth. "And you did?"

"Dude, sorry. I didn't think anything of it, and she can do these things with her mouth that would just cause you to lose your fucking mind."

"It's so nice to know that the *secret* of vampires existing is up for grabs to the first bimbo who gives you a blowjob," snarled Sally.

"If it helps, it was a really good blowjob."

"It doesn't!" she replied in a tone that said she'd gladly break my 'no killing the roommates' rule had she been able to. Right at that moment, I might have even been tempted to let her. Still, that wouldn't exactly get us out of this mess.

"Okay, enough! What's done is done," I Interrupted. "Tom, I accepted the fact that you're a fucking dumbass years ago. I guess I can't fault you for being you."

"I can," said Sally.

"Save it for later," I snapped.

"You know," Tom said, trying to change the subject. "It's kind of weird?"

"What is? I can think of about fifty weird things right now off the top of my head."

"Well, think about it," he continued. "Six months ago, if someone had told us they'd seen a ghost, we'd have laughed our asses off at them. But today...well, have you noticed how lately we can't take a crap without running into some creature straight out of a fairy tale?"

"Come to think of it, I guess you're right. That is a bit weird," I replied. "However, it's not really too relevant to our situation. For now, we should probably be wondering why we're here and why Sally and I can't move."

"I can answer that," said a voice from behind us.

* * *

The owner of the voice stepped in front of us. She was a cute brunette of average height and wearing a simple white dress. She had a pretty nice figure, along with bright blue eyes and what I guessed was at least a C-cup rack. I could see what Tom saw in her.

"Nice to meet you, Christy," I said dryly.

"Likewise, Bill. I've heard *a lot* about you," she said with a sly smile.

"So I've heard." I threw a glare at Tom.

She smiled at that. "Don't be mad at him. We've been aware of you for a while now. I just needed to confirm our suspicions."

"*We*?" I asked.

Before she could answer, though, Tom had to jump in and do his best to *help* the situation along. "Are you saying you just used me...like a piece of meat?" He looked thoughtful for a moment, and then added, "I guess I can live with that."

Christy walked over to him and playfully ruffled his hair. "And who says I'm through using you?" she asked with a wink.

"I don't suppose you'd mind just killing me now before I throw up in my mouth?" Sally commented.

Tom ignored her outburst and said to Christy, "Sorry, babe. As much as I like being used in that way, it's not cool when you mess with my buds. I'm thinking that might put a damper on our relationship...as in welcome to Dumpsville, population you."

She gave him a pouty look in return, but didn't remove her hand from his head. "Well then, lover, it's a good thing you won't remember any of this."

She started chanting under her breath. It was low, but it had an odd echo to it, almost as if she were hooked up to an amp set to reverb. Within a few seconds, the hand on Tom's head actually started to glow in a yellow light. His body convulsed once, and then his eyes glazed over and closed.

I was too stunned to speak for a second. Fortunately, Sally managed to blurt out what I should have. "What the fuck did you do to him?"

"Nothing much," the witch replied. "Just erased the last four hours from his memories and sent him off to LaLa land for a while."

"Guess that answers the question of whether you're good witch or a bad witch," snapped Sally.

I finally found my voice. "Are you sure he's okay? Because if he's not..."

"Don't worry, my dear Freewill," she replied. "We have no quarrel with him."

"There's that *we* word again."

"Me and my coven," she clarified.

"You do know you guys stole that one from us, right?" I shot back.

I heard the door click open behind us, and then a new voice answered my question, "Imitation is the sincerest form of flattery." This one I recognized.

"You've got to be fucking kidding me," I said as the newcomer walked in.

Christy bowed as he entered view. "Master, I have done as told."

"And you shall be rewarded, my child," said Harry Decker, stepping in front of me. He gave Christy a loving caress on her cheek before turning to face me.

"Son of a bitch," I hissed.

He in turn replied, "I bet you're wishing right now that you hadn't ruined my night."

* * *

"So let me get this straight, you're a witch, too?"

"*Wizard*," he corrected. "Women are witches, men are wizards."

"And either way, you're still an asshole. Although I guess that explains how you were able to hang on to that cushy job without doing dick."

"No. That's just knowing how to play corporate politics. No magic necessary. You might want to consider learning a few lessons there yourself," he snapped back.

"So what is all this?" I asked, gesturing around as best I could.

"This is what must be done," he answered cryptically.

"Please don't tell me that all of this is because Bill sent you home tonight with a giant case of the blue balls," Sally said.

"Don't be absurd, woman," Decker replied. "That little trollop (*oh yeah, those are fighting words*) is meaningless to me. But I knew if word got out that I was courting her, Mr. Ryder here would have to respond in some way." He turned back to me and continued, "And in case you're wondering, no magic was needed for that either. The whole office is more than aware of your pathetic little case of puppy love."

"The *whole* office?" I asked.

"You might as well wear a sandwich board with it written in block letters," he said with a sneer. "As it were, it turns out tonight was just a fortuitous coincidence that allowed me to accelerate my plans. It is as if fate itself has delivered you unto me."

Gan's eyes suddenly opened. "You should have let me kill him," she said, her tone implying she had been listening in on things. "I told you his kind would not be missed."

My mouth dropped open. "You knew he was a wizard, Gan?"

"Of course," she replied. "You did not?"

"Gan, if we get out of this, we need to have a little talk about this thing called assuming."

Decker interrupted, "It's safe to say that you won't be having that conversation."

Gan merely bared her fangs at that and replied, "In that, you are wrong, wizard."

* * *

Gan began to flex against her...whatever it was that was holding her in place. After a few seconds, flashes began flaring up and down her arms as she encountered the same resistance I had. Decker and Christy both smiled smugly as the smell of burning flesh began to permeate the room; however, those smiles began to crumble as Gan continued her assault, heedless of the fact that she was rapidly starting to turn all crispy. I have to say I was impressed...and a little dismayed that I was being shown up by someone who looked like a sixth grader.

"You cannot escape. Those are bonds of faith," spat Decker, but there was worry behind his voice.

"Then...perhaps..." Gan said, continuing to struggle, "you...need... stronger...faith." and with that, there was a flash of light – and suddenly she was standing on her feet. She looked like five miles of bad road, but an experienced vampire can take a lot of abuse before going down. Gan was apparently no exception to that.

She snarled and leapt at Decker to finish the job that, in hindsight, maybe I should have allowed her to do in the first place. As she did, I made a mental note to have a conversation with Sally about her lousy timing regarding humanity speeches.

Decker appeared to be caught completely surprised by the attack, but his pet witch, Christy, was not. She screamed, "Master!" and threw up her hands in a warding gesture. Whatever it was, it managed to snag Gan in mid-air just centimeters away from connecting with her target.

Gan struggled against it, but the witch made another gesture, barked something inarticulate, and suddenly Gan was no longer there.

"Gan!" I yelled as Christy slumped to the floor, apparently drained from the effort.

"What the hell did you do to her?" Sally snarled.

Decker ignored us and went to Christy's side to help her up.

She looked semi-stunned by whatever she had just done, but she managed to pant, "Forgive me, master. I only had time to send the child beast back."

"Back? Back *where*?" I snapped.

"Fear not, Mr. Ryder." Decker turned toward me. "Your little pet isn't harmed. My assistant merely reversed the spell that brought you all here. She's back in your apartment, safe, but in no position to cause us further interruption."

I let out a sigh of relief. Psycho or not, I felt a responsibility for Gan. There was also the fact that her getting dusted on my watch would most likely put the kibosh on any chance of talking the assassins out of killing me.

"Speaking of which," Sally said. "Why the hell are we here? What, you didn't think Bill's apartment was creepy enough for you guys? Trust me, I've seen it. It is."

Decker turned and answered in a slow voice, "Because this is where it all began."

* * *

"Not following you," Sally replied.

"This is where the Freewill was born, you simpleton of a slut," he spat back at her. Before she could open her mouth to reply, he continued, "Yes, we *know*. We've been aware of your coven and your kind for a *long* time. We've been watching you."

"So now you're a voyeur in addition to being an asshole?" she shot back. Go, Sally! I could see what she was trying to do. It was *Superhero 101*: piss off the villain until he started monologuing all about his grand scheme. Once he's distracted by his own delusions of grandeur, then *WHAM* – we bust out and take him down. I just wasn't sure how that last part was going to play itself out yet. Hopefully, it wasn't with "and now you know my plan so... *ZAP*" Fortunately for me, Sally was playing a game that I was qualified to be in the pro leagues for.

"Yo, Decker," I said. "I have a question for you."

"Yes, Freewill?" he replied with a sly grin. "How may I enlighten you?"

"Something that's been bugging me. What the fuck is up with wizards named Harry?" He looked confused, so I continued. "I mean, seriously, it seems like every freaking wizard I've heard of lately has been named Harry. There's you, *Harry Potter*, *Harry Dresden*, Harry Houdini..."

"I don't think that last one was a real wizard," commented Sally.

"Actually, he was," Christy replied.

"See!?" I said. "Do wizard mommies just have zero in the way of creativity, or is there something mystical about having a name that probably earned you multiple ass-kickings on the playground?"

"What does that have to do with anything?" Decker angrily asked.

"Listen, dude, I've played Dungeons and Dragons for the better part of a decade. I've run at least a dozen wizards...not a single Harry amongst them."

"This is irrelevant."

"Zoltar the Arcane...now there was a name for a wizard. And let's not forget about my fifteenth level gnome mage, Professor Blastingus..."

"Enough!" roared Decker. "I tire of your games, vampire."

"There was also Magnifico the Merciless, although I'm not so proud of that one..."

I was stopped as Harry grabbed me by the chin and moved his face to within inches of mine. "Do you want to know why you are going to die, or not?"

"Sure, as long as you pop a breath mint first." This was going swimmingly...at least as long as he didn't follow through with the killing me part.

"Six months ago, the portents all spoke of your coming." He backed up and began ranting. "The return of the vampire Freewills, who so long ago were wiped from the Earth."

"Wiped?"

"Yes. They didn't just disappear in a puff of smoke...or did you think that they had?"

"Well..." I said. Actually, I had never bothered to wonder. Now that he mentioned it, I guess immortals wouldn't just normally disappear unless something happened to them.

"What the portents did not tell us was that the reborn Freewill would be so...unimpressive," he continued.

"You apparently haven't seen Bill in action," commented Sally. Hard to tell if she was complimenting me or agreeing with him.

He ignored her and went on. "All of our divinings pointed to you, but we couldn't be sure. We couldn't risk warfare with the vampires over a nobody. Thus we have been watching you, waiting for confirmation."

"So you took a job at my place just to keep tabs on me?"

"Yes. Although the sign-on bonus wasn't half bad either," he replied. Asshole just had to rub it in. "However, I needn't have bothered. If I had known how readily your friend here would spill his guts in exchange for a little female companionship, I would have sent my protégé in sooner."

Let that be a lesson to you, my male friends. Never underestimate the power of the pussy.

He continued with his insane monologue, "Tonight only further confirmed your status...or did you think I hadn't noticed your little *transformation* outside of the cafe?"

"You saw that?"

"I see *many* things," he said as what looked like an electric charge passed behind his eyes. Ooh, spooky.

"I see things, too. For example, I saw your ass get shot down tonight," I shot back at him, but it was weak. The ball was back in his court.

He continued, his grin growing wider. "Thus I saw no reason to hesitate any longer. Our legends tell that your coming heralds disaster for my people. Thus if you are erased, that future cannot come to pass."

"So you're saying I'm gonna kill all the wizards? You know, it'd be funny if that happened, especially considering that before tonight I had nothing against you. Hell, I didn't even know you existed."

"Not you, fool," he replied.

"Not me what?"

"Not you! You aren't the one to bring disaster to us."

"But you just said..."

"I said your coming heralds it. There's a difference."

"Okay, I'm confused now," I said.

"Just now?" Sally asked. "I haven't understood a word of what this whackjob has been saying for at least ten minutes."

"ICONS!" he screamed.

"Huh?"

"Your coming foretells their return. If the Freewills shall ever return, so, too, shall the Icons of faith. It was they who decimated the Magi so long ago. If they return, they shall do so again," he raved.

Okay, I had heard of Icons. They were supposedly people of such great faith that their whole bodies became living, breathing weapons against vampires. They could turn us into French fries just by their touch, but they were supposed to be as rare as vampires like me, maybe even more so.

"I thought Icons fought vampires." I said with some confusion.

"Some did in the distant past. But then Christianity came. The vampires slunk off into the shadows before its wake and became nothing more than legends to the humans. My ancestors were not so fortunate," he said, a little touch of mania starting to enter his voice. "Once, we were like *deities* to the people. We protected them against your kind and the other scourges of the night, and in return they made us their priests, their wise-men, their *god kings*!"

"Let me guess," I interrupted. "Then this little thing called the Inquisition hit."

"Yes!" he snarled. "That and other uprisings like it. Those who had praised us suddenly turned on us. They called us tools of Satan and suffered us not to live. We fought back and might have won if not for the zealots...the Icons...amongst them. They were able to resist our powers and drag us from our many seats of power. We were hunted almost to extinction before we, too, managed to retreat into the relative safety of legend, where we have waited ever since."

"So let me get this straight," I said, "you think that my being here heralds the return of another group and that if you kill me it somehow cancels out them as well?"

"Yes."

"That is one of the stupidest fucking things I think I have ever heard."

"How dare you..."

"No, seriously," I interrupted. "It makes no sense. You have about the biggest, stupidest case of circular logic that I've ever seen. It's not much better than 'a duck has two legs, I have two legs, therefore I must be a duck.' Think about it. I'll wait. You are in marketing, after all."

"I did not expect you to understand. You are not even a man anymore; just an animal. What did you think that woman would ever see in *you*? She could no more love you than she could a beast," he said, a disdainful sneer on his face.

Ooh, that was low. I didn't want to do this, but now it was time to get nasty.

I tensed up and blurted out, "*Wingardium Leviosa!*" (*What? Hasn't everyone read those books by now?*)

"What?" he spat.

"*Accio*...err, asskicking?" I replied.

"Cut that out!"

I threw in a bad English accent to top things off. "Or what, you'll make me drink *polyjuice* potion?"

"I'll kill you right now."

"Oh no! *Avada Kedavra*...ugh!" I said, rolling my head back and playing dead.

"I do not find this amusing."

I lifted my head and shouted, "*Stupefy!* Oh wait, too late. Guess someone got you with that one already."

"Enough!" he screamed and threw up his hands. There was an electric jolt through the air, and suddenly I found myself flying back. I slammed into the wall and went down in a heap. I pretty much felt like I had just been put through a microwave, but a quick tense of my muscles confirmed that whatever he had just done had also broken his little containment spell.

I stood up and turned to face him and his little bitch of a witch, too.

I had no idea what the hell to do against them, but that didn't stop me from throwing them a grin of my own and saying, "Here I am, assholes. Rock you like a hurricane!"

And that's when the front door blew off its hinges.

Random Monster Encounter

WELL, EVEN IF that line did sound lame, the follow through was pretty damn badass. Pity it wasn't mine. Unfortunately, there was also nothing about it that boded well for me. Decker and his bullshit had hit at exactly the wrong time in my life. Yeah, okay, there probably wasn't actually a right time for a coven of witches to come along and declare that I needed to die so that they could go on frolicking naked in the woods during the full moon. I especially didn't need this crap right then, since it served to distract me from the assassins that were on a mission to turn my skull into an ashtray. I had been so preoccupied with Decker's loony ramblings that I had forgotten we were stuck in the loft, a place the assassins already had a heads-up about (*just ask Dusk Reaper*).

The front door, despite being of the heavy duty security variety, literally flew off its hinges and went slamming into the far wall. If anyone had been standing behind it, they would have been pancaked. Nergui stood in the doorway, flanked by his two death-dealing flunkies, Bang (*damn, that never stopped being funny*) and Cheng-gong.

"Give us the princess, and your death will be painless," Nergui said to me, ignoring the others in the room.

The odds were pretty skewed against me, no matter how you looked at them. Three assassins and two mages on team 'Fuck-up Bill's Day' versus just three allies on my side, all of whom were either restrained, unconscious, or both.

Fortunately, that whole *the enemy of my enemy is my friend* thing is mostly bullshit. Decker's ego was too big to allow the three bruisers at the door to do his dirty work for him. "The Freewill is mine, vampire filth," he hissed, bringing his hands up in a defensive gesture. Christy did likewise. Bunch of idiots. If Nergui killed me, then their insane little problem would be solved. Not that I was complaining if they wanted to fight it out, mind you. Still, what a pack of morons.

"His life is ours..." Nergui gave a sniff of the air and spat out, "*maapamba*. Leave now, and you will live." He and his three companions stepped into the room. They unsheathed nasty looking daggers, *silver* daggers.

I stepped back, not wanting any part of the sharp objects being brandished at me. "Sorry, Harry," I said to Decker. "They've got dibs. Good for you because I'm afraid of them. You...not so much."

"Then I shall teach you fear, beast," he snarled, pretty much right on cue. I tell you, some people are just no challenge.

Decker and Christy both murmured something unintelligible and gestured again. What can best be described as a distortion in the air appeared in front of them and then rushed forward to slam into my three would-be killers.

It looked impressive, like something right out of Hollywood, but it more or less did dick. The three vampires were pushed back and slammed into the wall, but none lost their footing. I don't think Harry was quite prepared for three elder vampire warriors. Guess he was still a first year at Hogwarts. Maybe he and Christy should go back to practicing their card tricks.

Though no damage appeared to be done, Decker was at least proving to be a distraction for the vamps. Nergui turned to Cheng-gong and gave a nod. Cheng threw his dagger. It landed hilt-deep in the floor at Decker's feet.

"That will be the only warning," Nergui said to him.

Decker glared back, a look of madness in his eyes. He did not like being casually dismissed, not one bit. He actually started to glow. It started out as a dim white light, but quickly turned an angry red.

What occurred next happened fast.

* * *

Nergui barked something, and Bang let loose with his dagger in my direction. However, right before the knife left his hand, Harry Decker let loose with...well, whatever he let loose with. The red glow leapt from him across the room, directly at Nergui. Cheng-gong uttered a shout of warning and dove in front of it. The blast hit him full on.

The backlash of it ruined Bang's aim. The dagger slammed into the wall not an inch from my face, close enough so that I felt the air it displaced as it flew by. I'd like to tell you that I just stood there rooted to the spot, an arrogant sneer on my face at the pathetic failed attack on me. The first part was true at least. I was rooted to the spot, all right, but the only thing that kept me from screaming and cowering like a little girl was the spectacle of what happened to Cheng.

Decker's attack enveloped him in the red glow, and Cheng-gong exploded in a shower of sparks and dust. Holy shit, the wizard had game after all. I never thought I would be happy that a bunch of assassins had burst in to try to kill me. I had no qualms about admitting that whatever Decker had done to Cheng would have likewise left me little more than dust in the wind.

This was turning serious. Unfortunately, it was almost over, too. The glow left Decker, and he collapsed to the ground with a glazed look in his eyes. Guess he had blown his load with that last attack. I'd keep that in mind for later...if there was a later. He had some nasty guns, but apparently limited ammunition. Good to know. If I could figure out a way to keep him from blasting me to ash on the first try, I'd be set.

He was no longer the problem, at least not until his batteries recharged; however, that still left two ancient vampires with a hard-on for some killing. Still, two was better than three. After this was all said and done, maybe I'd send a fruit basket to Decker's office. Or maybe that should be a funeral wreath instead, as he now had Nergui and Bang's full attention. That's the thing with teams. You somehow manage to kill Howling Mad Murdock, and you've still got Face, Hannibal, and BA Baracus to deal with. Both assassins faced the dazed wizard and hissed through their fangs. This was not going to be pretty.

Speaking of pretty, a gorgeous blonde projectile suddenly slammed into Nergui and Bang, taking them both off their feet. Way to go, Sally! The wonder twins' concentration on her bonds must have faltered as the battle started. Sally could have probably easily dispatched both of them but she wasn't stupid. She knew who the bigger threat here was.

As the three vampires went down in a heap, I heard Decker's voice wheeze, "This isn't finished, Freewill. (*yeah yeah, haven't heard that one before*) Get us out of here!"

Christy started to repeat the same movements she'd made back when she dismissed Gan. Before she could finish, though, I locked eyes with her. "Take them with you...*please*," I said.

She gave me a hard look back, but then her gaze softened and she looked away. A moment later her, Decker and my two bound roommates disappeared from the room. Thank God. Who knows, maybe she actually had some real feelings for Tom (*for whatever insane reason*). More likely, she knew that two helpless humans stood absolutely no chance of surviving. Whatever the reason, my roommates were out of there at least. The only potential problem was if they all went back to my apartment. A very angry Gan might be waiting for them. There was no time to worry about that, though. I had to be content with hoping for the best.

I ran to the pile of tangled vampires just as Nergui flung Sally off him. Bang had still not made it back to his feet, so I, in classic unsportsmanlike manner, kicked him in the face while he was still down. It was a solid connect, and he went flying, but I had no delusions that my strength was anywhere close to what was needed to make him stay down. Then again, maybe I could do something about that.

* * *

I bared my fangs and leapt at Bang. One bite, and I could maybe even the odds a little in this battle. Unfortunately, unlike my previous fights, I was up against opponents who knew full well what I was capable of. Nergui reached out while I was in mid-leap, grabbed my foot, and swung me so that I flew across the room.

"We know your tricks, Freewill. They will not work on us."

Well, isn't that just dandy...OOF!! I thought, slamming into a coffee table.

Having taken my fair share of throws in the past several months, I was able to roll with it a bit and get back to my feet in another second.

"I don't suppose the Khan would like to just, you know, discuss this?" I asked. Bang was back up and standing at Nergui's side. They both faced me. "I mean, this is really just a big misunderstanding. I wasn't even supposed to go to China." Yeah, I was babbling, and yes, I figured it was a long shot. However, it was also a distraction.

Sally was also on her feet again and once more going for Nergui's blindside. Sadly, you don't get to become a three-hundred-and-fifty-year-old assassin by being a dumbass. What we were doing was no doubt the oldest trick in their book.

As Sally threw a right cross at him, he turned and casually caught her by the arm. In one quick flick, he brought the dagger up and severed her hand at the wrist.

Before her newly unattached appendage could hit the floor, Nergui flung her toward me.

"SALLY!" I screamed just as she landed at my feet. Oh God, this wasn't good. I dropped to my knees to help her, although I wasn't sure what I could do. Her arm was spurting blood all over the place. She made a pained whimper, but appeared to be in too much shock to even cry out.

"It's okay. I'm here," I said, but there wasn't much comfort to give. If vampires could bleed to death (*could they?*), she was doing a good job of it.

"Take it," she whispered. I didn't understand. But then she held up her still spouting arm and repeated herself. She was actually offering her life blood to me.

"No...I can't," I stammered, feeling tears come to my eyes.

She gave me one of her typical Sally grins, and then whispered something else. I didn't quite make it out, but it sounded like "dumbass." Then her eyes rolled up in the back of her head, and she stopped moving.

This couldn't be happening. Sally and I were supposed to be an unbeatable team. Despite how she usually acted, she was one of the few people on the planet who had ever believed in me. My tears began to flow freely, and then I heard the two assassins in the room begin to advance.

Instantly, my grief extinguished itself, and that dull rage I had felt earlier began to rear its ugly head. This time, I decided to allow it to take me. My humanity be damned; these fuckers were going to pay.

I could feel something nasty inside of me clawing its way up. This thing was far darker than any Dr. Death persona I kept in the back of my head. I didn't know if demons existed, but if so I was sure one had taken up residence inside of me.

My fangs and claws extended, and I glanced down again to where Sally lay. That was enough to push me over the edge.

The change kept happening, and I could see by the looks on both their faces that they saw it, too. Nergui shouted something I couldn't understand, and both vampires came after me almost as quickly as thought itself. The only thing I knew was that it wouldn't be fast enough.

Unfortunately, I had no idea what happened next, as my vision went entirely to red.

Lend Me a Hand

THERE'S NOTHING LIKE a cool, refreshing breeze on a Fall night. Crisp and carrying just a hint of the winter weather ahead, but pleasant enough to be outside and still enjoy it. True, I'd never been much of an outdoors type. Anyone with eyes could figure that out by my pasty white skin (*even before I was undead*). This time of year was nice, though. No bugs, no sweating; just nice and comfortable. I wouldn't mind staying out there for a while.

Speaking of which, where the fuck was I anyway?

My head started to clear, and with it my vision. I looked around. It was still night. That was good; otherwise, my enjoyment of the breeze would've been quickly cut off by all the burning and screaming. Things like that tended to put a damper on the day trips as of late. Judging by the horizon, it was the wee hours of the morning, maybe an hour or so until daybreak. Still plenty of time to get indoors. Hey, I could actually see the horizon. Come to think of it, the entire view was pretty damn nice.

I tried to stand, wobbled a bit before finally doing so, and then realized why the view was so good. I was standing on top of some building. From what I could tell, I was at least twenty stories up, maybe more. Odd that I didn't remember stepping out for some pre-dawn stargazing.

There was a slight groan from off to my side. Considering the pitch, I wondered if maybe I hadn't brought some female companionship along. I walked over, still a little wobbly, and looked down to see Sally.

Aw, she looked like she was asleep...

And covered in blood...

And with her right arm ending in a stump...

Oh shit!

The memories of the past...however long ago that was, started to filter into my mind, snapping me out of my daze.

Oh God, Sally. Please don't be dead, I thought as I knelt down beside her. Well, okay, she was already dead, but I meant really dead. I reached down and put my hand on her throat to feel for a pulse. After about ten seconds of that, I mentally slapped myself upside the head. Duh! Vampires don't have pulses, regardless of their condition.

I needed to think this through. Remember your Boy Scout training, stupid! Oh yeah, I was a boy scout for all of two weeks before I got bored with it. Come on, what does one do when somebody's hand gets cut off by trained vampire assassins? Okay, pretty sure they don't have that one listed on WebMD. I got it: a tourniquet!

I started to pull off my belt so as to staunch Sally's bleeding stump, when I realized it wasn't doing so any longer. What had been a geyser of blood just a...however long ago, was now nothing, not even a drizzle. That wasn't good. No blood meant...No! Best not to think of that.

I looked closer. The stump wasn't bleeding because it had started to scab over. Her arm was at least partially trying to heal itself. Corpses didn't usually do that. Maybe there was still hope. Besides, didn't she just groan? Or was that the wind? Only one way to find out...

I thus did the only thing I could think of. If Sally was truly gone, it's not like it would have made things worse. So I turned her head toward me and gave her a hard slap across the face.

"Sally, wake up!" (*please!*)

Nothing. Okay, maybe I shouldn't have hit her hard enough to knock her brains out. I tried it again, slightly softer, but still enough to leave a handprint on her face. That time, I got a groan in response. Yes! She was still in there somewhere.

"Come on, Sally! You can do it. Those fuckers can't take you down that easily!" I said, feeling wetness welling up in my eyes. She started to come around. Her eyes were still closed, but I could see her trying to mouth something. I leaned in closer.

"Say that again. I didn't hear you."

A hoarse whisper met my ear, "Hit me again, and I'll gut you."

* * *

"Are you all right?" I asked as she started to finally come to...and yes, I realized what a dumb question it was, considering her new southpaw status. I figured it was a safer question than, "So, will you be going with a stainless steel hook or one of those nifty new titanium models?"

"What happened?" she asked while I helped her to a sitting position. She'd need some blood soon, but for now her vampire physiology seemed to be snapping her out of it. Vampires are tough fuckers to keep down if you don't manage to kill them outright.

"You were...(*God, please give me the strength to not say it*)...disarmed." (*Thanks for nothing, God*)

Sure it wasn't the most sporting thing to say, but it definitely brought Sally all the way out of her funk. Her eyes cleared and she gave me the ugliest of glares.

She held up the stump of her arm and stared at it, her eyes unreadable. Finally, she said in a small voice, "Shit..."

"Don't worry, they can do wonders with prosthetics these..."

"...it's gonna take weeks for that to grow back," she finished.

"It grows back?"

"Yeah. It's going to take a lot longer than usual, though. Fairly sure those assholes were using silver."

"Hey, as long as it'll grow back at all," I replied, my voice serious. "Most people would consider that a lucky thing."

"I guess so."

"So don't worry." I lightened my tone. "You'll be back to giving double happy endings at the massage parlor in no time." Her response was an eye-roll. Yeah, she was going to be fine.

"So where are we?" she asked, looking around.

"No idea. Top of some building, it looks like."

"Thanks, *Scooby Doo*. Nice to know you're around to solve all of life's mysteries," she quipped. "How did we get here? Did the assassins just decide to leave us alive?"

"I don't think so," I said, remembering back to the rage I felt when I thought she had been killed.

"Why?"

I explained what happened, maybe downplaying that it was her 'death' that caused me to Hulk out...no need to inflate her ego any more than it was. I told her how I felt that change come over me again and then everything went red.

"Scary. Guess there's more to this Freewill thing than either of us knows."

"Not sure I want to know. I'm not big on the whole *Jekyll and Hyde* thing playing itself out in my head."

"Whatever happened, it looks like you did a job on them, though," she said, indicating my clothes. I looked down and saw they were absolutely soaked with blood.

"Yours, probably."

"Some of it yes, but not all. It's not yours either," she replied.

"Let me guess, you can smell it?"

"You really need to practice this vampire thing a little more. You're starting to embarrass me with these stupid questions."

"Speaking of stupid things, we need to get out of here," I replied. "Sun's going to be coming up soon, and if we're still here yakking away when it does...well, that's just going to be pathetic."

"Agreed..." and then she mumbled something I didn't quite catch.

"What was that?"

She sighed and responded, "I said, 'Thanks for saving me'."

"I don't remember even saving myself."

"I know, but whatever it was you did, you remembered to take me with you when you did it. That tells me there was still some of *you* in there driving the school bus."

I hadn't thought of that. That actually made it a little less scary...not much, mind you, but it was enough for now.

* * *

We managed to get down to street level without being seen. The hatch leading down from the roof had been locked from the inside, leading me to believe I had somehow Spider-Manned my way up there. Locks aren't much of a deterrent for a pair of determined vampires, though. Fortunately for us, the stairwell was empty. Two blood-soaked intruders, one of whom had a gaping wound where her hand used to be, were bound to attract a little attention.

We were able to get our bearings, realizing we were a good mile downtown from the loft. Fortunately, there was a subway entrance less than a block away. We could use it to get into the tunnels, and thus the sewers, so we could make our way back unseen.

"Do you think it's safe?" I asked as we hopped the turnstiles (*screw you, New York MTA*) and made our way toward the dark underground.

"I don't think anywhere is particularly safe after last night. But I have a feeling that you gave the Chinese vamps a bloody nose, at the very least. They're probably lying low right now. As long as we don't get supremely unlucky and wander directly into them, we should be fine."

"Don't jinx us," I added.

"Point taken. Still, the smell down here should be enough to clog even the most sensitive vamp's nostrils," she said, turning down a maintenance tunnel.

"I can see what you mean," I said, sniffing the aromatic air. "Nothing like the smell of rancid ass to cover your tracks."

"Speaking of rancid things, I need to make a little pit stop," she said, suddenly slowing her pace.

"What are you talking about?"

She gestured toward a little nook close by. Inside of it, huddled under a moldy blanket, was a sleeping homeless man. Judging from the ripe smell, he was taking a nap with his good buddy *Jim Beam*.

In the darkness, I looked confusingly between Sally and the hobo before I realized that her fangs were extended and her eyes were turning black.

"Do you really have to?" I asked.

"Normally, this is a bit beneath my standards. But I've had a long day. You can turn around if it makes you uncomfortable."

I did. Sometimes, I can almost forget the whole undead predator of the night thing. This, however, was not destined to be one of those times.

* * *

When she had finished, she walked past me and started leading the way again.

"Feeling better?" I asked.

"Yes and no. It's going to take me at least a week to wash the taste of him out of my mouth."

"Did you really have to kill him?"

"Sorry to offend your bookish sensibilities, but I was almost wiped out," she replied. "Another few steps, and I'd have dropped again. I needed to fill up the old gas tank."

"Well, judging by the smell of that guy, you definitely went with the high octane." Damn, did I really just say that? I was definitely starting to get desensitized to this crap. That alone gave me a not-so-fresh feeling inside.

We continued to walk, Sally leading the way through the dripping tunnels. It seemed she had a purpose in mind.

"Where are we headed?" I finally asked.

"The office."

"As in the office the assassins already know about? The same office where they left you a gift basket full of severed heads?"

"The same," she answered.

"So you acknowledge you've either gone insane, suicidal, or both?"

"Perhaps a little of the first, but none of the second," she replied. "I set the security alarms before I left last time. These guys may be good, but I'm willing to bet they're about as technically adept as cavemen. If they're waiting for us, we'll have plenty of warning."

"You did clean up those heads before you left, right?"

"I put them into storage."

"*Storage*!? What for?"

"Waste not, want not. I'm debating maybe lining the walkway to my office with them. That should keep the complaints down a minimum."

"And yet," I mused, "I actually saved your crazy ass back there."

"Exactly. You need *someone* to live vicariously through."

* * *

After another half hour of traversing filth-ridden tunnels, things started to look familiar. I didn't spend too much time in the sewers myself, but I had still thought it prudent to know the emergency exits of all our properties nevertheless. We finally came to a ladder that went up to the basement of our destination. Every few feet, Sally would stop and reach out with her senses. So far, we were alone.

We got up and used a back stairwell to make it to our floor. Thankfully, it was still early enough so the regular businesses that shared the building weren't open yet.

"So why exactly are we here?" I asked.

"There's a supply closet and a shower in the back. We can get cleaned up and lay low until sundown."

"I couldn't help but notice the words *shower* and *we* in that exchange."

"Keep dreaming," she replied. "I'm gonna need to lose a lot more than one hand to go that loopy."

The alarms hadn't been tripped, so Sally let us in and locked the doors behind us. To quote an overused phrase, the place was quiet as a tomb. Once we had made a thorough casing of the joint and come to the conclusion that we were the only ones there, Sally walked into her office and sat down to relax. I followed her so that we could have a talk.

"After the sun goes down, I'm dropping you off at the safe house with the rest of the coven. Starlight can look after you," I said with a tone of finality.

Of course, with Sally I could have added "pretty please with sugar on top" and it wouldn't have made a bit of difference. She listened to orders every bit as well as Gan did. Must be a female thing. Thusly, she shook her head. "No way. I said I was sticking with you, and I meant it."

"You're done. You've had more than enough. Next time, you might not get so lucky. I'll make sure Gan is okay and then try to end this by myself."

"No chance."

"I'm serious, *lefty*," I said, indicating her stump. "You weren't a match for them before. You definitely aren't now."

"I know," she said.

"You do? Then why are you being so obstinate?"

"For starters, because I can be." She began rummaging through the desk with her remaining appendage. "Secondly, because I have a little friend to help equalize things." She pulled out and placed on her desk the biggest handgun I had ever seen. She smiled at me and said, "Desert Eagle, in case you were wondering."

"You plan on being attacked by some vampire rhinos?"

"If I am, this puppy'll have me covered. This thing will blow pieces of your buddies all the way back to China. Even better..." She pulled a spare clip out of another drawer and tossed it to me. I looked it over. The bullet protruding from the top had a shiny gleam to it.

"Are these...?"

"Silver bullets? You bet your ass. Cost me a pretty penny to have those babies made."

"You?"

"Okay, it cost the coven," she admitted.

"Yeah, about that...I thought you said the coven wasn't supposed to be armed."

"The coven isn't; *I* am," she said with a smile. "Don't tell me you haven't figured out by now that I have absolutely no issues with double standards."

Swords and Sorcerers

WE GOT OURSELVES cleaned up and presentable for walking the streets. In an odd bit of vanity, Sally found a pair of gloves and went about stuffing one with newspaper and then fitting it over her stump.

"That doesn't even remotely look real," I pointed out. "Looks like something you'd stick onto a Halloween dummy."

"You would know all about dummies, I guess. Besides, it doesn't need to pass Army inspection. However, there are people around here who see us coming and going all the time. One or two of the nosier ones might notice I had a hand yesterday, don't have one today – but voila, magically have one again soon enough."

I consider myself pretty smart, but Sally, ex-stripper or not, sometimes made me feel a teensy bit inadequate by how she always seemed to be thinking on her feet. Should our relationship ever turn sour, I'd be wise not to underestimate her. Oh, who was I kidding? If our relationship ever even looked like it was heading south, I'd be smart to stake her, leave her ashes in the sunlight, and then burn them when I was finished. Some enemies you just needed to take a *nuke it from orbit* attitude...it was the only way to be sure.

Still, Sally and I had all of eternity to plot against each other. For now, I was eager to get back to my apartment. Once I was sure she was fine and that the immediate danger was over, the fate of my roommates began to weigh heavily on my thoughts. I just hoped that Decker didn't have any plans as to taking his revenge out on them. There was also Gan to consider. If she got hungry enough, she wouldn't hesitate to notice the two walking refreshment stands sauntering around my apartment.

Once the sun was just barely down low enough for us to venture out safely, we made our move. There was no point in sitting around waiting to be picked off. We had taken plenty of time to lick our wounds (*sadly, Sally wasn't too keen on me licking anything of hers, though*), and that meant the assassins had probably done so as well. A new night meant the combatants would all be ready for action again.

We stuck to the underground as much as we could, but this time we used the subways themselves so as to stay with the crowds. Rush hour turned out to be a blessing for once; even had we been tracked, there were simply too many people milling about to make a move against us.

Once we were back in Brooklyn, I had Sally keep an eye out for Nergui and Bang. Her senses weren't nearly as acute as Gan's, but they were still better than mine. I wanted as much warning as possible in case we found ourselves walking into a situation. It turns out we did, just not one that I had expected.

* * *

We made it to my building, and I let us in. After climbing the stairs, we stopped outside of my door. I could hear voices coming from inside. I turned to Sally. "Smell any vamps?" She shook her head. "Smell any wizards?"

She shrugged. "I didn't the first time."

Oh well. I guess there are less manly ways to be dispatched than via a twentieth level chain lightning spell, I thought as I unlocked and opened the door.

"I'm telling you, *Glamdring* has the better feats," carried a voice from the living room, Ed's. What the?

"Dude, *Narsil* is the sword of legend. It fucked up *Sauron's* shit," responded Tom's voice.

"Yeah, and the piece of crap broke apart doing so," Ed said as we entered.

The living room was a bit out of place, as if a mess had been made and then hastily cleaned up; however, otherwise it looked fairly normal. Tom was sitting on the couch, and Ed was lounging in a chair. Neither seemed particularly...dead.

"What's up, Bill?" Tom asked, turning to us. "Sally, always a pleasure," he said with a wink. She couldn't help herself and eye-rolled him back – must be instinctive for her. "Maybe you can settle a debate. Ed and I are discussing which sword from *Lord of the Rings* was the most badass. I'm siding with the correct answer: Narsil."

"And you're a fucking retard for doing so," Ed replied. "Glamdring was *Gandalf's* sword...you know, the guy that even the Balrog couldn't snuff. Besides, think of what its name means...Foe Hammer. Tell me that's not the most badass thing in the world. Shit, if I ever start a death metal band, that's what I'm gonna call it: Foe Hammer."

"I will admit that could be a pretty good band name, despite your poor judgment of blades. Any thoughts on this, Bill?"

I was pretty much still stunned by the normalcy (*relatively speaking*) of it all, but I managed to squeak out, "I always kind of liked *Sting*."

"You are such a fag," Tom replied in a dry voice before turning back toward Ed.

"What do you think?" I whispered to Sally.

"I think I would be less embarrassed for them if we had found them skinned alive." It was a loaded question, and I should have expected a response like that.

"Um, guys," I said, trying to get their attention. Normally, I'd be more than up for a little weapon porn debate, but there was more than one game afoot, and I didn't want to get caught with my pants down again. "So...what's going on?"

"It's called a conversation," Ed replied.

"No, stupid," I said. "I mean, last night, this morning. You know, *what* happened today?"

They both looked at each other with a bit of a confused glance and then back toward me. Tom finally broke the silence. "Did we have a party or something last night?"

"A party?"

"Yeah, because I woke up on the floor, feeling like shit. The place was pretty trashed, too."

"Same here," Ed added. "It must have been a good one because I don't remember anything much past yesterday afternoon."

"Alright, enough of this beating around the bush," Sally said, stepping in front of me. "Is Gan here?"

"What's a Gan?" asked Tom.

"She better not be," Ed growled. "Bill, I thought you were gonna drop Frankenstein's daughter off with the coven."

"Well..." I started, but Sally cut me off.

"What about the wizard?"

"Now I have no idea what you're talking about," Ed replied.

"Oh yeah," Tom suddenly said. "Thanks for reminding me, Sally. Bill, there's something I wanted to tell you about Christy."

A look of murder appeared in Sally's eyes. She walked up to Tom and grabbed him by the shirt collar with her good hand. She pulled him to his feet and then some. I noticed his toes were just barely touching the floor as she spat at him, "Let me take a wild guess. She's a witch...and, oh yeah, you also just happened to spill the beans on Bill while you were getting your rocks off. Am I right?"

Tom's face was a mask of both surprise and a little terror, but he still managed to answer, "Wow. Good guess."

She dropped him onto the couch like a sack of potatoes.

There was silence in the room for a moment, and then Ed asked, "Having a bit of a day, are we?"

Sally turned toward him. She lifted her right arm and pulled off the glove. "You could say that."

* * *

"Holy shit! What happened!?" Ed cried, bolting to his feet.

Sally sarcastically spat in response, "A friend needed a hand, so I loaned them mine. What do you *think* happened?"

"Seriously. Sit down. Does it hurt? Can I get you anything?" Ed continued, showing some genuine concern. I had almost forgotten that just a few days ago, he had been out on a date with her.

"I'm fine," she replied, blowing off his entreaties. "Don't worry. It'll grow back."

"It will?"

"You can do that?" Tom asked me.

"If you even think about trying to snip something off me, I will do the same to you," I warned. I tolerated a lot from them as it were. No way was I planning on letting them lop off a finger just to see what would happen. "Besides, that isn't important right now." I caught a glare from Sally. "Of course it's important! I just meant we have other stuff to discuss right now."

"This seems pretty big to me, Bill," Ed said. "What else do we need to know about?"

"How does a vampire vs. wizard grudge match sound? The funny thing is, you guys had ringside seats and don't even know it."

Sally and I filled them in, starting with our adventure the previous night. Ed seemed both amazed by the story and a little pissed that he couldn't remember it. He seemed more upset by that little detail than by the fact that Tom's girlfriend had screwed with his head. It was a bit twisted, but I guess I could understand that. When *Godzilla* throws down with *Rodan*, you want to remember that shit.

Tom, on the other hand, seemed more concerned with the fact that his girlfriend had actually saved them in the end. Who knows, maybe there was actually something there. I had to temper his questions, though, by continually reminding him that she had put the whammy on us under the pretense of luring me to my death. I wasn't exactly an expert in these things, but even I knew something like that wasn't exactly a building block for a healthy relationship.

"Maybe it was a misunderstanding," he offered.

"When someone says, 'And now you must die, Freewill', it doesn't leave it open for much interpretation."

"Yeah, I guess so," he finally admitted. "I'm thinking she and I need to sit down and have a long talk about things."

"Talk!?" Sally snapped. "Are you that desperate for a piece of ass that you're actually considering having a little sit-down over lunch to discuss things with the same psycho witch who tried to kill your best friend last night?"

"Do you really want to know the answer to that?" Ed asked before turning to me. "And this Decker dude, he was actually dating your wannabe lady friend just to mess with you?"

"Yep."

"That's cold, man. Bet you wish you had let Gan gut the sucker."

"I don't know," I replied. "Maybe. But the whole thing is like a slippery slope. What if he had just been some normal guy out on a date?"

"If pigs had wings, they'd be eagles," Ed answered.

"All's fair in love and war," was Tom's response. Damn, my roommates just weren't being helpful at all. If I listened to their advice, I'd be Jack the Ripper within a week. Who'd have thought Sally's would have been the voice of sanity amongst us all? Oh well, best not to dwell on it too much now. That way leads to madness.

"Okay," I said, trying to get us back on track. "You know what happened to us...sorta. I'm still not sure what went down after Sally got turned into a southpaw.

But that's not important right now. What I'm curious about is what the hell happened to you two?"

Ed replied, "Like we said. No idea. We woke up with no memory of any of that. Gotta be honest, I'm still not one-hundred percent convinced that you and Sally aren't screwing with our heads just for the hell of it." She glared at him, showing him a little fang in the process. "Don't get me wrong, I believe you. It's just weird."

"Yeah," Tom agreed. "We woke up, and there was nobody else here. No vampire toddler, no wizards, nothing. Stuff was out of place, but it's not like back when Jeff trashed the place. Didn't look like there was a fight or anything. Although, there was one weird thing..."

"What?"

"Someone left us a new Playstation."

* * *

Tom's revelation did give us something to check. The games I had bought were all there, but the bags of clothing for Gan were missing. She had been here after all, although *when* she left and in *what* condition were still up for debate. I assumed she hadn't waited in ambush for Decker and Christy...there would have been blood splattered about, a lot of it probably, if that had happened. I hoped that the reverse didn't occur – that they had somehow managed to take her out of the equation. My fondness for Gan was limited, but seeing her become a casualty in a war she had nothing to do with wasn't what I wanted either.

"So what's the plan?" Tom finally asked.

"Gan is priority number one. We need to find her."

"Nice to see you care for the little hellion," quipped Ed.

"I care more about the damage she can do if she's not contained. As far as she's concerned, there are over eighteen million walking snacks in this city."

"Let's not forget that she's probably pissed to all hell," Sally added. "Those wizards did a job on her and then casually dismissed her. If that's not a mindset to put someone with the emotional stability of a preteen into rampage mode, I don't know what is."

"Almost forgot about that. If it were me, I'd probably be hunting those fuckers down right now."

"And she could do it, too," Sally continued. "Don't forget how easily she found you, Bill."

"Gives us a place to start, at least," I concluded. "Tom, give me Christy's address. We'll check there first."

"You're not going to hurt her are you?" he asked after some hesitation.

"We'll try not to." I looked at Sally. "*Won't we*? Seriously, Tom, she's not my favorite person on the planet right now but, when push came to shove, she got you and Ed out of danger. I promise I'll try to give her the benefit of the doubt."

"Maybe I should come, too?" he added.

"No!" blurted Sally. That wasn't too surprising. I knew that Tom drove her bugshit with his incessant comments, but this time she was in the right.

"Sally's got a point. We're gonna need to move fast. This isn't like last time, when we knew where shit was going down," I said.

"How about this?" Ed offered. "If you find out in advance where the action will be, you call us in."

I wanted to say no, but Sally spoke up first. "You still have that popgun?" she asked, no doubt referring to Ed's twelve-gauge.

"You bet."

"Then if we have enough warning, you're in." I gave her a disbelieving glare, but before I could say anything, she answered my unspoken question. "Don't give me that look. I'm not an idiot. Backup is backup, and as much as I hate to admit it, they helped just as much against Jeff as I did." Tom opened his mouth to speak, but Sally help up her hand to his face. "Doesn't mean I like it, though."

I jumped in before this turned into either a hug-fest or a homicide scene. "Ed, while we're doing that, can you find out Harry Decker's address?"

"What if he's not listed?"

"Call HR. They'll have him on file. Besides, Barbara there likes you. Lay on the sweet talk, and I'm sure she'll give you whatever you want."

"Barb the beast?" he replied with a look of horror. Barbara was the HR admin for our office. She was a sweetheart, but not exactly the easiest thing on the eyes.

"We must all make our sacrifices," I said with a solemn voice, which earned me a chuckle from Sally and a stare of death from Ed. I just hoped that his look was the deadliest thing I would be facing tonight. None of us had spoken about it, but we still knew the assassins were out there waiting for us.

Two Mongolian killers, a revenge-bent vampire princess dressed in expensive schoolgirl clothing, and a couple of whacked out magic users trying to fulfill an insane prophecy...

Damn, it was gonna be a long night.

Working Hard or Hardly Working

CHRISTY'S APARTMENT WAS our first stop. That was easy enough. As it turned out, she lived only a mile or so away from my place, a convenient location for Tom's girlfriend. Too bad she had to go and spoil it by being a backstabbing harpy. Oh well; nobody's perfect, I guess.

We easily made it past the front door security for her building. This was one of Sally's specialties. When you looked like she did, doors were opened for you...literally. We went up to Christy's floor and walked to her door. I then did the only obvious thing I could think of: I knocked.

"Step aside, idiot," Sally said. She gripped the doorknob with her left hand and started turning it. As the tumblers hit their limits, she kept putting on the pressure until the whole apparatus started groaning under the strain.

"Hold on a second," I said. "What if she has, I don't know, wards or stuff?"

"Wards?"

"Yeah. You know: circles of protection, explosive runes, that type of shit. I used that crap all the time in my game to keep thieves and the rest of the party away from my gold."

"I have no idea what the hell you're talking about. I don't speak dork."

"Fine. Be my guest." I made an *after-you* gesture to her and then backed several steps down the hall. If this thing opened up a fiery gateway to Hell, then at least I'd live long enough to shout, "I told you so!"

The lock cracked and...***KABOOM**!!!* Well, in my mind it did anyway, and let's face facts: if this were a game being run by my usual Dungeon Master, Dave, Sally would now probably be thoroughly ventilated. Instead, there was nothing. *Real world mages are rapidly starting to disappoint me*, I thought as the door just swung in.

Sally pushed it open all the way and then stepped through the doorway. She had no more than put her foot down when suddenly the door flew back at her face as if *Conan the Barbarian* had just decided to slam it shut. It crashed into her, and she went flying back into the opposite wall as the door clicked itself back shut again. I watched it happen, a smirk of amusement on my face – noting that my opinion of real world witches had risen back up a notch again.

Sally was dazed, but didn't seem to be otherwise worse for the wear. Thus, I didn't see any reason to fight the compulsion to stroll back up to her and say, "Told ya so."

* * *

279

Turns out that Christy wasn't home anyway. This didn't surprise me too much. I had considered it a long shot. If anything was going down tonight, chances are it would be in Manhattan. That was where my coven was headquartered. It was also where the assassins were hunting and all of last night's shit had gone down. Thus, I wasn't all too surprised to find us on a train heading back there. During most of the trip, I couldn't help but notice that Sally kept reaching inside her purse to stroke the enormous handgun within, all the while chanting, "Fucking witches!" It was an effort, but I somehow kept myself from grinning the entire time.

It turned out our timing was good. We had just gotten out of the subway, close to coven territory, when my cell phone rang. It was Ed.

"I've got Decker's home address for you."

"Good job," I replied. Ed gave it to me. Decker had an apartment in a building on the Upper West Side. I knew the area: monthly rents higher than most mortgage payments, twenty-four hour door service, and mostly home to executives, high paid professionals, and other assorted yuppie scum. It didn't surprise me in the least. I don't care what kind of dark wizard he thought he was, at the end of the day he was just another asshole corporate suit that more or less contributed nothing to society other than making the lives of people like me more difficult.

"You owe me," Ed groused.

"What happened?"

"I have to take Barbara out to lunch sometime this week."

"Aw, but you make such a cute couple."

Ed grumbled something back that would have made me blush had I been a good, God-fearing family man.

Sally, overhearing most of the conversation thanks to her vampire ears, said, "Tell him I'll make it up to him."

"What was that?" Ed asked.

"Sally said she'll send flowers to your wedding," I replied and hung up.

"That was mean," she commented. "As I said before, you're obviously jealous."

"Nonsense," I replied. "I just believe my roommates should stick to dating their own species."

"Oh. Then what about you and that girl you're still pining for?"

"That's different."

"How so?"

"What was that you were saying earlier...something about double standards?"

* * *

It turns out we didn't need to go all the way uptown. That was good. Too much smarm there for my personal tastes anyway.

We were walking toward another subway stop, passing through a section of midtown that was very familiar to me, when Sally suddenly sniffed the air and then stopped. "Gan's close," she said and pointed toward the various rooftops. "Up there somewhere."

I didn't really need to look. I knew where we were. Despite my doctor's note proclaiming my medical *condition*, I once more found myself back at work. Just great! Of all the places to have a potential showdown, it just had to be at the one where I could get reamed out for it by HR.

"Any idea where she is specifically?" I asked, mostly knowing what the answer would be.

"It's not like using a GPS," Sally complained. "I can sense that's she's close, which probably means she can sense us if she decides to try. If I had to guess, from what she did yesterday I'd say on top of one of these buildings." Of course, saying something like that in the middle of Manhattan was the equivalent of tracking an animal through the forest when the only clue you had was that it was 'near a tree'.

"Okay, then let's not worry about finding her. She'll come to us."

"Why?"

"Because I know where Decker is."

"How?" she asked.

"Because we both work right over there," I said, pointing across the street toward one of the buildings. "Welcome to my job, Sally. Please don't do anything to get me fired."

She just laughed. "Are you kidding? You walk in with me on your arm, and they'll probably give you a promotion." Yep, that's Sally. Humble as ever.

"I guess we should go up. If Gan is here, that means Decker's probably in his office. I know where that is."

"And what exactly are we going to do once we get there?"

"No idea. Maybe steal some office supplies?" I caught a glare for that. "Sorry. The good thing is that at this time of night, the place is going to be nearly deserted. Come five-thirty, if you're standing by the front doors you're liable to get trampled. The only people who are gonna be there at this hour are workaholics..."

"And wizards?"

"Apparently."

"So again I ask, what's the plan?"

"Make it up as we go along and hope for the best?" I offered.

"You must have been Napoleon in a former life to come up with that kind of strategy. Oh well, who wants to live forever?"

"Actually, I wouldn't mind it," I replied.

"*You*? Every minute that goes by without you getting dusted is utterly amazing to me."

* * *

We took the stairs. Yeah it was a pretty hefty walk up, but we decided the elevators were too risky. On the off chance that Decker somehow knew we were coming, I didn't want our bold plan to immediately end with "*and they went plunging downward, screaming toward their deaths*" before we even saw the guy. Fortunately, the stairs weren't really an issue. Vampire stamina is pretty damn good, after all (*despite whatever lies Gan might have said*).

"Once we get in, I'll go to his office. I want you to walk around and see if you can get rid of any stragglers."

"Snapping their necks would be fastest."

"Not funny," I replied. "Unless you come across Carl from the project management office...then it might be a *little* funny. Just use your feminine wiles. Chances are, most of the people still here are guys. Trust me when I say a little T&A would probably motivate them to fly down the stairs."

"Is that all I am to you, just a piece of meat?"

"Not at all. Without you around, who else would I rely on to piss away the coven's money?"

"Flatterer," she replied and then quieted down again as I pulled my employee ID from my wallet and let us in.

Nothing and no one greeted us upon entering. I was correct about the ghost-town nature of the place at this time of night. I sent Sally off to the right to do as I had asked, and then I walked straight toward Executive Row, where I knew Decker's office was. Part of my plan for Sally was to legitimately make sure there were no bystanders around. If the office turned into a battlefield, I didn't want any non-combatants to worry about. The other part was a contingency in case Decker was waiting for us. If so, he wouldn't get both myself and Sally with the first salvo. Not the best of plans. Then again, Decker hadn't exactly shown himself to be a strategic genius either so far. Thus, I hoped our mutual ineptitudes would cancel each other out.

I got to his office and heard voices coming from within. It seemed he wasn't alone. It was possible that Christy was with him. Both of them had proven to have limited endurance in battle (*although more than enough to take out a vamp*), but if they were together that could definitely tip the odds in their favor.

I put my ear to the door to listen.

"...can't put that out there. Yes Stefan, I know those are market rates, but I want some banners thrown in with that print ad."

Jesus Christ! All of that buildup in my mind, and the fucker was just on a conference call. Screw that! I opened his door, walked in, and plopped myself into one of the empty seats in front of his desk.

The party on the other line kept blathering on about print quality issues. Decker, on the other hand, just stared at me, obvious surprise on his face. Finally, never taking his eyes off me, he said, "Sorry, Stefan. I'll need to call you back tomorrow. The CEO just buzzed me on the other line, have to take it." He reached over and disconnected the call.

"Hey, Harry," I said casually. "Burning the old midnight oil?"

"Someone here has to get the job done," he replied with a guarded tone.

"Judging from last night, that obviously isn't you."

"Seems to be a lot of that going on," he drolled. "I'm surprised to see you. Those fellows who interrupted our chat looked a little out of your league."

"Nothing I couldn't handle," I lied.

"Let me guess: you ran like a little girl?"

"A lot of that going around, too," I shot back

"I suppose you're here to finish what we started. If so, you should know I'm not prepared for battle. It would be cold-blooded murder."

"What's a little murder amongst friends?" I quipped. "But sadly, no. You're not gonna believe this. Shit, *I* don't believe it. But for the second time in as many days, I'm actually trying to save your life."

He started to open his mouth to respond and, of course, that's when his office window exploded.

A View to Die For

THE SHATTERING GLASS muffled the soft *THFFT* noise that accompanied the shot, but it was audible to my enhanced undead hearing. Even had it not been, I probably would have still noticed the arrow sticking out of my shoulder. Even had I been too preoccupied to notice the arrow, I would have definitely noticed the silver arrowhead which was even now causing sparks to shoot from the wound in my arm. Goddamned assassins! Oh yeah, and also, "HOLY FUCKING SHIT!"

I was knocked backwards off the chair by the force of the impact. I was luckier than I had any reason to be. The windows on office buildings are pretty damn tough compared to your normal pane of house glass. I was betting the assassins hadn't known that when they shot at me. The glass had still given way against the projectile, but the course had been altered just enough so that Harry Decker wasn't sitting there having a meaningful conversation with a pile of ash.

After the initial flurry of glass shards washed over him, Decker dove over the desk and crouched down beneath, using it as cover. He wasn't entirely stupid. He had killed one of Nergui's buddies. He wasn't their prime target, but it didn't take a genius to figure out that they probably wouldn't bat an eye over turning him into collateral damage.

"You led them here, vampire!" he hissed at me while I was busy writhing in excruciating pain.

I gritted my teeth and replied, "Yeah, but you're the one who pissed them off." I grabbed the arrow and finally tore it free from my smoldering shoulder. If you're thinking that doing so probably hurt enough to make me wish I hadn't been born, you're correct. Hell, it hurt enough to make me wish that my *parents* hadn't been born. No wonder, the fucking thing was barbed. I now had a large, blood-spouting hole gouged into my shoulder that wouldn't be healing shut anytime soon. Oh yeah, this was going well.

I was busy trying to get my feet under me – and not cry like a little baby while doing so – when I heard another window shatter. This one was followed by what can best be described as cannon fire...Sally! Oh boy, no way was I not getting a pink-slip after this one.

But probably best to worry about unemployment later, like maybe when I wasn't in danger of becoming someone's hunting trophy. I took advantage of Sally's cover fire to crawl back into the main office. There was bound to be less chance of arrow-related incidents in there.

Despite my better judgment, I gestured for Decker to follow. He did, and together we ran to put at least one wall between us and that side of the building.

"Truce for now?" he suggested.

"Is there any chance of you pulling a *Dr. Evil* and stabbing me in the back?"

"I leave open the possibility," he replied. Hey, at least he was honest about it.

"Fair enough," I answered. "I don't suppose your protégé is around to provide us with any backup?"

"She has a cooking class tonight."

"Let me guess. Double double, toil and trouble?"

"French cuisine, actually."

I was going to respond with something appropriately pithy, but the whole loss of blood thing was starting to make me a bit light-headed. Fortunately, Sally saved me from my embarrassing lack of one-liners.

"We need to go. They're coming." As if in affirmation to her statement, there was the sound of more glass shattering. Sounded like maybe a floor or two below us.

"Jeez. What did they do, jump across?" I asked.

"Duh! It's faster than the elevator," she replied. "They'll be here any minute. I suggest we get going." She noticed my shoulder. "Can you run?"

"As long as I don't try any handstands."

"I have a better idea," Decker said. "Why don't you two provide a distraction to cover *my* escape?"

Before either of us could respond, there was a flash of light that sent me and Sally flying.

Oh well, he *did* warn me.

* * *

Sally was kind enough to break my fall with her...soft parts. Just in case you were curious, yes they are real, and they feel *wonderful*. What felt less wonderful was when she rudely shoved me off, but guess I can't fault her for that.

"Were we really *both* stupid enough to turn our backs on him?" she growled as she got to her feet.

"Yes. But at least we did it as a team," I said, being a glass-is-half-full kind of guy.

"Maybe we should just let Nergui finish us off," she commented.

"The hell with that! If I'm going down, I'm taking Lord fucking Voldemort with me." I got to my feet and started for the stairwell. "Time to put on our wizard-stomping boots."

"Up?"

"I'm pretty sure Harry didn't suddenly grow a pair and go down to meet them head on, so yes. Up it is. At least we can die with a good view."

"Speak for yourself. All I have is *you* to look at," she replied, opening the exit door and starting up.

Decker's footsteps could be heard above us. There weren't too many floors left in the building, so that meant he was probably headed for the roof. From below us, we could hear muffled Chinese voices coming up quickly. We were definitely the meat in this asshole sandwich.

"Give me the gun, Sally," I said. "Just do it, don't argue!" She paused for just a second, but then handed it to me. My shoulder hurt like a motherfucker, and blood was still pouring out of it, but at least I still had two hands with which to line up and take a shot. Sure, I had never fired a real gun before in my life, but I used to play a lot of *Duck Hunt* on my old NES. How much harder could it be? "Go and catch Decker. I'll try to slow down Nergui and Bang."

"The safety's still on, genius," she said with an eye-roll and then did as she was told. Yeah well, I'm sure I'd have figured that one out sooner or later.

She went after *Mr. Wizard* while I backed up to the next landing and stood my ground. I braced my feet and held the hand-cannon out ahead of me. Yeah, I felt like Dirty Harry. "Do you feel lucky, punk?" slipped out of my lips, along with my best mean sneer.

And that's when I saw something shiny come flying up the stairs, then turn and head right toward me. Fuck! Nobody told me they had goddamn boomerangs. It managed to slice my outer thigh before I could dive out of the way. It embedded itself into the wall. Some sort of curved throwing blade which was, of course, also made of silver. Christ, how much precious metal did these guys have? It must have taken them forever to get through customs. These guys weren't just assassins. They were pimps, too.

But that's okay...well, except for the new gash on my leg...I had some silver of my own. I stepped back into the stairwell and fired a warning shot down at them. No idea if it hit anything or not as the kickback from the gun caused it to slam up right into my face, knocking me on my ass.

As the stun of it wore off and the ringing in my ears subsided, I tried to get back up. Damn, think I chipped a tooth. I don't recall seeing that one happen in *Sudden Impact.*

Fine, Wild Bill Hickok I was not. Time for a new plan. I decided to make my stand with Sally after all. *It couldn't get much worse than this,* I thought, retreating up the stairs after her.

* * *

I was, of course, wrong. I reached the top floor and was about to open the roof access door when it came blasting off its hinges straight into me. It crushed me like a bug against the opposing wall. The breath was forced out of me, and I was pretty sure I heard a few ribs crack in the process. This was definitely not going according to any plan. I had been beaten up, bloodied, and still hadn't gotten off much offense of my own. As soon as the world stopped spinning, I was going to be mighty pissed.

The door gave a groan as I pushed it off me. Wait, doors don't groan. I lifted the broken door and saw the reason why. I chucked it down the stairs (no reason to make Nergui's mission any easier) and bent down to check on Sally. She was a mess. I had caught the ass end of the force blast, but she had gotten the main course. Her arms were skewed at multiple crazy angles, and judging by the way she was bent over, I'd have guessed her spine might possibly be broken as well. She looked like a dump truck had run her over and then backed up to do it again; however, if she was making noise, then she was still alive. I wasn't about to let anyone change that, especially not a backstabbing prick like Decker.

I could feel that rage welling up inside of me again. No! Now was not the time. Who knows what would happen by the time I woke up again, *if* I woke up again? Sure, things always seemed to work out for *Bruce Banner*, but I had a sneaking suspicion any alter-ego my subconscious tried to conjure would be somewhat less than trustworthy. I took a few deep breaths and tried to keep a level head, but it was hard going.

Fortunately for me, though, distractions were plentiful.

I was snapped back to reality as I heard the door I had tossed down the stairs being shoved aside. A split second later, another of those Mongolian batarangs came flying up the stairs at me. Down was definitely not an option.

The blade went wide and struck the door frame instead of something more fragile...like myself. Thinking quickly, I wrenched it free (*cutting my fingers in the process...oh joy!*). I probably couldn't throw a knife any better than I could shoot, but it gave me more of an arsenal than I had before.

"Sorry, Sally," I whispered, picking her up and tossing her over my good shoulder like a sack of potatoes. Hopefully it wouldn't mess her up much worse than she already was. Besides, leaving her for

Nergui to find just wasn't an option. I wasn't in particularly good shape myself, but I didn't think I had far to go. I just hoped I had enough in me for a quick burst of speed.

I waited.

And, as expected, I didn't have to wait for long. Nergui's voice floated up to me from just one flight below. "It is over, Freewill. Make your death an honorable one."

Honor this, fucker, I thought in return. Okay, time to make or break. "Catch me if you can, assholes!" I screamed with insane glee, bursting through the doorway onto the rooftop at the fastest speed I could manage.

* * *

I didn't go straight. I'm not *that* stupid. Instead, upon stepping out and making a target of myself, I did a little razzle-dazzle and jumped to the left, toward some large air conditioning units. The blast came a split second later. I could feel the air displace as it roared across the roof and toward the doorway just as Nergui and Bang stepped through.

I'll give credit where credit is due: those vamps were fast motherfuckers...just not fast enough. They attempted to sidestep the blast and both wound up being only partially successful at it. Nergui was caught fairly full on. He slammed into the right side of the door frame and then was blasted straight through it. A similar blast a few moments ago had nearly turned Sally into a puddle of vampire-colored paint; however,

Nergui had three extra centuries of badassery on his side. I imagined he'd probably tumble down a few flights of stairs and then be right up in my shit all over again.

Bang had caught the periphery of the blast as he tried to leap in my direction. It had sent him spinning out of control, causing him to bounce off the rooftop a couple times before skidding to a halt against an antenna array, bending it in the process. *sigh* It's not like cell service doesn't already suck enough in the city as it is. Next time you're in midtown and you can't get five bars, I guess you can blame me.

Still hidden behind the A/C unit, I put Sally down on the rooftop. It would provide her some cover, and if not, I hoped that the various combatants would show at least a little chivalry to the downed lady. Unfortunately, if I just stayed where I was, standing over her like a protective mother bear guarding its cubs, I'd be easy pickings. At best, I needed to take out a few of my many enemies. At the very least, I needed to be a distraction for her.

I peeked around the corner and saw Decker at the far edge of the roof. He was down on one knee, breathing hard. Much like the night before, the expenditure of power had temporarily drained his batteries.

"I thought you said you weren't in any condition to fight!" I yelled at him, still from behind my cover. No use tempting fate in case he had another shot left in him.

"I lied," he panted in return – an asshole to the very end. The question was; should I pick him off or try to take out one of the Khan's lackeys? At the time being they seemed the far greater of the...hell, I had lost count of all the evils by that point.

I stuffed Sally's gun in the waistband of my pants. No point in shooting wildly, as I was pretty sure I couldn't hit the sky if I aimed at it. A small part of me was sure it would go off and blow away my balls, along with a good chunk of my lower body, but fate actually surprised me for once and left me intact, or as intact as I was. Fucking silver weapons. If it weren't for them, I'd have been all healed up by now and ready for round two; instead, I had a gimpy arm, a bleeding leg, and a chest cavity that felt like a sumo wrestler was sitting on it every time I tried to breathe.

I hefted the silvered knife. I could probably throw it no better than I could shoot, but in close quarters I wouldn't need to. I turned left and charged toward where Bang was just now getting to his feet. He had gotten the wind knocked out of him by Decker's *Power Word: Fuck You* spell. He reached his feet, and I almost instinctively skidded to a halt. The guy was seriously messed up, and from the look of things, not by any magic hex. Everything was starting to scar over thanks to his quick healing, but the damage was still quite evident. He was missing his right eye and had a good gouge taking out of that side of his face. There were likewise deep tears and scratches across every part of his torso that I could see. Though apparently functional, one of his arms had an odd cant to it, as if it were missing a sizable chunk from the bicep. In short, Bang was pretty *banged* up.

I remembered back to the night before, right before blacking out. Had I caused that damage to him? As Decker and Christy had been long gone by then, it seemed the only logical answer. Unless, that is, Nergui had decided to take out his frustrations at my escape on his friend. Fucked up culture or not, though, that didn't seem to make much sense. In the movies, the bad guys are always shooting their incompetent lackeys, but in real life you don't snuff the hired help, at least not until the job is done.

Bang saw me coming and attempted to strike a defensive pose, but it was too late. I flung myself at him and slammed into his midsection. He went down with me on top, and we skidded across the roof a good ten feet before coming to a stop.

"Having a good time in the city!?" I yelled, slamming my left fist into his jaw. "Here's a little souvenir for you!" I raised the knife and brought it down toward his chest. It was just about then that the rational voices in my head spoke up and reminded me that I had absolutely no idea what I was doing. They always like to do that during times like these. Well okay, I haven't exactly had too many times like *this*. Tussling with a centuries old assassin wasn't exactly a normal thing, even in *my* life. Oh well, another thing to add to my resume.

Bang had other ideas, though. Despite his injuries, he still managed to catch me by the wrist before I could do more than prick his skin with the blade. I put my other hand on top and started bearing down. Vampiric strength is a badass thing; however, it doesn't mean much if the person you're fighting has it, too, except multiplied by several times. I couldn't budge him. In fact, the fucker had the nerve to start smiling at me. He said something glib sounding in that gibberish Chinese of his. I didn't need to understand him to know I had just been burned.

"Oh yeah? Your boss is James T. Kirk's bitch!" I lamely spat back. If he had spoken English...and had a working knowledge of the dorkier aspects of American pop culture...it would have been pretty damn insulting, believe me.

I heard noises behind me. I turned my head to check and saw that Nergui had once again emerged onto the rooftop. Decker had regained his feet as well and appeared to be steeling himself for another salvo of spells. Good, they were keeping each other occupied for the moment. I was just about to turn back to Bang when movement caught my eye. It was Sally. She was actually trying...and mostly failing...to get back to her feet. Fucking crazy bitch.

"STAY D..." I started to yell, right before doing the opposite myself. I had stupidly allowed myself to be distracted against a vampire who, unlike me, knew what he was doing. He had gotten his other arm free, and with the added leverage, literally threw me off him. I really needed to enlist in the Army or sign myself up again for self-defense classes. Spending all of eternity being on the receiving end of shit like this did not sound like fun to me.

Oh, and in case you're wondering, being thrown through the air isn't a particularly fun thing either. It is considerably less amusing when it involves a rooftop that happens to be a couple hundred feet above street level. A birds-eye view of what was waiting for you, one short trip at terminal velocity later, would be enough to give anyone a slight case of vertigo. A vampire with a fear of heights would almost be chuckle worthy if I weren't the one it was happening to.

I was almost about to count my lucky stars (*and believe me, it wouldn't have been a particularly high count*) that Bang's throw was going to leave me a few feet short of the edge, when I realized I had failed to take into account the bounce factor. Ah yes, momentum. Kind of wished I hadn't blown off so many physics classes back in college; otherwise, I might have remembered the whole *bodies in motion tend to stay in motion* thing. Not that it would have done me much good. Knowledge of the laws of physics doesn't necessarily mean an ability to break them...at least outside of *The Matrix* (*which I was pretty sure I wasn't in, given the utter lack of leather-clad chicks named Trinity coming to my aid*).

I slammed down and tumbled toward the edge. The knife flew from my grip, and a barely intelligible, but highly audible, "OH SHIT!" escaped from my lips. I didn't know if a drop from this height would kill me, but it was a fair certainty that it would mess up my day in more ways than one.

There was only one chance. As my legs slid out over the edge, I slammed my fingers down into the rooftop as hard as my vampire strength would allow and tried to dig in. Some days, I curse having been turned into a vampire; that exact moment was not one of those times. I managed to sink them in just enough to stop myself before the bulk of my weight carried me over. I was going to be picking roofing tar out from beneath my fingernails for a month, but considering the alternative, I'd be happy to do it.

Unfortunately for me, the alternative was very much still a possibility. I had just barely stopped myself from going over when I looked up to see Bang standing over me. That same asshole smile was still on his face as he reared back to punt my head off.

* * *

At the speed of thought, dull anger flooded through me. I had been there before, or at least one of my old *Dungeons and Dragons* characters had. It had been a difficult campaign, fighting our way through the Accursed Pass of the Blood Mountains. Following a particularly nasty encounter with a pack of Hill Giants, my character was left with a broken leg. In game terms, this meant that the DM saddled me with a bunch of bullshit negative modifiers to all of my scores, including speed. Afterwards, while climbing a cliff face toward our final destination, my character's injuries had slowed the party down enough so that we lost the element of surprise. The others were pissed at me. Thus, when my ranger finally reached the top of the cliff and was pulling himself up, my friend, Mike, walked his barbarian over to me and said, "Sorry, but you've become a burden," right before kicking me in the face, sending my character plummeting to his death. Bunch of assholes! They all had a good laugh about it and even stopped on the return trip to loot my corpse. It was one of those indignities that one did not so easily forget.

No fucking way was I letting some shithead named Bang do the same thing to me again. He'd have to find some other sucker to loot a +3 flaming sword from...or something like that, anyway.

As his foot came straight at my head, I let go of my precarious grip on the rooftop and grabbed his leg with both hands. His foot still slammed into my face, but my mouth, or more precisely *my fangs*, was waiting for it.

I bit into the soft leather of his boot. My teeth had no problem going through the material to the flesh inside. Just for the record, at no point did it taste particularly good. I chomped down on his toes and hung on for dear life. Bang started screaming and tried to back up. It was enough for one of my legs to lift over the edge and find purchase to push myself up with.

Bang lost his balance and fell on his back, but it also freed his other leg to kick out at me. He managed to score a glancing blow, but it was enough to make me let go. Rather than risk a repeat performance, I instead rolled out of his range.

He howled while cradling his injured foot. It gave me enough time to get back to my feet. We locked eyes as I did so. The smile was gone from his face, but it was spreading on mine. I complemented the gesture by spitting out two of his toes toward him. It's not like I was planning on swallowing them anyway. Sadly, it was mostly a psych-out maneuver. I had gotten a little of his blood from the ordeal, but it was barely enough for a quick recharge to even my normal levels. I was still way out of my league here. On the upside, though, Bang wouldn't be competing on *Dancing with the Stars* anytime soon.

Or maybe I spoke too soon. He did a quick kip-up and was suddenly on his feet again. A few missing toes wasn't exactly a mortal wound for someone like him. Even worse, he then drew one of those silver daggers he and his buddies seemed to favor. Guess he got a lot of *bang* for his buck out of those (*I kill me*). The grin was still gone from his face, but the look that was there made me wish that it wasn't. This time, he meant to finish the job.

What's a Little Murder Amongst Friends

I KNEW THE stare down was a ruse. I had seen how fast vampires could move. Any second, Bang would be on me quicker than I could blink my eyes. His power, speed, and experience eclipsed mine by many times over, and he was more than aware of it. However, he still hesitated. I had given him more of a fight than he had expected so far, and apparently gave him a *lot* more than he bargained for the previous night. That was it! I was an X-factor as far as he was concerned. He wasn't entirely sure what I could do and was thus playing things a bit more cautiously than he might otherwise. Maybe I could use that.

I tried my best to keep a grin on my face. Best to let him think I wasn't afraid of him. I was, though, and he could probably see it my eyes...thus I put on the ol' vamp face. I extended my fangs and claws, then I blackened my eyes (*I was starting to get pretty good at this*). Bang actually took a small step back. All vampires can do that stuff. It was pretty par for the course. However, something allowed me to take it further. I was the Freewill of vampire legend, after all. Too bad I had absolutely no fucking idea what that meant or how to control it. That moment of extreme anger I'd felt earlier had passed. In its place was weariness from my wounds and a slight desire to piss myself out of the fear of getting my head lopped off; in other words, I had nothing.

CLANG or maybe not. I apparently still had one crazy ass bitch of a guardian angel. A metal grate flew out of nowhere, slamming into the back of Bang's head. Sally! I turned my head, and sure enough it had been her. Somehow she was still in the game, although just barely. The effort appeared to be all that she had in her. She attempted to give me a thumbs-up with her still very disjointed arms, but instead just fell back down. Still, if she could mount an offense in her fucked-up state, I wasn't about to let it go to waste.

I closed in and swung my claws. They sliced a nasty-looking furrow across Bang's chest. I repeated the action with my other hand, and he let out a grunt of pain. I needed to keep it up. If I tore into him enough, even he would go down...probably. I reared back to do it again, maybe a nice slice out of his throat would give him something to think about.

But then I just stopped. I didn't *mean* to stop. I had every intention of following through on my attack, but my body stopped responding the way I wanted it to. It was curious, but the spreading heat in my midsection gave me my first clue. I looked down to see Bang's dagger several inches deep in my stomach. Yeah, that would do it.

Before I could come up with a suitably clever response to being gutted, Bang backhanded me, and I went tumbling away, my blood spraying out in an arch as the knife pulled free. I finally came to a stop face-down on the rooftop. Considering the sizable hole in my stomach, it was not the most comfortable of positions to be in. It was made even less fun due to the butt of the desert eagle digging in dangerously close to where some of my insides were trying to make their way out. Wait a second...I still had the gun! I was a suck shot, but it was better than nothing.

Unfortunately, I shouldn't have been worrying about my front, my back, or even the shooting lessons I needed to take. I should have been more worried about my head. I felt rough fingers grab a handful of my hair and jerk me upright to my knees. The hand forced my chin up so that I got a pretty good look at the sky. It was partly cloudy, probably low chance of rain. Sadly, there was high chance of my death. I saw the same dagger that had just been used to fillet me, enter into my view. Bang was slowly lowering it to my throat when a shrill shriek pierced the air.

* * *

I had heard a similar scream the night before. It was an almost animalistic battle cry in a high pitch that only a feral cat or a pre-teen girl could manage. Gan! About time she decided to join this party. Pity it was probably too late to do me any good. Oh well, I had been meaning to lose a few pounds one of these days anyway. This was one way to ensure I stopped procrastinating about it. Besides, throughout my life I had suffered from a poor body image, so maybe I wouldn't miss it all that much anyway.

I didn't feel the blade biting into me, though. The hand holding the knife was hesitating. I craned my eyes up as far as they would go, and I could just barely make out Bang's head. It was turned toward the direction of the scream. He hadn't been expecting Gan.

No time to waste! I fumbled with my right hand for the gun, but my grip was slippery with blood. The first time I tried to pull it out, I rammed it straight into my wound instead. **FUCK**! Talk about a wake-up call! I needed to remember in the future not to bring cold steel into contact with my intestinal tract.

On the second try, I got the weapon free. Without thinking, I lifted it up and pointed it back over my shoulder to where I thought Bang was standing. I pulled the trigger (*Bang, meet a bigger *bang**), and for a second there thought I had blown my own head off, so loud was the explosion. Now I know why people wear ear plugs when they go shooting. The kickback from the gun tore it from my fingers (*and almost dislocated my shoulder*). It went clattering away, still smoking from the shot I had made – not that I could hear the clattering. In fact, it was probably going to be a while before I could hear *anything*.

I flopped down again face-first onto the roof, the wound in my stomach again sending fresh waves of pain through me. Wait! I was free. Bang had let me go. Guess the shot had surprised him. Hey, maybe I even managed to wing him. I rolled over onto my back to check and saw him standing there above me, knife still in hand, but minus most of his head.

Whoa. *Hope there weren't any low flying aircraft passing overhead when I pulled the trigger,* was all I had time to think before his body burst into flame and a shower of Bang dust fell upon me. Ewww, some of him got into my mouth. I was going to be investing heavily in *Listerine* after this one.

Still, dental hygiene was a concern for later. At that moment, I needed to concentrate on not dying from my injuries. I tried to stand, doubled over in pain for a few moments, and then managed to right myself. I put my hand over my stomach to try and staunch the blood flow. It was still going pretty good, although most of my other injuries had at least slowed to a minor drip.

I looked around. Still no sign of Gan. Wait! There was a small blur on the rooftop next over. It was moving fast, but I caught a glimpse of a flower pattern. There was no mistaking one of the overpriced dresses Sally had purchased the other day. If she hadn't been moving like the wind and screeching like a banshee, she might have looked cute in it...for an ancient little hell-beast, that is.

Gan reached the edge of the roof, maybe some five floors lower than the one we were on, and kept going. She leapt the distance between the two and then fell out of my sight. What the hell? I lurched over to the edge and looked down. Wow, she was actually scaling the side of the building, using her claws to gain purchase, and moving pretty damn fast at it, too. She'd be up at our level within the space of moments. Good, I could use a little backup...even if I had to promise to marry her to get it.

Unfortunately, I wasn't sure I had a few moments. A muffled sound caught my attention, and I turned around to check it out. I saw Decker down on the ground, the hilt of one of Nergui's daggers sticking out of his leg. He was rolling around, screaming (*I think, my hearing still wasn't quite back to full yet*), and more or less being pretty obvious about the fact that he was out of the fight. Oh crap. Where the hell did that gun fly off to?

Nergui said something to the downed Decker, which I didn't quite catch. He then turned and looked in my direction. A look of surprise crossed his face, as he no doubt noticed the fine dusting of Bang coating the area. He closed his eyes for a moment, appeared to mouth something, and then he opened them, meeting my gaze. He gave a respectful nod and started to walk slowly in my direction. He appeared to have taken a pretty good pounding from Decker and was noticeably limping; however, he didn't seem to be in any great hurry either. No wonder. I didn't really have too many places left to run.

Still, there was no point in making it easy on the guy. I held onto my still bleeding stomach and hobbled over to where Sally was. She had again somehow managed to make it to her feet. She nodded as I approached and started to say something, but I gave her a shove, which put her back down where she had been.

I leaned in and said in a low but firm voice, "Stay down and out of the way. He's after me. The moment you have an opening, you get to the stairwell and get the hell out of here. For once, do as I say, *please*!"

She looked as if she were about to mouth off, but then she averted her gaze and gave me a single nod of her head. I was half-amazed. Personally, I had given her about a ninety-five percent chance of telling me to go fuck myself. Maybe I should play the lottery when this is all over.

That would have to wait, though. For right then, I had a game of Russian roulette to finish...or was that Mongolian roulette? Whatever the case, in this version of the game five of the chambers held bullets and only one kept me from losing my head. Oh well, in the words of Han Solo, "*Never tell me the odds.*"

Sally stayed down and scuttled out of sight. As for me, I ran – or at least tried to. If Nergui wanted me, he'd have to catch me first. Fuck that whole *stand there and take it like a man* crap. I'm more of a *he who fights and runs away* guy anyway. Unfortunately, the running part may have been a bit of a stretch. It was more like a gimp trot. Sorry, but I'd like to see anyone take a pig-sticker to the gut and then try running the Boston Marathon.

Fortunately, most rooftops of office buildings aren't the wide open expanses you might expect. There were plenty of obstacles, my plan being to keep them between myself and Nergui for as long as it took Sally to get out of there. Nergui, no dummy, saw what I was trying to do and put a little more oomph into his limp.

"Do you really wish to die this way?" he called to me. Hey, I could hear again. Good to know my vampire healing wasn't entirely on the fritz today.

"Actually, I'm trying to *avoid* dying this way."

"You only delay your fate by seconds," he said, coming around an air vent I had just moved behind.

"That's a few more moments to figure out how to kick your ass," I replied without much conviction. As it were, I wasn't exactly breaking the four-minute mile, and I could already feel myself starting to slow down. Too much blood loss was starting to take its toll. Another few minutes, and I'd be done for; however, even those few extra minutes were denied me.

* * *

Something heavy thudded into my leg. In my current condition, it was more than enough to trip me up. Down I went. I looked around for what had hit me and saw Nergui's dagger. However, it hadn't come from Nergui. If it had, it would have buried itself six inches into the back of my neck. No, this was a sloppy throw. What had hit me was the hilt, not the blade. I looked to my right. Fuck! In my insistence to run away from Nergui, I didn't notice my path had taken me close to Decker. He was still on the ground, one hand over where Nergui's knife had been just a few moments ago. He gave me a smile and flipped me the bird with his free hand. What a dick! Unfortunately for him, though, I wasn't the only one who had seen what happened.

I turned my head and saw that Gan had finally made it onto the rooftop. She screamed something in her native tongue. No idea what it was, but it sounded decisively unfriendly. She looked between myself and Decker, then launched herself in his direction. It wasn't *quite* the assist I had been hoping for. I guess she was still a little pissed from him barbecuing her the night before. That tended to cloud a person's judgment.

Unfortunately, I didn't see what happened next, as rough hands grabbed me by the back of my shirt and hauled me to my feet. "For kidnapping the princess, you must die. But I give you the honor of dying like a man, Freewill," Nergui said in my ear.

"Wait! Kidnapping? I..." I didn't get a chance to finish as I was flung face-first into the side of one of the large, steel...yeah, definitely steel, ouch!...A/C units I had been previously using for cover.

CRUNCH! *Oh well,* I thought woozily, slumping to the ground, *It's not like I was all that pretty to begin with.* Time for a good, long nap? Yeah, that sounded dandy. Sadly, I was again rudely hauled back to my feet.

"Nap time over already?" I muttered. I managed to crack my eyes open to see Nergui's face looking back at me. Unlike Bang, there was no grin or snide Chinese comment. He didn't look particularly happy about this at all. It was just business for him. I could almost respect that, if his business hadn't involved bringing my head back to the Khan as a trophy.

"Your..." Before he could finish that thought, I was dropped back down again. I was starting to dislike the feeling of the rooftop against my bruised and battered body.

Hold on, what just happened? I shook my head to clear it. It helped, a little at least. When I looked up, I saw that Nergui was busy trying to dislodge something from his back...that something being Sally: stump, broken bones, and all. That bitch! Guess she decided that I could take my orders and shove it after all. On the other hand, maybe I shouldn't be too hard on her, as she had done more to save my ass in the past ten minutes than I really deserved. If we lived through this, she could keep the black Amex. She had earned it.

She hung on with all she had, but it wasn't enough. Nergui grabbed her arms and started to pry her off. That was when Sally crossed the line from crazy to batshit fucking insane. Before he could completely shake her off, she raised her head, extended her fangs, and bit down into the side of his neck. I couldn't believe what I was seeing. She had told me what would happen if a normal (*as in: not me*) vampire did something like that, and yet she was still doing it...to save me.

Blood immediately started spurting from his neck, and still she bit down harder. The look on Nergui's face was a combination of shock and pain. He couldn't believe what she was doing either. I used the moment to pull myself back to my feet. If she could take enough blood out of him, he could potentially weaken to the point where he might be beatable...emphasis on *might*.

* * *

As I got to my feet, I saw flashes of light from the corner of my eye. At first, I thought it might have just been me, seeing as I was on the verge of passing out and all. Then I realized that it must have been Decker. He was putting up a fight against Gan, but there definitely didn't seem to be as much behind it as there had been earlier. Too bad, so sad for him. I'd be sure to send flowers to his funeral or maybe just piss on his grave, depending on which mood struck me at the time.

My immediate priority, though, was still Nergui and the Sally-shaped growth that was still digging at his neck. She was definitely taking a toll on him. That was Sally, alright. She could drain the will to live from any man, one way or the other. Nergui wasn't quite out of it yet, but he wasn't moving quite as spryly as he had been. Unfortunately, that was when Sally stopped.

She raised her head from his neck and looked at me. She gave me a sheepish smile and then projectile vomited a large gout of blood. If you've seen *The Exorcist*, you have a good idea of how this went. Gross is definitely one word for it. Unfortunately for her, it didn't end there. Her eyes rolled into the back of her head, and suddenly she fell from Nergui's back. She landed on the ground and started violently convulsing, more blood spraying from her mouth. I wished I could do something to help her, but there was nothing I could think of. No, that wasn't right. I could make sure she hadn't taken on this kind of suffering in vain. I could finish off Nergui and end this...for her.

Nergui was still too stunned from Sally's attack to notice me again. He was holding his hands to his neck, trying to staunch the massive flow of blood. It gave me a chance.

I didn't have a lot left, but I summoned what I could. I rushed forward, and just as his eyes were again turning toward me, I nailed him with a double-fisted upper cut. It was a clean, solid hit, and Nergui went flying. If luck was with me, the fucker would have a nice dislocated jaw to show for it.

It wasn't.

He flew a good fifteen feet through the air and landed in a heap...right next to the knife that Decker had thrown at me just moments earlier. You've got to be fucking kidding me!

Nergui's hand closed on the hilt. He slowly rolled to his feet as I looked for cover against what I knew was coming. Unfortunately, I was spent. Whatever I had summoned for that hit had truly been all that I had left to give. My body felt like it was encased in Jell-O...and not in a good 'wrestling with topless chicks' kind of way either.

The next few seconds were like a slow motion scene from a movie. Several things happened at once, and it was like time slowed down for a heartbeat or two to let it all unfold. I heard Gan's voice scream out, "BILL!" as Nergui steadied himself. I turned my head and saw her toss Decker to the side like a piece of garbage. I glanced back to find that Nergui had flipped the knife so that the blade was in his hand. He started to pull his arm back. Out of the corner of my eye, I saw a tiny flower patterned blur moving almost faster than I would have thought possible. Nergui's arm snapped forward, and I saw the blade leave his hand. His aim was true. I saw where it was headed, but for some reason my body refused to respond with much more than a few twitches in the direction I was trying to will it toward. Stupid body!

Then, just like that, time suddenly snapped back to its normal speed. The blade closed in on my heart just as that flowery blur leapt in front of me. There was a dull thud, and then Gan's tiny body slammed into me with more than enough force to take me off my feet. I went down, and she landed on top of me.

"*Princess*! No!" I heard Nergui's voice scream right before he trailed back off into his native language. Whatever he was saying sounded frantic, but I could no more understand it than if he had been trying to communicate in clicks and whistles.

"Thanks for the save, Gan. Now get off me," I said in a weak voice. She didn't move. That's when I finally understood what had happened.

I gently rolled her off me and managed to get to a sitting position. What I saw confirmed my fears: the silver blade was stuck up to its hilt in Gan's chest. She wasn't moving.

"*Why*!?" yelled Nergui. He ran to her other side and dropped to his knees. "Why would she do that?"

"Oh, Gan," I said with a sad sigh, gently stroking her cheek. "What have you done?"

Nergui slapped my hand away. "Do not touch her, kidnapper!"

"Are you fucking for real!?" I snapped back with more strength than I thought I had left. "Does it *look* like I kidnapped her? Would she take a knife for me if I had kidnapped her!?"

"But my master said..."

"Your master was wrong! Think about it. Gan came here after me. I didn't ask her to."

"But why? She had everything..." he said, anguish in his voice.

"Apparently not," I replied, and then decided it was best to sugar coat the next part and leave my opinions out of it. "Gan got it in her mind that she wanted me as her mate." He gave me a dubious look in return. "Yeah, I thought it was weird, too...err, I mean she came all this way, and I'm obviously not worthy of her."

He was silent for a moment as this sank in. Finally, he appeared to come to a decision as he looked me in the eye. "I...I am..." he seemed to struggle with the word, "sorry, Freewill. Had I known, I would have acted...different."

"Even though the Khan ordered otherwise?" I asked, not bothering to cover the doubt in my voice.

"The Khan is wise, but he does not know all."

I was tempted to point out that, from what Gan had told me, the Khan knew all about this part. It was beginning to become obvious that he put out the hit on me in a fit of asshole anger. But then again, I also didn't see the point in mentioning such to Nergui, as it was doubtful it would help the situation any.

"I had pledged to bring back your head to him," he continued with downcast eyes. "However, because of my foolishness, I shall only be returning with the body of his daughter and my worthless life as penance."

There was a moment of silence that passed between us as this started to sink in. But then my subconscious decided to speak up again, as it often did. For once, it actually had something useful to say.

"*Body?*" I suddenly spoke up as the thought hit me. He raised his eyebrows at that. "Nergui, why do we still even have a body? Shouldn't she be ash by now?"

His eyes widened in surprise. We both looked at Gan, and then back at each other. Then we smelled it...the silver! Smoke had started wafting from the wound in her chest. Jesus Christ, we were a pack of idiots!

"Pull it out!" I yelled, but Nergui was way ahead of me. He grabbed the blade of the knife and yanked it from Gan's body. There was a spurt of sparks, followed by a spray of blood, and then, just barely audible, the barest of gasps from her mouth. She was still with us.

It should have been obvious, had we not been morons. If you kill a vampire, you get dust, end of story; anything less meant the deed wasn't done. Nergui's aim hadn't been quite as good as I had thought. He had somehow just barely missed her heart. Sally's attack had done its job after all.

"How do we help her?" I asked, not really knowing much outside of maybe hoping she healed from the wound. Sadly, the silvered blade meant that her recovery would be slowed down considerably.

Again, though, Nergui was more prepared than I. He reached to his side and unclipped what appeared to be a water-skin. He uncorked it and tilted it over Gan's lips. A familiar red liquid poured forth from it into her mouth. Even unconscious, she instinctively started swallowing gulps of it.

"This will help," he said, administering the blood. After a few good swallows from Gan, he pulled the skin away. He reached into a pocket and produced a small glass vial. It looked vaguely familiar. He poured the viscous contents into the water-skin, gave it a shake to mix, and then proceeded to feed more of it to Gan.

"Isn't that...?"

Nergui nodded in response. "It will allow her to sleep and heal."

"It will also keep her from running off if she starts feeling better," I pointed out. Nergui gave me a knowing smile and nodded again. He wasn't stupid. "What now?" I asked, just in case we were getting back to that 'trying to kill me' part again. One can never be too paranoid with these things.

"I will return with the princess, and we will let the Khan know the truth," he replied. I was tempted to point out that the fat fuck already knew the truth and that this whole thing was just one gigantic hissy fit from him, but I refrained. That would probably be kicking the hornets' nest. "I am certain that once the truth is made known to *all*, the great Khan will show mercy and rescind his order," he finished. As I said, Nergui wasn't stupid. I saw what he was getting at. If the findings of the investigation were made fairly public knowledge, then the Khan would have no choice but to call off the dogs. Nobody would give a damn about him killing a vampire of my age, but they might take some exception to killing the legendary Freewill just for shits and giggles.

"Will Gan be okay?"

"She is his daughter," was his answer, and probably the only one he needed to give. Gan was the Khan's family, and hundreds of years old or not, people tended to tolerate a lot of crap from family.

"I guess the only thing left to do is clean up here and make sure we both don't drop dead in the process."

He nodded and then winced as he put his hand to his still oozing neck. "Your friend surprised me. She must care a great deal about you to have done this."

Oh shit! I almost forgot about Sally in the aftermath of what happened to Gan. I pulled myself weakly to my feet and limped over to check on her. She was still in the same spot. She was curled into a fetal ball and shaking, a few retching noises still escaping from her lips. In short, she didn't look particularly well. I needed to get her out of here and back to where she could be properly cared for.

I picked her up in my arms and looked back. Nergui had done the same for Gan. As I started slowly walking toward the stairwell, I heard a low murmur coming from Sally. I was amazed that she was still conscious, if just barely. I bent my head to hers and asked her to repeat herself.

"Remember," she said with a wheeze, "when I said that being near you was the safest place to be?"

"Yes."

"Need to rethink that," she whispered with a slight smile, and then was quiet again.

I started to chuckle when I suddenly remembered how she had gotten her original injuries...for this evening, at least. I looked around, scanning the rooftop...nothing.

"Where's Decker?" I asked Nergui.

"Decker?"

"The wizard," I clarified.

"Did the princess not dispatch him?"

"I thought so..." I trailed off. Then where the hell was he? Did wizards turn to dust like vampires? No, probably not. No convenient buckets of water around either. What a world!

That's when I noticed it. There was a thin trail of blood leading into the stairwell entrance. It appeared to go downward. Son of a bitch! "I don't believe it. After all that..." but Nergui held up a hand to silence me from saying more.

"Hush." He appeared to be listening to something. "We must go now," he said, walking past me and starting down the stairs.

His hearing was much more sensitive than mine. For a moment, I didn't notice anything, and then...sirens. The cops. How could they have...Decker! I would have bet anything on it. Not only had the fucker betrayed me, attacked us, and then done his best to trip me up when I was running from Nergui, but now he had run downstairs and called the police on us, too. Goddamn, what a prick!

The Epic Epilogue

THE BATTLE HAD ended on a sour note. Fortunately, the vampire community's *contributions* to the NYPD would help ensure that things weren't traced back to us. Decker probably knew that, too, not to mention I'm fairly sure he wanted the wizarding world exposed to the general public about as much as we wanted vampires to show up on the six o'clock news. Still, it had been one last kick in the balls from him before the asshole got away.

On the upside, at least the battle was over. Sally and Gan had survived the ordeal, albeit barely. As for myself, I was happy to report I'd live to get back into trouble for another day. What I didn't know then was that *another day* wasn't as far off on the horizon as I assumed.

After we escaped from...well, my job I guess, we quickly made our way underground. I'm sure we looked quite the sight to any onlookers. But between the weirdness of our appearance and the fact that we were all mostly covered in blood and grime, I wasn't too worried about any positive IDs anytime soon. After traveling a few blocks through the sewer tunnels, we split up. Nergui told me that he wanted to waste no time getting back. He was going to immediately work on making arrangements for himself and Gan to head home to Asia. Can't say I was all too sorry to see him and his still unconscious bundle of 'joy' depart from my life.

That done, my main concern turned to Sally. Vampire strength or not, I was at the end of my endurance. She was starting to feel pretty heavy by the time I made it back to coven territory. I more or less just barely managed to stumble back to the loft, but make it back I did, and I only dropped Sally once...maybe twice, along the way.

There was plenty of refrigerated blood in the larder underneath the loft, and I managed to get two pints of it down Sally's throat. It was touch and go for a few minutes there, but somehow she managed to keep it down without yakking all over me. I mean, yeah I had gotten plenty of gore on me during the previous few hours, but that would have just been nasty.

At last, I put her in one of the loft's two bedrooms and gave a call to the safe house in Brooklyn. The 'All Clear' was given, and the remaining members of the coven were soon on their way back. Thank God for that, because I was done.

I must have finally passed out because when I opened my eyes again, I saw that several members of the coven were milling about the room. I checked on Sally and found Starlight in the room with her. She had taken charge with regards to Sally's care. Seeing that she was in good hands, I gave my roommates a quick call to let them know I was still amongst the living, or undead, or however you want to put it. I then grabbed the spare bedroom and let blissful unconsciousness take me away again.

I was out for a good twelve hours. Sally was down for eighteen before she started to stir. Her attitude took another four or so to wake up, but when it did, I knew she was going to be fine. As her wounds, outside of her missing hand, hadn't been caused by silver weapons, her cuts were already closed and her bones were starting to mend. It was still going to be a while before she was doing much more than attempting to sit upright. Regardless, before the night was through she was already barking out orders again and taking charge.

Right before dawn, my roommate, Ed, showed up. He claimed it was to give me a ride back home, and I wasn't about to argue with that. Unlike Sally's, my wounds were taking their sweet time to heal, and I was still pretty banged up. I had no qualms about bypassing an hour-long subway ride. Still, I'm not a complete idiot. He was partially there for me, but he was also checking in on Sally. Oh well, if he insisted on living dangerously, who was I to argue?

* * *

The next day passed well enough. At the very least, no assassins, wizards, or love-struck preteen psychos showed up to darken our doorstep. By the late afternoon, I felt more or less myself again. I was

324

probably going to hold off on any duels to the death for a couple days; however, I felt good enough to bundle myself up in layers of day clothes and head back to Manhattan to check on things. I was still coven leader, at least on paper. Considering the events of the past several days, it was probably a good idea to not be a stranger. The coven would need to be rebuilt, and that was a duty I couldn't shirk, no matter how much I wanted to.

I arrived at the loft just as the sun was setting and found a few coven vamps hanging around, but no Sally. They told me she had returned to the office. I was just thinking it was a good sign for her health when my cell phone rang. Speaking of the devil, it was her.

"Where the hell have you been?" she barked. "I've been trying to reach you for the past hour." There was still a wheezy quality to her voice, but she sounded a lot stronger than she had the previous night.

"Good to hear you're feeling better," I replied.

"I'm just dandy," she growled. "Get your ass over here as soon as you can." With that, she hung up.

"Love you, too," I said cheerfully into the now dead line. *Yep, good to be back to normal*, I thought as I headed to the door.

The office wasn't far. It took me no more than fifteen minutes to get there. The place was still a disaster. Vampires were scurrying back and forth, straightening things up. At least I saw that the desks that usually controlled the hotline were unmanned. I had no doubt that Sally would have it up and running again in no time, but it was nice to know that the vulnerable of the city could have at least a minor reprieve from being served up as the daily special.

The only area of the floor that appeared to be back to normal was...you guessed it...Sally's office. What a surprise. Even less of a surprise, I saw that Starlight was back to manning the desk outside of it. I sighed as I approached. "Hey, Star. I see Sally got you again."

"Hi, Bill," she replied. I noticed that she was showing distinctly less skittishness toward me than she normally did. After the last few days, I was probably the least of the evils she had been dealing with. That was good. I didn't mind it at all.

"Do I need to send you on another *coffee break*?" I asked with an even voice.

She actually met my gaze to answer, "No. I volunteered this time. Lets me keep an eye on her." She hooked a thumb toward Sally's door. I smiled at that. Having a mother hen looking out for her was probably driving Sally nuts.

I excused myself and let myself into Sally's office unannounced. Leadership has its perks, after all. Her normal super comfy executive chair was pushed off to the side. Sally sat behind her desk in a wheelchair, an IV of blood attached and flowing into her arm. She did not look amused.

"Starlight?" I asked, indicating the setup.

"Who else? She wouldn't stop badgering me until I let her strap me in to this contraption."

"Looks good on you. Matches your eyes," I quipped.

She held up the stump of her right arm toward me. It looked much better than it previously had. I could have sworn I already saw tiny little finger nubs starting to grow from it. "You probably can't tell," she said, "but I'm giving you the ghost finger."

"Good to see your stunning personality wasn't amputated."

"Quite true, but enough of my sunny disposition," she said, putting on a serious tone. "We have a problem...more specifically, *you* have a problem."

"What a surprise," I commented. "What now?"

"Got a call from Boston about an hour ago. It was about Gan and Nergui."

"Oh, don't tell me she escaped again."

"Worse. They made it back."

"Why is that worse?"

She shook her head. "They made it back to *nothing*. The Khan's camp was completely destroyed."

"Are they okay?"

"Yeah. There are plenty of nomadic covens in that region. They hooked up with a few of them."

"So what the hell happened?" I demanded

"No idea. It was all over by the time they got back. Sounds like whatever was fighting them won." Shit! I had completely forgotten about the alma or whatever they were. I pulled out my cell phone and started typing a message. She saw me and asked, "What are you doing?"

"I'm texting Ed. You just reminded me of something we were supposed to look into."

"Tell him I said 'Hi'."

"Tell him yourself," I said, putting my phone away again. "So Gan's fine?"

"Yep."

"That's good."

"For *them*, yes. For you..." she trailed off in a low voice.

"Me what?"

"The word from Boston is that they're blaming you for this."

"WHAT!?"

"The Khan sent three of his warriors to retrieve Gan from you."

"I'm pretty well aware of that."

"So..." she continued in a slow voice, "since they were here and not there, the Khan's forces were depleted."

"Oh," I replied, comprehension sinking in. "But it was just three guys."

"Three of the Khan's *best* warriors," she corrected. "While they were in China doing their duty, everything was hunky-dory. Once they left, not so much. You can do the math."

"So what's the bottom line?" I asked, feeling my good mood instantly evaporate.

"Just rumblings and rumors so far, from what I can hear."

"Let me guess...more assassins are coming. A lot more."

"No. It's *worse*."

I put my hand up to rub my temples and sighed, "Define 'worse'."

"They're expecting you to *fix* things."

* * *

I got off the subway and walked toward home, the beginnings of a migraine starting to form. Fix things? How the fuck was I supposed to fix things? I didn't even know what things there were to fix. Sally said she'd keep me posted as more news became available, but I was sorely tempted to toss my cell phone down a sewer and change my home number. I doubted any further news would be very much in my favor.

I didn't know the half of it.

I arrived at my apartment and let myself in. I immediately froze in the doorway at the scene that greeted me. Tom was sitting on the couch. That in and of itself wasn't too shocking. The fact that he had his face glued to a witch, who had just days before kidnapped us all, was the thing that had me just a wee bit disconcerted.

I stood in the doorway for a moment while they continued to play tongue-hockey, oblivious of me. Finally, I cleared my throat. They both stopped what they were doing and looked in my direction. Christy's face held a fairly shocked expression. Tom's looked like a mouse that had gotten caught with the cheese.

"Sorry, didn't mean to interrupt you," I said in a frigid voice.

"It's cool, dude," replied Tom easily. "We talked things out."

"Talked things out," I repeated to myself. I closed the door and walked over to our kitchen nook. I had a feeling I was going to need to drink something a lot stronger than blood before the night was out. "And what exactly did you two *love birds* talk out?"

"Christy's sorry about what happened. Right, hon?" he said. She nodded vigorously in reply. "We decided to try to work things out, but first rule going forward is the apartment is off limits."

"Off limits?" I queried, waving my hands in their general direction.

"Well, not for *this*," he explained.

"Oh. So what you're saying is that she'll only try to kill me again when I'm not here. Is that right, Christy?"

She gave me a sheepish smile in return and opened her mouth to speak, but I held my hand up. "Give me a second. I have a feeling I'm gonna need a drink for this." I opened the fridge and grabbed a pint of chilled blood.

While I was contemplating adding a shot or three of Jack Daniels to it, Tom tried to change the subject, "Oh yeah, almost forgot. You got a call while you were out."

"From who?"

"Caller ID said it was your job."

"Great," I replied. What now?

For a while there, I had been afraid that the whole battle at my workplace would be traced back and dumped squarely onto my lap; however, a few quick phone calls to some of my programming buddies the day before had confirmed that the damage was being blamed on nameless vandals, possibly corporate sabotage. Hell, they hadn't even closed the place for any longer than it took to replace the broken windows. I never thought I would be so glad that the vampire nation kept the cops in their back pocket.

Still, what would they be calling for now? I put down my drink and pressed play on the machine. Whatever it was, I was almost hoping that it would put me in an even worse mood for the reaming I was about to give Tom and his little succubus.

*Bill, it's Jim. Call me when you get this. Just got word from HR. The VP of Marketing filed a harassment complaint against you. What the hell is that about? Call me. *beep**

I couldn't even process that for a second. I just stood there, stunned. The motherfucker complained about me to HR!?

I heard Christy say, "I should probably go."

For once, even Tom had a clue. "Yeah, that might be best," he said, getting up to walk her to the door. She beat a hasty retreat. Probably for the best, but apparently not for the last, considering the state I had caught her and my roommate in.

Once he had shown her out, he walked up to me, but I again held up my hand. "If you even imply the words *sexual* harassment..." I let the threat hang in the air.

I was interrupted from the tirade I felt building up by Ed walking out of his bedroom. "I heard you come in," he mentioned. If he heard that, he no doubt heard what else had gone on. He wisely mentioned none of it. "Here," he said, handing me a piece of paper.

"What's this?" I asked without looking down at it.

"I looked up alma for you."

I looked down at the paper. It was a printout of a webpage. "Is this Wikipedia?"

"Yep, came right up in Google. Not exactly the heavy research I was expecting."

I scanned the entry. "You've got to be kidding me!"

"Nope."

"What is it?" Tom asked.

"Alma," Ed explained, "is the Mongolian name for *Bigfoot*."

"No fucking way!"

Ed shrugged. "That's pretty much what I thought."

"You're telling me that the vampires are in a war against Sasquatch?" I replied in a stunned voice. I then took a few minutes to fill them in on what Sally had just told me.

"Sounds like the vampires are in a *losing* war against Sasquatch," Ed commented when I was done.

I nodded. "Yeah, and apparently they're expecting me to be their General Custer."

"That is fucking cool!" Tom exclaimed, but then quickly added, "I don't mean the thing with you, Bill. But seriously, vampires versus bigfoot? I'd pay to see that shit."

"Don't forget the wizards," I pointed out with a sigh. Jesus Christ, how did I find myself in this position? I put my head down on the counter.

"Maybe we should give you a few moments," said Ed, leading Tom toward the living room.

"Why bother?" I said, standing up straight. I picked up the phone and started dialing.

"What are you doing?"

"Calling work. It's still early. Jim might still be around. Who knows, maybe he'll have something else to say to *brighten* my day." That last part came out as a growl as my temper began to fray. I had gone through far too much in the past couple days for life to suddenly decide that it needed to take a mega-dump on me. I barely even noticed when a familiar female voice answered the phone.

"Hopskotchgames. Jim Floskie's office."

"Is Jim in?" I asked, rubbing my temple with my free hand.

"Bill?" replied Sheila's voice. "Sorry, he already left for the night."

"Figures," I commented without much gusto. "I'll call back tomorrow."

"He's out. Taking a personal day."

"That's just great," I commented with a sigh.

"Sorry," she said in an understanding voice. "Hey, I heard what happened."

"You did? Let me guess, the whole office knows," I replied, starting to feel a dull throb of anger in the back of my head.

"Don't worry about it. Nothing's going to happen to you."

"Really?"

"I doubt it," she replied and then lightened her tone a bit. "So what did you do, hit on him in the men's room?"

"Of course not!"

"I'm just kidding. I know that," she said with a laugh. "Besides, I'm sure most people here will stick up for you. Harry doesn't exactly have too many fans."

"No?"

"You haven't been around here much lately; I have. Trust me on this. He's not exactly Mr. Popularity."

"You seemed to be getting along with him."

"Oh, please," she said dismissively. "I was just letting him buy me a drink after work. Truth be told..." she lowered her voice to a whisper, "I kind of think he's a bit of an asshole, actually. In fact, I might even tell HR that he's probably just doing this because he's pissed off at you about the other night. You should have heard the stuff he was ranting about after you left. It was weird."

"I bet," I muttered. "I meant...what about you? Were you mad at me, too?"

"For what?"

"For...ruining...I mean, for the other night?"

"Not at all. I'll admit that it was a little odd (*a little?*), but I know how it is. I have a nephew. We've done some weird things together. I thought it was kind of sweet that you were spending time with your family.

As for the rest of it, I might even owe you a bit of thanks."

"Thanks?"

"If you hadn't shown up, I'm pretty sure Harry would have tried weaseling his way up to my apartment." She gave another chuckle. "So in a way, I guess you were my knight in shining armor."

"Really?"

"You keep asking that. Yes, really."

"Thank you," I replied, a bit dumbfounded, but nevertheless feeling the first traces of brightness shining into my otherwise not-so-hot day. "I really appreciate that."

"No problem, Bill. Anytime," she said, the warmth never leaving her voice.

"Sheila..." I had meant to say 'goodbye'. Maybe it was her tone, or maybe the past few days had just left me too tired to psyche myself out. Whatever the reason, my mouth decided it had a mind of its own, and what came out instead was, "what do you think about maybe grabbing a cup of coffee with me sometime?"

There was a pause on the other end, which was just as well because time suddenly stopped for me. Holy shit, did I actually just say that? I rewound my mental tape...yes, I did. I wasn't even thinking about it. It just kind of slipped out. Great! Now, not only did I have the Draculas, Sasquatch, an asshole wizard, and an HR department to deal with. I could also add being shot down to my ever growing list of mental baggage. What the fuck was I thinking?

"Sure. It'll be fun," came her reply.

My mind went completely blank. Who was I talking to? What were they agreeing with? I had no idea. It was like my brain decided to do a core dump and was still rebooting itself. I looked up, unable to say a word. I saw Tom and Ed staring back at me. They both had their mouths agape. Finally, Ed started miming the words "*thank you*" and "*hang up*" to me. Oh...oh yeah.

"That's great, Sheila. Thanks. We'll...set something up." Okay, I needed to end this before I ventured back into social retard territory.

"Sounds good."

"I'll talk to you...soon!" I said and then quickly hung up the phone before my tongue could spit out anything stupid sounding.

There was a stillness in the room for a moment, then I numbly walked over to the living room and plopped myself down on the couch.

Finally, Ed broke the silence. He had a big grin on his face. "Congratulations, man. You *actually* did it."

"I did, didn't I?" I said, it starting to sink in. "I can't believe it."

"*You* can't?" asked Tom. "I thought I was going to have to listen to you pine for her until I died of old age."

"Oh yeah, speaking of which, it looks like you owe me twenty bucks," Ed replied to him.

"For once, I'm happy to pay up," Tom said, walking over to the kitchen to grab a beer. "Who would have thought it? Today, Bill, you are finally a man."

We all chucked at that, me more so at the irony of the statement. Then Ed said, "Seriously, I'm proud of you." He clapped me on the shoulder and then got up. He started to walk toward his room before turning back toward me. "Bit of advice, though?"

"What?" I asked, the grin still on my face.

"Maybe next time, wait until after your *sexual* harassment case is finished before asking out a co-worker."

"Asshole," I replied with a smile.

I couldn't believe it. Here I was, a mountain of supernatural evil about to come down on my head like an avalanche, and the only thing I could think about was that I had finally taken a step forward with the girl of my dreams. It wasn't much. Heck, I wasn't even sure it would be considered a date. Still, it was more progress than I had made in all the time I had known her. It was a victory, no matter how small.

I decided to put my feet up and enjoy it. In a short while, Bigfoot could crash through the wall followed by the *Loch Ness Monster* and *Zontar the Thing from Venus*, for all I cared. Not for right now, though. For at least the next five minutes, all was right with my world. I could live with that.

THE END

Bill Ryder will return in:
The Mourning Woods: (The Tome of Bill, Part 3)

Can't wait for more Bill? Follow his ongoing
misadventures on Facebook at:
www.facebook.com/BilltheVampire

Author's Note

Let's face facts: sequels are scary business. And no, I don't just mean horror sequels. I mean *any* sequel, and for many different reasons. The thing is; they're scary for both the audience and the writer. For the audience, it's always the same: will this live up to the expectations set in the previous chapter? Will I wind up with a *Godfather part 2,* or will I suffer through *Batman and Robin*? Even worse than that last example...and one of the cruelest things that one human can inflict upon another...is the sequel in name only (cue scary music!) because, let's face facts, nobody wants to pay good money to see *Halloween: Season of the Witch* and find out that it has absolutely nothing to do with Michael Myers. As for others, well let's just say that the less said about *Highlander: the Quickening*, the better.

So, too, can sequels be a nightmare for the creators. Can we capture that same magic again? Can we expand upon the world we've created? Can we remember to follow the rules we set? Have those rules written us into a corner? Can we stay true to the characters we've already created? This last one in particular can be difficult because are they truly our characters anymore?

From a legal perspective, this one is easy to answer. There's no doubt that Marvel is within their *legal* rights to undo Peter Parker's marriage to Mary Jane with but a single issue; however, that doesn't mean millions of comic book fans won't storm their offices with pitchforks and torches after they do so. Roland Emmerich and Dean Devlin were well within their rights to present a Godzilla that didn't breathe fire, but as a diehard Godzilla fan I know in my heart that there is a special place in Hell reserved for both of them in doing so.

Thus, therein lies the fear. As a writer, I've breathed life into these characters, loved them, nurtured them, and want to continue to do so; however, there's a fine line because, in some ways, the second they were born they'd already outgrown me. The returning characters in this book aren't mine anymore; they're ours. All I can hope is that I've done right by them again.

If not, you can find me sitting out on my backyard deck, patiently awaiting the tarring and feathering that I know will be coming for me someday.

Still, until such time as the angry mobs descend to tear me limb from limb, I hope you enjoyed these further adventures of Bill Ryder and his friends. I had a hell of a time tagging along with them on this journey. I hope you did, too.

Rick G.

About the Author

Rick Gualtieri lives alone in central New Jersey with only his wife, three kids, and countless pets to both keep him company and constantly plot against him. When he's not busy monkey-clicking out words, he can typically be found jealously guarding his collection of vintage Transformers from all who would seek to defile them.

Defilers beware!

Rick Gualtieri is the author of:

Bill The Vampire (The Tome of Bill - 1)
Scary Dead Things (The Tome of Bill - 2)
The Mourning Woods (The Tome of Bill - 3)
Holier Than Thou (The Tome of Bill - 4)
Sunset Strip: A Tale From The Tome Of Bill
Goddamned Freaky Monsters (The Tome of Bill - 5)
Half A Prayer (The Tome of Bill - 6)
Bigfoot Hunters
The Poptart Manifesto

To contact Rick (with either undying praise or rude comments) please visit:

Rick's Website:
www.rickgualtieri.com

Facebook Page:
facebook.com/RickGualtieriAuthor

Twitter:
twitter.com/RickGualtieri

Bonus Chapter

The Mourning Woods
The Tome of Bill, part 3

THAT'S PRETTY MUCH how it was for the next two days as we made our way further north. Eventually the towns became fewer and much farther in between. When not driving, Ed joined me in trying to stay as busy as possible. Unfortunately, cell service was starting to become spotty in the long stretches of...well...Canadian nothingness.

Tom, for his part, continued to push himself further up Sally's list of people to kill. Despite looking absolutely fine, he continued to whine about becoming one of the undead. When I pointed out that both Sally and I were amongst that number and neither of us (*especially her*) looked worse for wear, it only increased the whining. "Yeah, but you guys are vampires, the undead elite. I'm going to be a disgusting corpse, forever in search of brains."

"When you finally find some, I hope they stick," Sally replied.

"Personally," I said, "I think you should be more worried about your dick rotting off."

"Seriously, Bill," Ed asked. "Do you think Christy would even notice?"

"Nah, probably not," I replied, eliciting laughter.

"That's right, joke about it now," Tom said, morosely. "Just don't go looking for any mercy once the zombie apocalypse starts."

* * *

Eventually we were forced to start using our fuel surplus. We stopped along the side of the road at the northern tip of Saskatchewan – or whatever the fuck they call it – to refuel. It was about midnight, cold as fuck, and utterly desolate. While Tom and Ed went to grab some gas from the trailer, I got out to stretch.

"Don't wander off," Sally said from still inside the car. She was bundled up in a parka and looked like the world's most expensive Eskimo hooker.

"Yes, Mom," I replied. Her warning aside, I started to walk toward the tree line. It had been a couple of hours since our last stop and "little Dr. Death" was feeling the need for a piss break.

As I walked, I glanced up. It was truly marvelous how the night sky looked when there wasn't any city around to muck it up. Even had my vampire night vision not been up to snuff, the stars were bright enough to make things passable. At least out in the open they were.

I entered the tree line and the gloom settled around me. Even though my vampire eyes cut through the darkness, the density of the brush made it difficult to see more than a few feet in any direction.

Once I was out of sight of the car, I found a suitable looking tree and unzipped to do my business. Ah! Few things are as reinvigorating as a good piss after a long drive.

I was almost finished, when a sound caught my attention. Thinking it was one of my roommates, I called out, "Go find your own garden, guys. This one is already watered."

There was no response, save the crunch of more foliage. My thoughts immediately turned to Sally. She had been in the car as long as the rest of us. Maybe she needed a "rest break" too. While the thought of her squatting amongst the trees was definitely humorous, I had no intention of getting caught with my dick hanging out. I'm not sure what comment she would have, but I'm certain it wouldn't be kind.

I quickly zipped up, and that's when I heard another crunch. Whereas before the sound was hard to pinpoint, this one was close enough for me to tell it was coming from the opposite direction of the car. Another crack. Closer and it sounded big.

I reminded myself that was probably bullshit. It was absolutely quiet out there. In such solitude, a fox could step on a twig and it would sound like cannon fire. I was probably psyching myself out for nothing.

Suddenly there was a snort from directly in front of me. Brush obscured my vision, but I could make out a shape beyond it and it was bigger than me...a lot bigger.

Oh, crap. I hadn't even considered that I might run into the Alma, Sasquatch, Grendel, or whatever the fuck they were called. What if they were making a preemptive strike to take me out? I wouldn't put it past the filthy, shit-flinging fuckers.

I began to back up. I had gotten a taste of what these guys could do when I was over in China. I wasn't about to underestimate them. The shape in the woods matched me step for step. I began to crouch down in a defensive stance – learned from countless hours of kung-fu movies – when it stepped from the brush and I found myself staring into two large, brown, and not overly intelligent eyes. A set of antlers nearly four feet wide sat atop a large head. A fucking moose.

I breathed a sigh of relief and chuckled as it just stood there, dumbly chewing its cud or whatever the fuck a moose chews on. Damn. There I was, almost shitting myself and for what, an oversized deer? On the up side, it was the first one I had ever seen outside of a zoo. Now that the scare was over, it was actually kind of cool.

Figuring a photo would make for a neat souvenir, I pulled my phone from my pocket. I aimed the camera and pushed the button. The flash went off causing the moose to jump in surprise. It made an angry snort and then, without further warning, charged straight at me. Oh, fuck! Forget what I said about Bigfoot. Being trampled by the equivalent of a freight train on legs wasn't particularly high on my list. I turned and ran.

Judging by the crashing sounds behind me, the moose was following.

Thank God, vampires are fast. Used to be, I was the fat kid in high school who came in dead last in every single track event. Nowadays, though, there wasn't an Olympic sprinter alive who could keep up with me once I got going. There were just two problems. For starters, this wasn't ideal terrain for me to go all out in. Secondly, my pursuer had both the home field advantage as well as an extra set of legs. I had just burst from the tree line, I could see the car ahead, when this deficiency became painfully clear.

I was mowed over from behind. It felt like a bus plowed into me. I went down, but was that enough for my moosey friend? Of course not. I felt a pair of hooves slam into my back. The air was forced from my lungs and I was pretty sure I could feel some of my favorite body parts cracking. Then the fucker did it again. It was stomping the shit out of me.

* * *

The Mourning Woods

Available in ebook and paperback.